Praise for the Soul Seekers by Alyson Noël

"Daire and her boyfriend Dace are back to restore the balance of good and evil after saving her grandmother and her soul. Dace is deliciously yummy, and if I say so myself, so is his evil brother Cade. It's a bit more fast-paced than *Fated* was, and it's setting up the series to have longevity. If only it wasn't so long again until the next installment!" —*Night Owl Reviews* (4.5 stars—Top Pick!)

"Noël uses her New Mexico setting to weave in Native American mythology such as spirit animals and skinwalking. An intriguing story."
—*Kirkus Reviews*

"Daire and Dace's chemistry is intense and sizzling. Whenever they are by each other, sparks fly. And the other characters add flavor to this highly addictive read. I couldn't put this book down!"
—*Young Adult Books Central*

"Alyson Noël paints a magical New Mexican landscape."
—*New Mexico Style*

"Noël does a terrific job of slowly unspooling secrets and motivations with writing that is both charismatic and spunky."
—*Los Angeles Times*

"A rush of romance will sweep you away in this hauntingly mystical read. I'm already as addicted to Daire and Dace as I was to Ever and Damen. Next book, please!"
—Janet, teen reader from Kentucky for *Justine* magazine

"An adventurous page-turner. Dreams and reality bleed into each other in this dangerous and edgy romance. Another home-run series for Alyson Noël!"
—Anna, teen reader from NY for *Justine* magazine

"Emotional, fast-paced, romantic. I love Alyson Noël's lushly descriptive writing—I could hear the beating of the crow's wings, feel the blue-eyed boy's embrace, and smell Paloma's coffee in this new Soul Seekers series."
                    —Catherine, teen reader from Florida for *Justine* magazine

"With fantastic characters and an amazing plot, *Fated* will suck you in and leave you breathless. Noël is a master with words . . . with passion and thrills around each corner, this book is a must-read."
                                        —*RT Book Reviews* (Top Pick!)

"Atmospheric and enjoyable . . . Noël's many fans will be eager to find out what happens next."   —*Publishers Weekly*

"Readers will feel the pull of Daire's quest just as forcefully as Daire herself does, and will count the days until the release of *Echo*."
                                —*Shelf Awareness, Maximum Shelf*

"A fast and enjoyable read . . . with some very unique plot twists and balance among the romance, conflict, and family relationships."
                                                    —*Deseret News*

"Two boys, one light and one dark, factor heavily into the intriguing, twisting story line, which is sure to draw Noël's numerous fans."
                                                        —*Booklist*

"Another captivating series from Alyson Noël. *Fated* did an excellent job setting up everything for the next books in the series. . . . I'm really looking forward to seeing where this series goes!"
                                                    —*The Story Siren*

"I found myself unable to put this book down, completely captivated by the narration and the beautifully crafted world. It was a refreshing YA fantasy with new elements I've never seen before."
                                —*Love, Literature, Art and Reason*

also by alyson noël

mystic

alyson noël

st. martin's griffin ≈ new york

This is a work of fiction. All of the characters, organizations, and events portrayed in this novel are either products of the author's imagination or are used fictitiously.

www.stmartins.com

Design by Anna Gorovoy

Library of Congress Cataloging-in-Publication Data

Noël, Alyson.
   Mystic / Alyson Noël.—First edition. (The Soul Seekers ; 3)
      pages   cm
   ISBN 978-0-312-57567-0 (paperback)
   ISBN 978-0-312-66488-6 (hardcover)
   ISBN 978-1-250-02078-9 (e-book)
  1. Supernatural—Fiction. 2. Soul—Fiction. 3. Dead—Fiction.
4. Love—Fiction. 5. Indians of North America—New Mexico—
Fiction. 6. New Mexico—Fiction. I. Title.
  PZ7.N67185Mys 2013
  dc23

                         2013003450

St. Martin's Griffin books may be purchased for educational, business, or promotional use. For information on bulk purchases, please contact Macmillan Corporate and Premium Sales Department at 1-800-221-7945 extension 5442 or write specialmarkets@macmillan.com.

First Edition: May 2013

10 9 8 7 6 5 4 3 2 1

In memory of Shaun Daniel Winegar
1966–2012

Animal Spirit Guides

Jaguar

Jaguar represents power, grace, and stealth. Jaguar teaches us the benefits of silence, concentration, and deep contemplation. Having enhanced physical abilities to feel and see its prey, Jaguar inspires us to be more sensitive to the people around us. With its eerie unyielding stare, the spirit of the Jaguar leads to a greater depth of vision and inner knowledge. Able to bring down prey many times its own size, Jaguar reflects power beyond the individual, a power enhanced by the intimate connection with all, the spirit, and imminent rebirth.

Monkey

Monkey represents perseverance, fluidity in motion, and balance. Monkey teaches us to adjust our course quickly when confronted with new information. A brilliant shape-shifter, Monkey prompts us to explore who we are and who we choose to be. Intelligent and adaptable, the spirit of the Monkey instructs us to reject rigid thinking and to be open to new perspectives, approaches, and experiences. A naturally curious and social creature, Monkey encourages learning, creative problem solving, and communicating in a concise and straightforward manner.

Raccoon

Raccoon represents disguise, dexterity, and adaptability. Raccoon teaches us how to be dexterous in the many faces of self we reveal. Disguised by its mask, the spirit of the Raccoon is not one of a thief, but rather one of mystery, a tool of transformation allowing us to achieve altered states for healing and magick. Having powerful nimble claws, Raccoon encourages us to be creative with our hands, and its ability to live anywhere reminds us to be flexible and adaptable in any situation we find ourselves in.

Squirrel

Squirrel represents trust, thrift, and preparedness. Squirrel teaches us to gather resources and prepare for the future without accumulating things from the past, such as worries and fears. A very active and energetic animal, Squirrel reminds us that in our quest to achieve our goals we need to take time to socialize and rest. With much of its time spent gathering and storing food, the spirit of the Squirrel informs us of the importance of balance between giving and receiving. Able to scurry up the side of a tree to evade a predator, Squirrel cautions us that danger is best avoided by climbing to a higher place.

Red Fox

Red Fox represents wisdom, invisibility, and discretion. Red Fox teaches us to be in harmony with our surroundings, through stillness and quiet we can blend in almost to the point of invisibility. With its highly developed sense of smell, Red Fox encourages us to sniff out every situation and person, avoiding those that we sense are trouble. Using its keen eyesight to hunt under the cover of darkness, the spirit of the Red Fox encourages us to see beyond our present situation and into the realm of spirit. Mentally agile, Red Fox guides us to rely on the power of our instincts and to freely call on our creative force.

It is only with the heart that one can see rightly; what is essential is invisible to the eye. —Antoine de Saint-Exupéry

house
of light
and
shadow

one

Daire

I wake to a room gone suddenly bright as Axel calls to me from his place by the door.

He pauses. Allowing time for me to gather myself, begin the slow crawl from slumber, before he makes his way to my bedside. His approach heralded by the soft hum of his breath rising and falling—the muffled hush of his feet crossing the smooth limestone floor.

His voice is a melody.

His movements an inspired choreography.

Still, when he stands by my side and places a tentative hand on my shoulder, I shrink from his touch and squinch my eyes shut. Stretching back to the dream where I cling to the memory of Dace's embrace. The sweep of his fingers moving over my flesh . . . the press of his lips meeting mine . . . desperate to lose myself in the glittering burn of his kaleidoscope eyes, reflecting my image thousands of times. Preferring the fantasy of Dace and me blissfully reunited at the Enchanted Spring, to the barren truth that awaits me.

"Daire, please. I know you're awake." Axel keeps his tone light, as though he's not the least bit annoyed by the game. "I will gladly sit here all day if that's what it takes." He claims a space on my mattress and waits for me to acknowledge him.

"You have the patience of a saint," I snap, reluctantly forfeiting the dream and accepting it for the ghost that it is. My eyes widening at the sight of Axel's anxious lavender gaze. Caught by the way it darkens to a deep stormy amethyst, before turning as clear and luminous as the day we first met.

The day our first words were spoken, formalities exchanged.

The day he swept me into his arms and rocketed me high into the sky. Piercing through the glorious silken spun web that yielded to a world of bright golden light.

So unlike the prior times—once deep underwater—once in a haunted Moroccan square—back when I was naïve enough to disregard the events as coincidence.

"I'm hardly a saint." His fingers spear through his shock of blond hair that swoops over his brow and falls in loose curls past his cheek. A move I've observed countless times, and yet, it's no less enchanting than the first. The platinum strands seamlessly blending into a complexion so fair, smooth, and translucent, I can't help but think (and not for the first time) that between the pastel eyes and porcelain skin, he appears so exquisite, so strikingly angelic, the only things missing are a halo and wings.

"If not a saint, then an angel, perhaps?" The question hangs heavy between us, not nearly as jokey as it might seem on the surface. Here in the Upperworld, anything is possible, and I'm eager to get to the truth of this strange situation I find myself in. "Or a spirit guide, maybe? Perhaps even *my* spirit guide?"

My gaze narrows on his as I silently ponder the unspoken questions:

Am I a convalescent or a captive?

Is he saving me or enslaving me?

Assured by the way he flinches, the way he tears his gaze away, that he heard the thoughts as well as the words.

"What if I told you I was none of those things?"

"Then I'd suspect you were lying," I say in a voice that's strong and sure. Wanting him to know that while I may be at a physical disadvantage, dependent on his willingness to take care of me and tend to my wounds, my will is still strong. My days as an invalid are nearing an end.

He lowers his chin, sending a tumble of blond curls sailing over his forehead, down past the finely sculpted bridge of his nose, before landing at the perfect bow of his lips. "If you insist on a label, and clearly you do, then I guess you could say I'm a Mystic." He runs his palms down the crisp white tunic he wears.

"A Mystic?" My tone is as stark as my face.

He nods, making great study of the abstract, Georgia O'Keeffe–style painting of a vibrant blue lake on the far side of the room, before settling on the small, glass-tiled pool where I often bathe in a modest white gown as Axel rinses the suds from my shoulders and hair.

"Define Mystic," I say. Despite a number of prior attempts, this is the most I've ever gotten out of him, and I plan to push it as far as I can.

"One who is initiated into esoteric mysteries." He turns to me, clearly pleased with his explanation, but I'm far from satisfied.

"Would you care to elaborate, or are you being purposely vague?" I lift my chin, quirk a brow, surprised to find my sarcasm tested by the shock of his luminous grin. A grin that begins at the tip of his chin and creeps all the way to the haphazard part in his hair. A grin so open, kind, and authentic, it takes all of my will to curb the impulse to return it.

"I'm being purposely vague, there's no use denying it. So now, if the interrogation is over, perhaps we can talk about you?" Misreading my silence for surrender, he leans closer. "How are you feeling?" he asks, studying me with a concerned eye and a cool palm that travels from my brow to my cheek. Searching for signs of the fever and chills that have plagued me since I arrived in this place.

"The interrogation is *never* over. You should know that by now." I pull away from his touch, striving for a stern voice and the expression to match. Resolved to get at least a few of the answers I seek. "What exactly is a Mystic?" I demand.

He shutters his eyes, sighing when he says, "I'm afraid it's of a scope that is far beyond human comprehension."

"Try me." I frown. Glare. Commit to waiting for however long it takes to get him to properly answer me. But all I get in return is a view of Axel's grin. "C'mon, Axel," I plead. "Why won't you tell me what it means? Is everyone in the Upperworld a Mystic? And if so, where are they? Why haven't I seen anyone but you the whole time I've been here?"

He commits to the silence, leaving the questions to hang heavy between us.

"Fine." I breathe a frustrated sigh. "But don't think this is over. You can evade me for now, but I'll find out eventually. You're not the only stubborn one around here." I do my best to rebuff the lure of his charm, but it's no use. Even when he's not smiling, chucking a self-conscious hand through his hair, or engaging in any of his other well-practiced gestures from the "Handbook of Disarming Moves," he radiates such an abundance of genuine kindness, benevolence, and undeniable charisma, it's not long before I fold. "So, in the spirit of cooperation—which, by the way, is something you could stand to learn a thing or two about—I will answer your question by saying my fever has finally broke."

I watch as his fingers move from his lap to my cheek and then back to his lap. Captured by the way his movements cast the most glorious veil of light, bearing no hint of darkness or shadow.

"And my memory is returning," I add, noting the fleeting flicker of worry that crosses his face as his gaze returns to the painting.

"And exactly what do these memories reveal?" he asks, his voice as quiet and uncertain as I've ever heard.

I hesitate, needing a moment to decide what to say. Torn between the desire to pretend to know more than I do—if for no other reason than to gain some semblance of an upper hand—and admitting I know very little in the hope that he'll finally explain how he came to find me dying in the Lowerworld with my own athame turned against me. The double-edged blade bisecting my heart as Cade Richter moved to stake claim on my soul.

"I know there was a struggle. I know that I lost. And I was hoping you could fill in the blanks." I stare hard at his profile, willing him to turn to me, acknowledge me, but for the longest time, he favors the wall. "Fine," I say. "Keep your secrets for now. It's not like I won't find out eventually. But, if nothing else, can you please just tell me whether or not Dace is okay? I'm thinking that if I'm here in the Upperworld with you, then everyone in the Middleworld probably assumes that I'm dead. Which means that the prophecy was averted. Which also means that Dace is alive— that I was able to save him. *Right?*"

Axel clamps his lips so tightly it takes all of my will to keep from grabbing hold of his shoulders and shaking him until he responds. Allowing an annoyingly long drag of time to loll before he says, "I'm not keeping secrets, Daire. It's just I see no point in reliving the past when the present awaits."

"It's the past that got me here!" I cry, instantly regretting the hysterical ring to my words. I'm getting worked up. I need to rein it in. Need to rebuild my strength. These emotional outbursts never result in anything good. "How long have I been here?" I ask, casually broaching the question as though I'm only mildly curious. My attempts at keeping track have left me confused. Most of my time is spent sleeping, and the light seeping through the curtain-covered window never seems to change all that much, making it impossible to count the succession of days.

"Linear time does not exist here." Axel shrugs. "But then you already knew that." He brings a hand close to my chest, ready to move on to more pressing concerns. "May I?" His hand hovers uncertainly, awaiting permission to proceed, despite the fact that as my only caretaker this is hardly the first time he's done this.

I nestle my cheek against the pile of downy pillows with soft silken cases he's placed under my head. Embarrassed by the rush of blood that creeps up my neck and floods my cheeks as he loosens my robe until my wound is exposed.

"It's healing nicely." He skims a finger along the jagged, puckered line of angry red flesh he coaxed back together with his platinum needle and spool of golden thread. His touch reverberating straight through my core, all the way to the invisible network of scars hidden under the surface, where he worked his magick and reassembled my heart.

"How soon can I return?" I ask. It's the same question I always ask.

And like always, Axel defers. Grabbing a small glass jar from the nightstand, he repeats his usual mantra of "Not yet," as he removes the lid and places it on the glass-topped table beside me. "But soon . . . very soon . . ."

He dips a finger into the fragrant blue ointment, about to apply it to the wound, when I catch him at the wrist and push his hand away.

"I don't want it to fade," I say, rendered nearly breathless from the effort it takes to resist him. Fielding his skeptical look, I add, "Now that I remember, I can't afford to forget what landed me here."

He mutters under his breath. Some archaic language with slurred vowels and hard consonants I don't understand. Then he abandons the jar, pulls my robe closed, and with a sigh of resignation, says, "If you're entertaining thoughts of revenge, I'd advise you to quit. You'll only lower yourself to Cade's level, squelch your potential, and establish yourself as his equal. Is that what you want?"

"It's not revenge that motivates me." I clench my hands into fists, my actions betraying my words. "It's love. Dace is my only concern." At the mention of his name, my heart clenches in pain. Imagining the grief he must be feeling, not knowing the full truth of what really happened that night.

And while the exact events may continue to elude me as well, one thing is sure: I saved him.

I died so that Dace could live.

Except that I'm not really dead.

He just thinks that I am.

"Best not to think about that either." Axel turns his back in dismissal. "You need to get well. That's why you're here." He scoops an uncertain hand through his hair.

"Is that the *only* reason I'm here?" I prop myself higher onto my pillows, and stare hard at his back. It's an uncomfortable subject, but I need to know once and for all.

Why did he save me?

And what does he expect in return?

"What are you really asking me, Daire?" He faces me with a gaze so open, so direct, I'm instantly silenced. No longer sure how to phrase what I most want to say.

Is he a crazy stalker who took advantage of a moment of weakness in order to abduct me?

Or is he truly a Good Samaritan, a Mystic, as he claims, with only my best interests at heart?

While he's always treated me with kindness and respect, I can't help but suspect that his motives aren't entirely altruistic.

We fall into an uncomfortable, sagging silence. The kind that used to spur me to say something stupid, crack a dumb joke, but no more. I'm no longer that girl. The new Daire is patient.

She's willing to wait.

She has no other choice.

But when Axel makes for the door, I instantly regret having pushed it too far. He can't leave. Not yet. He's not the only one with an agenda here.

I lift myself until I'm almost fully upright, making an exaggerated show of breathing heavily and gritting my teeth. And just as I'd hoped, an instant later he's right back beside me.

Patience. You can do this. It's like Paloma taught you: Think from the end.

"Don't push it, Daire." Axel's fingers grab hold of my shoulders as he lowers me back toward my pillows. "Just because the fever broke doesn't mean that you're healed."

I nod as though I wouldn't dream of questioning his wisdom, the irrefutable truth of his words. "I guess I'm just feeling a little restless," I say, aiming for chagrin and hoping I'm not overdoing it. "I'm not used to being bedridden and weak, and that makes me a pretty poor patient." I make a guilty face. "It's just that, if I've any hope of leaving this place, I'll need to work on regaining my strength. The longer I lie here, the more my muscles will deteriorate. So, maybe I could try to walk for a bit. What do you think?"

I hold my breath and shoot him my most hopeful look, aiming to convince without coming off as rehearsed.

When he doesn't reply fast enough for my liking, I struggle to sit up again. Grimacing and gritting until I'm propped flushed and breathless against the headboard, begging, "Please. I need to get up and move around—take a short walk. But I need your help. I can't do it alone." I force myself to swallow the lie, but the bitterness sticks to my tongue. "C'mon, Axel, didn't you promise to heal me, rehabilitate me? Isn't that what you said?"

His brow knits, his lips pull into a frown, and I know that I've won. That he sees what I want him to see—me, clammy, breathless, and pale—making demands that betray my abilities.

I suck in a lungful of air, curl my fingers around the side of the mattress, and attempt to swing my legs over the edge. The sight of it causing him to say, "Clearly nothing I say will change your mind."

"Clearly," I whisper, indulging a small, secret smile when he secures an arm around my waist and eases me to my feet until my body is wedged hard against his.

His touch providing a reassuring strength that leaves me uneasy, reminding me of the moment he saved me. The way his lips pressed hard against mine as he snatched me from the fingers of death—restoring my life with a kiss.

The question is why?

Why me?

And, more importantly, now that he's saved me, why is he hiding me?

Not a single person has dropped by the whole time I've been here. And often, when he thinks I'm asleep, I watch through slitted lids as he peers through the curtains, fingers twitching nervously at the thought of being seen.

While there's no denying the amount of care and devotion he's paid me, his reluctance to answer my questions leads me to believe his motives aren't nearly as pure as they seem. That they have less to do with his inner moral compass, and more to do with the simple fact that, for whatever reason, he couldn't bear to lose me.

Like he has a personal stake in my being.

Like I mean far more to him than I rightfully should.

A suspicion that leaves me uneasy.

My heart belongs to Dace. And if what I suspect of Axel is true, then he's turned my life into a debt I can never repay.

"Do you think you could manifest a cane?" I ask, and despite having seen him work his magick plenty of times, I still stare in unabashed wonder when a beautiful, carved-ivory cane instantly appears in my hand.

"I hope no elephants were injured in the making of this?" I grip the handle hard, testing its strength by shifting my full weight upon it.

"It came from the ether just as it will return to the ether as soon as you're through with it." He loosens his grip on my waist and allows me some space, while he hovers nearby, ready to catch me at the first hint of trouble. "So, now that you're up, where do you go from here?" His eyes glint in a way I can't read.

Is it amusement? Pride? Is it possible that he's on to me—sees right through my charade?

"You gotta have a goal, Daire. You can't hit a target you can't see."

"The door." I tip my head toward the large wooden doors with elaborate carvings as though I just now thought of it. As though I haven't spent every waking moment imagining my palms pressed hard against them, pushing toward freedom.

I slide a slow foot before me, careful to keep my weight evenly distributed. No use injuring myself further just to prove a point. Aware of Axel shadowing me, his moves perfectly mirroring mine. Until the next step when my gait falters, my legs quiver in protest, and he slips a steady arm around me and props me hard against his chest.

"You'll get there, Daire. Not to worry," he says, as I sigh in defeat, allowing my body to sag in surrender as he lowers me back to my sickbed and tucks the blankets around me. "It's just going to take a little longer than you'd like, that's all."

I give an obedient nod and slide my lids shut. Appearing to be lulled back to sleep by his whispered promise of *soon, very soon* . . .

Until the door closes behind him and I leap from my bed.

two

Dace

Dark.

The word sounds in my head. Drums in my ears. Jolting me out of the sweet anesthetized void, and back to the harsh glare of wakefulness again.

Like a leaky faucet, it pauses, gathers, and then drops once again.

Dark.

It's the first word I've heard for . . . how many days? It's impossible to tell. With no trace of sun or moon, with only a dreary canopy of sticky gray sludge hanging overhead, time isn't marked here in the way that I'm used to.

Still, I'm glad for the company. Glad I'm no longer left to fend for myself in this strange, foreign land.

I try to crack an eye open. See who has joined me. But a thick coating of crud has glued my lids shut, and it takes a bit of digging with bloodstained fingers to break it all up.

"Who's there?" I call, my voice coarse and strange. A result of the festering wound on my neck. "Show yourself!" I roll to my left and survey my surroundings, only to find no one there. Then I roll to my right and confirm the same thing.

It's just me.

Only me.

With nothing but this bleak and barren landscape for company.

Dark.

I heave a deep sigh and flop onto my back. Tempted to laugh at my foolishness, but the mirth just won't come. It died along with all the other virtues I once held in high regard.

Things like faith, hope, charity, and love have no place here.

Though love was surprisingly stubborn. It put up a good fight.

Long after the others were lost, it's love that held on.

Determined to stick well past the point when my heart became a cold, bitter stone.

Long past the point when my memories of Daire railed against me, turning into an enemy existing solely to taunt me. A crafty, cunning adversary with a surplus of patience, willing to wait for just the right moment—when exhaustion turns to despair—to strike hard and fast. Able to devastate with a few happy images that are welcome at first—quick takes of Daire laughing, Daire loving, before fast-forwarding straight to the moment when her eyes shone with fear once she saw how I'd changed. Accurately guessing the embarrassing truth of the reckless choice that I made. How I sacrificed my soul in an attempt to save her, by becoming like Cade.

Still, it was her face I clung to when death came to claim me.

It was her face that cushioned the fall.

But now that I'm no longer at home with the living—now that I've no place among the dead—it's her face that haunts me.

Daire is gone.

Dead and gone.

In my attempt to save her, I failed her. And now, in the place where my soul once thrived, lives only regret.

Dark.

I bite hard on my tongue. Cover my ears with blood-caked hands. Still the word sounds again.

And that's when I get it.

That's when I realize that it doesn't sound from outside of me—it's a word conceived in my head.

The sound repeats. Becoming more insistent each time, as the enormity of my situation becomes clear.

The darkness it speaks of is thrumming inside me.

My fingers slip down my torso, seeking the blood-crusted gash where I plunged Daire's athame deep into my gut, willing to sacrifice my own life in order to end my brother's. An act of martyrdom ultimately denied me when, at the very last second, Coyote stepped in. Catching Cade's departing soul in his snout and forcing it back into him, while allowing mine to drift free . . .

Still, we are connected in miraculous ways, and one thing's for sure—if Cade lives, I live.

Or at least some semblance of me.

Dark.

There's no use pretending. No one will find me. I will rot in this place and I deserve nothing less.

I shutter my eyes, fold my hands over my chest, and wait for the numbing wave of unconsciousness again.

three

Daire

I've barely cleared the bed when my head grows dizzy and my vision swirls with stars so insistent, I'm forced to grab hold of the nightstand and wait for the moment to pass. Dismayed to find myself nearly as helpless as I was with Axel. Guess it wasn't all just an act.

Still, I can't let that stop me. Can't afford to be swayed by the pain. Driven by my need to break out of here and ensure Cade stays contained, I press on until I'm putting a solid distance between me and the bed.

Whoever said that pain is a great teacher was spot-on. I've grown more in my time here than I did in the past sixteen years.

I make for the armoire on the far side of the room, hoping my clothes are still there. But other than some filmy, white, ethereal gown with thin straps, a square neck, and swirls of light beading cascading down the front, the cupboard is empty.

I jerk the gown from the hanger and frown. The style veers so far from my usual look of skinny jeans, scrunchy boots, and clingy tank tops worn under my favorite green army jacket, I'm reluctant to try it. It's the kind of dress usually reserved for debutant balls or weddings, which does nothing to lessen my fears over Axel's intentions.

Clearly he manifested it for me. I'm the only one here.

The question is why?

Did he really plan to make me his bride?

With no other option, I lose the robe and tug on the gown until its silky white fabric skims over my hips and flutters well past my knees, before landing with a flounce at my ankles. Then I heave a deep breath and peer into the mirror, shocked to see the stark image staring back. Axel has taken great care to steer me away from all reflective surfaces, and up until now, I had no interest in looking. But now that I've started, I can't seem to stop. And I wonder if my family and friends will notice just how much I've changed.

My hair is darker. The color of my lips deeper. Which in turn makes my skin appear even paler. And though my cheeks are sharper, far more defined and hollow than they once were, it's the eyes that capture me most. The irises deepened into a dark feverish emerald that burns with a craving for revenge.

Despite telling Axel that it's love that drives me, my need for vengeance runs a close race.

I continue the inventory. Noting a body that's thinner, weaker, though not nearly as battered as when I arrived. Other than the vivid red scar peeking free of the gown's deep neckline, there's no sign of the violence Cade did me. The kind of heinous acts he will never get the chance to repeat. I will learn from my failures, and use those same lessons to fuel my success. And if it's the last thing I do, I *will* retaliate. I will see that Cade pays.

My reverie broken by the sound of muffled footsteps coming from the other side of the door, I freeze in place. Fearing for what Axel might do if he finds me like this.

If he truly does have my best interests at heart, I imagine he'll be incredibly hurt to learn I've deceived him.

And if not . . .

A moment later, the sound fades and I hurry the search for my belongings. Relieved to find the soft buckskin pouch Paloma gave me, and the key on the long black cord that symbolizes Dace and my love. Though sadly, Django's black jacket, one of the few tangible pieces I had of my dad, has gone missing. Either left behind in the Lowerworld, or so damaged from my battle with Cade, Axel disposed of it along with the rest of my things.

I slip the talismans over my head and glance inside the pouch. Ensuring the stone Raven, the Raven feather, Django's Bear, the small aquamarine I gleaned from the falls, and the polished turquoise heart Dace gave me as my Secret Santa gift, are all there, though doubting their magick remains.

Paloma insisted the pouch be kept carefully guarded, and well within reach. Claimed no other person must ever look inside it, or its power will be lost.

Not only has it been out of my sight since the night I arrived, but I'm willing to bet Axel peeked the first chance he got.

Nevertheless, I tuck the pouch inside the dress, then nestle the small gold key underneath. Relishing the harsh chill of metal on flesh. The way it clings, cold and alien, to the scar that bisects my chest.

Another reminder of all that I've lost.

As dressed and ready as I'll ever be, I rush to the window and peek past the curtains. Ensuring it's clear before I move for the door and press my palms hard against it just like I envisioned countless times before.

Except this time when I give the doors a good shove, they remain stubbornly fixed.

I push again.

And again.

Thrusting my body wildly against the ornately carved wood, only to discover they've been bolted from the outside.

I race for the window, in search of a latch, but find none.

I grasp the ceramic pitcher Axel uses for water, and slam it hard against the pane, only to learn the glass is shatterproof.

I race to all four corners of the room, desperately seeking a way out, but there is no escape.

I'm trapped.

Imprisoned.

My worst fear confirmed.

Axel is both saving me and enslaving me.

He was my only way in—and now my only way out.

I slump to the floor in defeat. Left with no other option but to change back into the robe, return to bed, and continue the ruse until I come up with a much better plan. A plan that could take days, maybe even weeks to evolve. Yet, with no other choice, I heave myself up, grab the dress from the hem, and begin to slip it over my head. Dragging the buckskin pouch along with it, until I notice the trail of warmth it leaves in its wake.

It's a sign. I've no doubt. Wouldn't be the first time the amulet sought to get my attention.

I tug the dress back in place, and fold my fingers tightly around the pouch. Aware of my damaged heart pounding hard against my chest as I call upon the spirit of many generations of Santos ancestors. Summoning the collective wisdom of Valentina, Esperanto, Piann, Mayra, Maria, Diego, Gabriela, Alejandro, and Django, before I go quiet and still and wait for a sign of their presence.

Their message promptly delivered in frantically whispered words that sound in my head.

What lies outside of you is no match for what lies within you. You must be willing to do that which you believe you're not capable of.

While the meaning is clear, the problem is, I'm no longer sure what I'm capable of.

I thought I could avert the prophecy, and maybe I did. But Axel's refusal to discuss it leaves me uneasy.

I also thought I was ready to slay Cade—ready and willing and perfectly able. And though the memory is still hazy, there's no denying the way I hesitated the moment I pressed the knife to his throat. Watching him bleed under my hand was nothing like I expected. It was less like slaying a beast, and more like murdering a human.

It's a mistake I won't make again.

Though one thing is clear, if I want to return to Enchantment I'll have to act fast. And while it's tempting to forge a less resistant path by trying to convince Axel to release me, I can't risk it not working.

I need a plan that's solid and sure.

I need a plan that doesn't rely on Axel's consent.

You must be willing to do that which you believe you're not capable of.

I reach for the heavy wooden chair fronting the desk, and drag it to the other side of the door where I press my back flush to the wall, and wait.

Envisioning the scenario from start to finish.

Seeing myself fulfill the act without hesitation.

Without an ounce of regret.

Resolved to do whatever it takes to get out of this place.

four

Dace

When the murkiness gives way to darkness, I can't help but spread my arms wide and embrace it like the savior it is.

Longing to melt into it.

Disappear in it.

Hardly able to believe that after all of this time, after all of the mental anguish of remembering, deliverance has come.

My breath slackens. My pulse dims. With the soul already gone, it won't be long before the body and mind are claimed too.

But when the darkness above me narrows and shifts, I realize the mistake. What I mistook for salvation, is merely a shadow.

Funny how just when I gave up on being discovered, someone has found me.

"Well, I'll be. If it isn't Dace Whitefeather. It is you, isn't it?"

The voice is familiar. The face is obscured.

"So this is where you've been all this time. Should've known you weren't dead."

I swipe a hand across my brow, roll into a sitting position, and take a full inventory. Counting a cheap black suit, a severely starched white shirt frayed at the collar and cuffs, and a ridiculously skinny black tie.

"Should've known she was lying."

He clucks his tongue against the roof of his mouth, as my gaze drops to his feet. Noting worn shoes that, despite a recent polish, are pocked with a cross-hatching of scuff marks.

"This was supposed to have been taken care of weeks ago. Now the whole thing's delayed. She'll pay for this. Make no mistake. She will not get away with it. There's a fiery place in hell with her name on it."

The last bit prompts the curtain to rise in the theater of my mind as a long-ago slide show unspools. The face in my memory no longer an exact match for the one that looms before me, but recognizable all the same in the way of the long, crooked slant of a nose that hangs like a hook toward a pair of bloodless mean lips turned crueler by time. But the eyes are the real attraction, just as they were back then. Still wild. Still crazy. Still hinting at the uncorked fanaticism lurking within.

Suriel Youngblood. Phyre's doomsayer father.

"Never send a girl to do a man's job." He shakes his head and rakes a hand through his carefully coiffed and greased hair, before he slips a large black duffle from his shoulder and drops it to the dirt where he kneels down beside it in a chorus of cracking knee joints. He retrieves a brand-new Bible with a white leather cover with one hand, and an iron stake along with what can only be described as an oversized mallet with the other.

I remain rooted in place. Watching with only the mildest curiosity, as he approaches me with his collection of unfathomable tools. Suddenly made aware of just how abnormal I've become.

A normal person wouldn't lie back and wait.

A normal person would take one look at this madman and choose to either fight or flee.

But I'm no longer normal.

No longer human.

I'm empty.

Soulless.

And if he's here to release me, I have no plans to stop him.

"Been down here demon hunting all day," he says, as though I deserve an explanation for his crashing my party. "Usually there's no shortage of them. This part of the Middleworld rarely disappoints. The deeper the dimension, the bleaker the landscape, the better the bounty. I've been at it off and on for years. These are some of the best slaying grounds that I've found. Though today's been quiet. Must've walked for miles before I stumbled upon you." He shakes his head, pulls his lips back, and hocks a wad of spit that lands smack between us. "Second I saw you I knew exactly why I was called here. He works in mysterious ways. He does indeed. Just like Him to present such a monumental find in such a beautifully simplistic way."

While I have no idea what he's going on about, I don't care enough to ask him to elaborate. I just lie back and watch as he stoops by my side. Face contorted in crazed and earnest conviction, as he presses the Bible hard to my chest and holds it in place with the spike's razor-sharp tip. A stake that's filthy, well-used. Bearing a heavy crusting of what can only be the remains of his previous kills.

"You think I'm a vampire?" I peer at him through narrowed lids, amused by the idea. I always knew he was delusional, but I guess I never realized just how deeply disturbed he really is.

Taking great care to center the mallet's fat head flat against the stake, he throws his head back and enters into a loud and thunderous sermon that roars through the land. Same kind of zealous Armageddon talk he used to preach about on the street corners back when I was a kid. Back when everyone either rolled their eyes and laughed or chose to hurry past.

Guess I never listened well enough to realize that all of this time, the sermons were directed at me.

Convinced that my entrance into the world marked the beginning of the End Times he's been preaching about for the better part of his life, he's spent the last sixteen years planning my demise.

"Vampire, demon, sorcerer, skinwalker—what's the difference?" His eyes roll skyward, as though addressing an invisible friend. "Satan, Lucifer, the devil, the deceiver, the fallen, Beelzebub, Mephistopheles—they're merely titles, names. Evil is as evil does. There is no use making distinctions. All you need to know is that the Last Days are upon us. The signs are everywhere! Twice now, a flock of ravens fell from above. And it was only days ago when the sky opened wide and purged a torrent of fire."

I close my eyes and groan. Wishing he'd just shut the hell up and do it already. But when he continues to drone on and on, raging about six-toed cats, and a whole slew of other superstitious non-sense, I can't help but say, "I hate to break it to you, Suriel, but not a single thing you've mentioned is a sign of anything other than my brother showing off his impressive supply of magick tricks."

If he heard me, he chooses to ignore it. His voice pitches higher and higher until it overrides mine. "The Shining Days of Glory are among us! Sinners will burn—the righteous ascend! But in order for those glorious days to commence, evil must be slayed, and that son, means you . . ."

He repositions the stake so it's resting dead center over my chest. The tip gouging into a holy book he's grossly misinterpreted. And when he flings the mallet back and slams it down hard, I watch in fascination, as though it's happening to someone other than me.

The stake screws into the book, resulting in a muffled groan as it gouges a hole in the white leather cover. Grinding its way through shiny gold lettering until it breaks through and begins shredding the pages inside.

I wait for the sting of the razor-sharp tip to impale my flesh, but there's still an inch of paper stretching between me and deliv-erance. The progress much slower than I'd anticipated.

He pulls away, centers his hand once again, and I squeeze my eyes shut, eager for the release soon to come. Having no idea where I'll end up. What sort of place would admit someone as dark and soulless as me? Yet clinging to the dream of redemption—of landing in the place where Daire rests.

He shoves his knee hard against my rib cage, pinning me down as though I might try to flee. Then he returns to the grim business of slaying. Pounding the stake over and over, the effort causing fat beads of sweat to pool on his brow, as his arm grows shaky, his aim poor.

"You can do this," I whisper, figuring he could use the encouragement. "I completely understand and I won't try to fight you."

He drives the stake harder until my nostrils jam with the stench of metal burning through paper. His voice rising, eyes rolling in his head, as he cries, "Good shall overcome evil! I will drive the Word straight into your soul. Though make no mistake, it's too late to save it. There is no Grace for a blasphemer like you!"

Yeah, whatever. Just make it quick. Daire is out there somewhere, and I really need to find her . . .

I heave my chest higher, hoping to speed things along. Biting back a grin at the first pinch of contact, the moment when the sting of sharp metal grinds into my flesh.

Won't be much longer . . .

The stake gouges harder, deeper, slowing only slightly when it butts against bone.

I grit my teeth hard, commit to the pain, and prepare for the end. One more blow should see that it's done.

His sour breath blasts hard against my cheeks as he grasps a fistful of my hair and drags my face closer to his. "Look at me, sinner!" He shrieks, flecks of saliva showering my cheeks. "I want to look into the face of evil. I want to see the life force snuffed from your demon eyes!"

I do as he says, hoping it'll speed things along. My desperate gaze meeting his crazed one, only to watch as he screams, "Where the hell did it go?" He jerks my head higher, ripping a chunk of hair straight from my scalp. "What the hell happened to it? What did you do with it?" He butts his nose against mine.

"I don't know what you're talking about." I groan, frustrated, breathless, aware of a warm stream of blood surging down my sides. I heave my torso up, keeping it taut, as I thrust deeper into the stake.

If he won't end this, I will.

"Your soul!" He screams, waving the mallet carelessly above me. "What did you do with your soul? Where is it? What have you done with it?"

Oh. That.

I close my eyes in defeat. Sink deeper into the dirt. "It's gone. Lost. I heaved a last breath, and it went. But then I heaved another breath and . . ." There's no use explaining it. No need to tell him about my connection to Cade. And how the mere act of Coyote saving his soul has kept me alive without mine. I press my cheek to the ground, saying, "I have no idea where it went."

Suriel grunts. Shifts his weight off, and gets to his feet. Muttering a long stream of curses as he slams his tools back into his bag and makes to leave.

"Wait! Come back!" I shout, staring in anguish at his retreating form. "Finish what you started! You can't stop now—not after coming all this way!"

"It's the *soul* that I need. You're no good to me now." He shoots me a look of disdain. "The Last Days are upon us—I shall not be defeated! If I can't snuff your soul, I'll get Cade's. You were both conjured by evil—as far as I'm concerned, you're one and the same."

He leaves me with blood seeping from my chest—hope seeping from my heart. My dream of being reunited with Daire gone, just like *that*.

Suriel may be crazy, but he's smarter than most people think. Able to see the very thing most everyone else has sought to deny—the mystical connection between Cade and me.

I roll to my side, steeple my palms tightly against the wound at my chest.

I was so close. So damn close.

Yet, while it may not have ended in the way that I wished, there is comfort in knowing it's just a matter of time before it will.

When Cade goes, I go.

Maybe then I'll find peace.

Maybe then I'll find Daire.

five

Xotichl

"It doesn't seem right."

"What doesn't?" Auden reaches for my shoulder and gives it a squeeze. Temporarily abandoning his search for the perfect parking place to comfort me.

"This." I flip a hand toward the windshield. "Coming to the Rabbit Hole. After everything that's happened, it feels wrong to hang out here. "

"We can leave if you want." Auden's touch is gentle, though his tone betrays his concern. "But I thought you said you wanted to come here so we could keep an eye on things?"

"I did." I heave a deep exhale. "And while I still think it's important to maintain a presence, without Daire and Dace, it's just not the same." My voice hitches. My throat clamps on a sob. It's been doing that a lot lately. Every time I think of my long-lost friends. Which is pretty much every second of every day.

Lost.

It's the only word I can use.

Lost is bad, no getting around it, but dead is much worse.

The night Daire made it snow, on Christmas Eve, I was sure she was gone for good. The snow was so vibrant, falling in a rainbow of hues, I assumed it was her final good-bye, and mistook it for her elegy.

But now I'm no longer sure. Guided by something that's more than a feeling, stronger than a hunch—a sort of inner knowing that Daire and Dace are still out there. Somewhere. It's the kind of gut instinct I've learned to hone and trust. Though without any physical proof, I'm reluctant to voice it. The few times I've tried resulted in awkward pats on the arm, followed by empty words of encouragement. Everyone quick to placate the poor little blind girl who can't see what to everyone else is so clear.

They assume I live in a lonely world of darkness, but they couldn't be more wrong. While I may not see things the same way as the sighted, I'm able to grasp the kinds of things that for most remain hidden from view. The world is far richer, and much more vibrant than most people realize—a vibrating sphere of lush streams of color and pulsating swirls of energy.

Thoughts, feelings, music, people, animals, nature, inanimate objects—they're all made of energy. Modern physics has proven what the ancient mystics have known for eons. And thanks to my regular sessions with Paloma, I've witnessed it firsthand.

It was my mom's idea to seek help from Daire's *abuela*. Impressed by her reputation as a healer, she figured it was worth a try to see if Paloma could reverse the blindness that struck when I was a child. But while Paloma was unable to restore my sight, she did teach me how to access my inner vision, also known as blind sight. And after months of working together with only the smallest bits of progress, it all came together the day she asked Auden to join us.

I'll never forget the way she flattened my palm against a speaker she'd hooked up to Auden's guitar. How after he strummed a few chords, the most glorious burst of colors blazed into the space just before me.

Auden often jokes that he loved me first. That he fell for me the second he walked in the door and saw me waiting for him in

Paloma's office. At that very moment he knew he'd have to do something big to impress me, so he wooed me with song. Pouring all of his emotions into his guitar strings, hoping I'd be able to glean how he felt.

All I know is it worked. We've been together ever since.

It's funny how people always make a point to assure me that he's really, really cute. As if I can't see for myself.

As if I have no idea that his love for me glows in the sincerest shade of purple.

That his words are spoken in a deep and true orange.

And when he kisses me, the air swells with sparkling bubbles of pinks, silvers, and reds that swirl about the top of our heads.

It wasn't long after, when I started to see other things too. And while it was confusing at first, it didn't take long to determine that lies are always delivered in a dark, greasy yellow that clings to the person's lips long after they've silenced. While praise, when it's sincere, shines a bright shiny silver that showers the giver as well as the receiver. And the last few days, I've watched with concern as Paloma's sadness over Daire and Dace's absence has turned her usual benevolent shimmering blue energy into a dark, sludgy gray.

"I'm afraid it will never be the same, flower." Auden swerves into a space, kills the engine, and pulls me against him so tightly, the ribbing of his heavy wool sweater imprints on my cheek. His voice reduced to a whisper, his lips tickling the curve of my ear, he says, "But we have to go on. Whether we like it or not, we have to adjust." He kisses my temple, my cheek, my lips.

"And what about Cade?" The words are muffled against him but I know that he heard. "What if he shows up? What then?" I curl my fingers under the hem of his sweater, and flatten my palm against a warm patch of skin.

"I wouldn't worry about that." Auden leans into me, his lips teasing mine. "No one's seen him since that night. But if he does show, we're ready for him, right?"

I pull away and tilt my face toward his, relieved to see a stream of orange flowing from his mouth. He believes what he says. He's not trying to humor me.

"Just because *we* haven't seen him doesn't mean no one else has." My voice rings with certainty, despite having no tangible evidence with which to back it. "At the very least, I bet his creepy Coyote has seen him. And since his dad, Leandro, doesn't seem the slightest bit concerned, I can only assume he's seen him too. Besides, let's not forget that Cade is not just a demonic psychopath, he's also a complete and total egomaniac who would never deny himself the opportunity to gloat. It's one of his greatest pleasures. He pretty much lives for it."

Auden starts to speak, but he's stopped by a knock on the driver's side window, accompanied by a female voice calling, "Hey—any room for a third wheel?" A moment later the door opens and closes as Lita's energy fills the backseat of the car. "Sheesh, it's totally freezing out there." She claps her mitten-covered hands together in an attempt to warm herself up. "Makes me wonder if this snow will ever stop."

I sigh. Auden mumbles in agreement. And we all fall quiet again.

It's been snowing steadily since Christmas Eve, and even though we like to complain about it and all the inconveniences that go along with it, deep down inside we dread the day it will cease. As long as the flakes continue to fall, we have a connection to Daire. But if she doesn't return by the time the earth warms, the snow melts, and spring is sprung, well, what then?

"So, any news? Any news about, you know, anything?" Lita asks, reluctant to actually voice what all of us are thinking: *What happened? Where are they? Will we ever see them again?*

We've spent countless hours poring over the most minute details of that night. Attempting to piece it together and discover some hidden clue we might've missed at first glance. But the fact is, we all saw the same thing: Daire sprinting into the club, warning us to run, to get as far from the Rabbit Hole as we possibly could. The sky was bleeding fire, she said. The prophecy had begun. Her last words to me being: *"I'm going to stop this. Fix this. If it's the last thing I do."* Then she jerked free of my grip, made for the vortex, and no one ever saw her again.

I shake my head, clearing it of the memory as I twist toward Lita and say, "No news in the two hours since we last spoke." I do my best to chase it with a grin, though it doesn't come as easily as it should.

She breathes a sigh so heavy and deep, I'm instantly reminded of just how much, and how quickly she's changed. It wasn't long ago when she was the undisputed queen of Milagro High. The uber-popular, snooty, mean girl everyone openly admired and feared. The kind of girl who would never even consider acknowledging someone like me. But then Daire came along and brought us all together. Her arrival in Enchantment may have incited Cade's actions, but it also changed our lives in some really good ways.

"So, what do we do? How do we handle this?" Lita asks. The question chased by the click of her compact opening, followed by the sticky swish of her lip gloss wand moving over her lips.

"You're Milagro royalty, what would you suggest?" Auden laces his fingers with mine.

"Former royalty. I gave up the crown, remember?" Lita snaps the compact closed, and dumps it along with her lip gloss into the abyss of her purse.

"And look who's wearing it now," Auden says, and I know from the tone in his voice, the shift in the air, that Phyre is here.

Lita sniffs, gathers her stuff, and props open the door. "Good," she says. "Let her have it." She climbs out of the car. "If she wants everyone to notice her, I'll be the first in line. I don't trust that girl for a second, and I plan to watch her every move from this moment on. And, for the record, Daire didn't trust her either. Which means I'm going to do whatever it takes to figure out just what

she's up to—why she's back in Enchantment. If for no other reason than to honor Daire's memory."

"Don't do anything reckless," Auden warns.

"Who me? Reckless?" Lita laughs. Coming around to my door
when she says, "You coming, flower? We have reconnaissance
to do."

"Hey, I'm the only one who gets to call my flower, flower!"
Auden pulls me close and plants a sweet kiss on the top of my
head.

"That's probably for the best," Lita says. "It felt kinda weird.
Anyway, we better *vamanos*. We can't afford to miss the show
now that the main act is here."

"Right behind you," I say, as Auden and I slip free of the car.
Following Lita into the surreal swirl of the Rabbit Hole's energy.

six

Daire

I hate to admit it, but waiting is not a skill that comes naturally to me.

Although it starts off well enough, it's not long before I grow antsy. And once my body starts fidgeting, it's not long before my mind gets fidgety too. My head hosting a never-ending parade of self-defeating thoughts. Doubting my abilities. Questioning my strategy. Worried that I might've judged Axel too harshly. That I'm being paranoid. That I got it all wrong.

After all, he did save me.

He did stop Cade from stealing my soul.

Not to mention how he's cared for me, healed me, without once asking for anything in return.

And yet, every time the long list of possible misinterpretations stacks up against me, all I have to do is take one look at this creepy, bride-like gown that I'm wearing, and just like *that*, I'm resolved to go through with my plan.

Reminded of something Paloma once said, that patience is the companion of wisdom, I settle into waiting again. Using the time to scrutinize every last detail, all too aware that there's only one shot at getting this right. If I hesitate, if I falter even slightly, all will be lost.

Axel is bigger. Stronger. With magickal abilities that far surpass mine.

There's no room for mistakes.

The gravel crunches and shifts just outside the door.

The bolt groans and recedes.

I press against the wall, tighten my grip on the chair, and watch as the door opens wide and Axel crosses the limestone floor to my bed.

He calls out my name. Gently shakes the lump he's mistaken for me. Having no idea that I've repurposed my robe along with the stack of clean towels he left for my bath to resemble the sleeping version of me, until it collapses under his touch.

He turns, lavender gaze widening in confusion when he finds me lurking behind with the chair angled high.

"Daire?"

It's the last thing he says before I center the chair and heave it down hard on his head. Already racing toward freedom when he crumples into an unconscious heap at my feet, I spare one last look at his unmoving form, mouth a silent apology, and bolt the door firmly behind me.

seven

Xotichl

After countless laps around the club, Lita returns to our table, plunks her purse on an empty stool, claims the seat across from Auden and me, and says, "No sign of Cade. And believe me, I looked everywhere I could. Including Leandro's office, which was awkward to say the least, mostly because he was in there. I even checked the bathroom. I wouldn't put it past Cade to peek under the stalls. But nope, *nada, niente.*"

"And Phyre?" I lean toward her, straining to hear over the music.

"Phyre's just . . . Phyre. I mean, I get that she's gorgeous and all, but she's also completely weird and totally untrustworthy. Which is why I can't understand why everyone's so enamored with her."

"I'm not sure everyone sees her as weird and untrustworthy," I say, as Auden taps his thumb nervously against mine. A sure sign that he's more anxious about his meeting with the record exec than he lets on. "I think that's just us."

"Well, it wasn't all that long ago when Daire was new and no one liked her," Lita says. And before I can chime in with the reason, she adds, "Then again, that was mostly my fault since I pretty much turned everyone against her. Anyway, it sure would be nice if we could get some *new* boys in this town. You guys must be so tired of my third-wheel self always hanging around."

Auden and I both start to refute it, but Lita's quick to shush us.

"Oh, please. Don't even try to deny it. Believe me, I feel the same way. And I'd be more than willing to change it, but unfortunately this is Enchantment. Which means there's not one single datable boy in this town." She breathes a wistful sigh. "You know what this is?" She pauses, but it's not so we can guess, it's meant for dramatic effect. "This is my karma." She bumps her palm against the table for emphasis.

"Your karma for what?" I move closer to Auden and rest my head on his shoulder. Trying to temper his nerves with a nice wave of calm.

"For being a mega-bitch. For pegging everyone I didn't approve of as an uncool loser."

"You thought I was uncool?" Auden feigns dismay at her words.

"Well, being the lead singer in the only decent band in this town did give you a certain edge . . . but anyway, let's face it, I was a witch."

"You were, indeed," I say, seeing no point in denying what we already know.

"And I'm pretty sure I'm paying for all of that nastiness now."

"You're serious?" I laugh. I can't help it. While I definitely believe in karma, that's not really the best example of it.

"What's so funny?" Lita's energy flares, her tone is more than a little defensive. "It's true, what goes around comes around."

"So, what you're saying is that there are no new boys in Enchantment because you used to be really mean to everyone you deemed unworthy of you. It has nothing to do with Enchantment being a totally undesirable place to live, with falling house prices, no good job opportunities, and an evil family of Coyotes at the helm of it all."

Lita groans. "Well, when you put it like that, it sounds a lot less like karma, and a lot more like narcissism. Like I think the world revolves around me."

"Not the world," Auden says. "Just Enchantment."

"Well, it used to revolve around me, or at least that's what I thought. It wasn't that long ago when I branded Dace as a giant dork, I was hating on Daire, and Cade Richter rocked my world. And now that I've awakened, I can't help but feel like I missed out all those years by not giving people like you, Auden, and Dace a chance. I was so caught up in my image, and being popular, and all . . ." Her voice fades as she shifts in her seat. "And yeah, as much as I hate to admit it, I was so totally and completely caught up in maintaining my relationship with Cade, I couldn't conceive of anything else. It's like I was possessed. And it's so weird how like, one minute I was totally obsessed, and then the next, just like *that,* I was completely and totally over him."

I sit with her words, wondering how to respond. Taking a chance on the truth when I say, "Actually, it's not as strange as you think . . ." Auden stiffens beside me, urging me to proceed with caution when he presses his thumb hard against mine. Daire was always intent on protecting Lita from the truth, and she wanted me to protect her too. But Daire's no longer here, and without her, we're left to fend for ourselves. Which means the more people who know the truth about this town, and the Richters who run it, the better.

Lita slides her elbows toward me. I can tell by the shift in her energy, the creak of her seat. "Well, don't stop now," she says. "You've got my full attention."

"Okay. But listen, instead of getting ready to order another soda, what do you say we get out of here?"

"How'd you know I was going to order another soda?"

"I heard you pull some bills from your wallet."

"Seriously?"

I shrug. Amused by how easy it is for a blind person to impress the sighted.

"Sheesh. There really is something to that blind sight stuff, isn't there? Anyway, fine by me. This place gives me the creeps. It's filled with too many old memories and most of them bad. So, where are you guys taking me, 'cause it's not like we have a whole lot of choices."

"You sure about this?" Auden asks, the words spoken in a conflicted shade of puce that dissipates with a quick nod of my head. "Well, I would go with you, but I have to meet someone. So, Lita, I'm trusting you to take good care of my flower and get her home safely." He plants a soft, sweet, lingering kiss on my lips, as Lita jangles her keys in annoyance. The only public displays of affection she can tolerate are her own.

"So where is it?" she says, leading me away from Auden. "Where are we going? Is this like a girls' night out?"

"Something like that." I exit the club alongside her. "I figured since it's still kind of early, we can head over to Paloma's. If you're going to learn the truth about this town, you should hear it from the one person who can best explain it."

eight

Daire

The moment the door slams between me and Axel, I run.

Problem is, I have no real direction in mind.

Although the plan was perfectly executed, went off without a hitch, I never really thought past the moment I'd make it outside.

Other than crashing through the veil of light, and waking up in my sickbed, I have no recollection of anything outside of the room Axel kept me in. No recollection how we arrived here, much less how I might leave.

A bed of purple stones, like tumbled bits of amethyst, roll and shift under my feet as I race toward a glossy red bridge that leads to a grove of jacaranda trees with oversized blooms, where I lean against one of the trunks and spare a few moments to rest. Reminding myself that while there's no doubt I need to put some serious mileage between Axel and me, I also need to maintain my strength. Running around like a maniac will only serve to deplete my energy.

I fight to steady my breath as I gaze all around. Struck by how the surrounding Upperworld landscape is just as Paloma described it—an enchanting, breathtaking world bathed in a glorious, soft golden light.

Like the Lowerworld on steroids.

Paloma also told me that it's far more difficult to access than the Lowerworld, even for the most gifted Seeker.

Well, thanks to Axel, the accessing part was a breeze. The question remains, how to leave?

I close my eyes and go silent and still, seeking the answer within. If the Upperworld truly is a place of love and light and benevolence and magick, as Paloma claimed, then surely some of my powers must still be working.

When the back of my dress begins to flutter, softly nudging me forward, I take it as a sign that Wind is now with me. Though I still sneak a quick glance over my shoulder to ensure it really is my guiding element, and not the force of Axel rushing toward me.

If he really is a mystical being, he won't stay down long. Which is good on the one hand because it means I didn't kill him—but bad on the other because the second he recovers he'll surely come after me.

With my dress insistently swirling at my knees, I peer back toward the place where I came, only to find the beautiful meadow with its shiny red bridge and amethyst path . . . and nothing beyond.

No sign of a small cottage with large, bolted doors and shatterproof windows.

No sign of the place I was held prisoner for days on end.

The place I once found so formidable, vanished as though it never existed.

Did Axel somehow enchant it or cloak it so that only he could find it?

The thought alone is enough to spur me away from the trees and toward another beautiful bridge, this one painted a rich, vibrant cobalt, where I come across the first people I've seen since I fled.

I consider asking them for assistance, but discard the thought just as quickly. While the Upperworld is rumored to be friendly, the fact is, I'm a stranger in a strange land. I don't know the rules. I can't take the chance. So I tuck my chin to my chest and jog briskly past. Only to have one of them say, "Slow down, newbie— there's no reason to hurry!" as the other one laughs.

Newbie?

I shirk free of the thought. Can't afford to engage.

My heart is still damaged, my stamina fading. I need to use what little energy remains on getting the heck out of here before Axel awakes.

I sift through my memory. Try to dredge up anything I might've forgotten about how we arrived. Remembering the feel of Axel's arms folding around me . . . rocketing me high into the sky, until we pierced through a glorious, silken spun web, bursting into a world of bright golden light . . .

And then . . .

And then?

There's a big empty gap yawning between that first glimpse of the light and the moment I awoke in the bed. Though while the memory may be irretrievable, one thing is sure: If I flew upward to get here, I'll have to glide downward to return.

I shift my search for something that descends—anything—a ladder, a slide, a large tree with long roots. And it's only a moment later when Wind stirs, prodding me toward a warm, incandescent glow beaming off to the right that looks a lot like the golden web that landed me here.

I race toward it without question, convinced it's my exit. So mesmerized by the inviting way it pulsates before me, I nearly miss the group of girls cutting my path.

"Slow down!" one of them calls, but I keep my chin lowered and brush past.

Gaining a handful of steps between us, when she says, "Daire?"

I push my legs faster, causing my heart to quiver in protest.

Just two more steps and I'm there . . .

"Daire Lyons-Santos?"

I pretend not to hear. If she knows my name, that can't be a good thing. It might mean she's connected to Axel.

She rushes up from behind me. Her movements quicker, lighter, more fluid than mine, she catches me by the shoulder with ease and spins me until I'm staring into a pair of deeply appraising eyes that remind me of the color of the sea at sunrise. Her silvery/pink gaze so astonishing, it's a moment before I manage to take in her soft brown skin, long, dark ringlets, and the tall lithe body clothed in a dress that's a close match to mine. Only instead of stark white, hers is the same shade as her eyes.

"It is you, isn't it?" she says, her surprise at finding me here visibly marked on her face. Though while it's clear she knows me, I have no idea who she is. "What are you doing here? Where have you been? I've been searching everywhere—I lost track of you in all of the chaos." She tugs on the slim strap of my dress. "And why are you wearing this? Who gave this to you?"

I duck free of her grip and take a step back. While I have no idea what's going on, or why my dress could be of any concern to her, I know better than to answer.

I chance a quick glance over my shoulder, needing to reach that shimmering veil more than ever. Regretting the act the moment she catches me looking.

"Oh, no," she says, closing the space between us with one fluid step. "I don't know how you got here, Daire. Or how this even happened, but you cannot go back there. Not now. Not ever." Her friends call to her, asking if they should wait, but she waves them away and returns her focus to me. "Come, Daire. Come with me." Her fingers circle my wrist. Her gaze locks on mine. "I'm here to help. There's nothing to be afraid of. It won't take long to get this all sorted out."

I nod like I mean it. Going so far as to return her smile in a bid to win her confidence. While I'm sure she means well, she has no idea what's really going on. No idea what's at stake back home.

No idea of what Axel has done.

And I'm in no mood to enlighten her.

She turns on her heel and tugs on my arm, and I pretend to drop my resistance and follow along. My willingness to obey causing her to slacken her grip just enough to allow me to jerk free and bolt toward the veil, using every ounce of strength that I have.

Aware of her voice calling out from behind me—high-pitched and frantic, urging me to stop.

But it's too late for that.

I'm already soaring, diving, bursting through the web.

Already in gravity's clutches, plunging toward earth.

burnt
offerings

nine

Xotichl

After several knocks on Paloma's front door go unanswered, Lita and I head around back where we find her tending to a bed of strange hybrid plants that continue to thrive no matter the season.

I tilt my chin high and take a long, greedy inhale. Filling my nose with their lush fragrant scent before I say, "I'm a day early and I brought company." I nod in Lita's direction. "I hope that's okay?" The question asked more out of politeness than any real concern that Paloma would turn us away. She likes having us around. Sees us as a link to Daire, much like we see her.

She grasps the basket of medicinal night blooms and struggles to stand. The scene unfolding before me in a grim, sludgy, stream of energy with a luminous glow at the tip of her fingers.

"Here, let me get that." Lita rushes up beside her in a streak of vibrant orange that veers toward Paloma's listless gray. The contrast providing a bitter reminder of just how frail Paloma's become in the past few days.

While she never fully recovered after her soul was returned, and while there's no doubt that Daire's disappearance has taken a toll on each of us, Paloma's clearly the most affected of all.

Despite having firsthand knowledge of the hazards of being a Seeker, she holds herself responsible for the loss of her granddaughter. And no matter how many times I remind her that the prophecy was in motion, that it couldn't be stopped, it doesn't do much to alleviate the guilt.

Lita takes the basket and helps Paloma to the back door as I follow them inside. Moving past a kitchen that's rife with the scent of something healthy and delicious warming in the oven, past the continuous crackle and pop of the wood-burning kiva fireplace, and up the ramp to her office where she settles us at the old wooden table, before she returns to the kitchen to grab us a snack.

"I could get used to this," Lita says, when Paloma places a steaming cup of ginger tea and a vegan cardamom cupcake before us. "What do you say tomorrow, same time, same place, same snack?"

We all laugh a little longer than the joke actually merits. Hungry for an excuse to lighten our emotional loads.

"Aren't you going to have some?" Lita asks, when Paloma joins us at the table.

"I am fasting until she returns," she says. "These are Daire's favorite. I make a fresh batch every day, so they'll be here when she comes back."

Lita falls silent, busying herself with her cupcake and tea, as I lean toward Paloma, and say, "I brought Lita because I think it's time she learns the truth of this town, and I figured you're the best one to explain it."

The muted squeak of her finger running circles around the rim of her mug tells me I need a better way to sell this.

"With Daire missing—" I pause, needing a moment to collect myself before I continue. No matter how many times I say it, it doesn't become any easier. "There's no other Seeker to replace her. Which means we're all going to have to pitch in and do our part. But we can't protect each other if some of us don't even know what they need protecting from."

Paloma remains quiet for so long, I'm on the verge of begging, when she says, "I suppose you're right." Her voice, like her energy, is weary but resigned. "So, where do you suggest I begin?"

"How about the beginning," Lita says. "I've got a feeling the history of this town is nothing like they taught us in school."

Paloma nods in assent and settles into her chair, relaying a story so strange I keep careful watch over Lita's energy to see how she's handling it. And to my surprise, she's not nearly as shocked as I assumed she would be.

"I knew it!" Lita cries, the second Paloma's story ends. Smacking the table for emphasis, which from my end looks like a sharp streak of orange merging into a stagnant stream of brown. *"I so totally knew it."* She over-enunciates every word. "I mean, maybe I didn't know that all of the Richters, also known as El Coyote, are pretty much evil to the core. And maybe I didn't know that Cade could turn into an actual demon because he's basically the spawn of a demon and contrived by black magick. And maybe I didn't know that this town is filled with secret portals, or vortexes, or whatever you call them . . ."

"So, what exactly did you know?" I ask, unable to keep from grinning.

"I knew that Cade was bad news. I knew there was something very dark about him. And I feel like hurling every time I think of all of the things that I . . . that we . . ." She steadies her breath, rubs her palms against the table, and starts again. "Anyway, as for that creepy coyote of his, I've seen it. More than once. And the first time I saw its eyes glowing red, I screamed bloody murder and ran. But then Cade told me some made-up story about how he found him abandoned as a pup and decided to rescue him, train him, and keep him as a pet, and . . . ugh. I can't even tell you how disappointed I am in myself for being so charmed by all that. I can't believe I actually believed him!"

"Don't be so hard on yourself." Paloma slides away from the table, the chair's legs scraping hard against the tiled floor. "The

Richters know how to alter perception. They altered yours, as well as most everyone else in this town."

"Everyone except Xotichl." Lita swivels toward me. "How come you never fell for his act?"

"Cade can't get to me." I duck my head, take a sip of my tea. "None of the Richters can. It's the benefit of being blind."

"Are you saying he *glamoured* me?" Lita's voice pitches so high, she practically squeaks. "That he looked into my eyes and hypnotized me like the vampires do on TV?" She's torn between fascination and outrage, as demonstrated by the way her energy sparks and flares.

"Not exactly," Paloma says. "They need the benefit of your sight in order to alter the way you perceive things. It's an esoteric practice that very few have been able to master. As the story goes, before they happened upon the secrets of this particular skill, they were average, if not honorable, citizens. Or at least until they became warped by the power. They grew increasingly greedy, acquisitive, drunk on their own authority. No matter how much damage they do, the people continue to perceive them as a family worthy of their awe and respect. All too happy to toil away for the Richters' various interests, while spending all of their earnings eating and drinking in their bar and other establishments. It's a terrible cycle ensuring they remain forever indebted. You know the saying: *Absolute power corrupts absolutely*? The Richters are a prime example of that."

"And Cade is the worst of them all, having spent the last year stealing bits of people's souls, which he then fed to his dead ancestors in order to resurrect them and do his bidding," I say, wanting Lita to know that while her falling for Cade wasn't exactly her fault, the truth is far worse than she thinks.

"Are you seriously telling me that he used my soul to fuel some godforsaken, Richter zombie?"

If I thought she squeaked before, it was nothing compared to how that sounded.

"Not all of it. Just a piece," I say, instantly regretting being so blunt. It's a lot to swallow in just one gulp. I need to break her in slowly.

"It was returned to you on the Day of the Dead when Daire convinced the Bone Keeper to release them," Paloma says. "You've probably noticed a few changes since then."

"The same day I broke up with Cade!" Lita gasps, and then, as though it just now registered, she says, "Wait—did you say, *the Bone Keeper*?" The squeaking reaches an all new high. "Now you're telling me there's such a thing as a Bone Keeper too?"

"She has a skull face, she feeds off the stars, and she wears a black leather corset, stiletto boots, and a snake skirt," I tell her. "Well, according to legend, anyway. Though Daire did confirm it."

"So . . . she's a goth?"

"Probably the original goth," I laugh. "Oh, and the snake skirt is made of real snakes that slither around her waist and legs. And those same snakes did the soul retrieving by slipping down the Richters' throats and—" I pause, watching as Lita's energy fades into something horrible and bleak. So much for my attempt to rein it in.

"Okay, so, in a nutshell, the Richters are evil, Dace and Daire are good, spirit animals are not superstition, they're real, there are three worlds—a Lowerworld, an Upperworld, and this one, the Middleworld, and—" Lita pauses, hesitant to actually say it. "And a piece of my soul was stolen by my ex-boyfriend, which he then used to reanimate a dead ancestor, until it was rescued by a snake, and found its way back to me?"

"In a nutshell," I say, my voice small and regretful.

"Sheesh. And to think I've lived my whole life here, and the entire time I didn't have the slightest clue of what was really going on."

"Most people only see what they want to see," Paloma says. "It's only when they can no longer afford that luxury that they see what they must."

"Anything else I need to know?" Lita asks. "What about vampires and werewolves—oh, and fairies? Where do they fit in—are they real too?"

"While I can't speak for them, I can say that Daire's the one who made it snow." I grin at the memory, imagining the triumph she must have felt when the flakes began to fall after so many failed attempts.

"And Cade is responsible for making the sky bleed fire," Paloma says.

The words so unexpected, I lean toward her, as Lita grumbles, "Figures."

"How so?" I ask, listening intently as Paloma rises from the table, goes to an old locked cupboard, and retrieves a heavy tome she places in the middle of the table.

"The Codex," I whisper, voice laced with awe, as the vivid colors of its energy blooms in the space before me.

"Codex? What's a codex?" Lita swivels her focus between Paloma and me.

"A codex is an ancient text. This particular codex was created by Valentina—"

"One of the first of the Santos family Seekers," Paloma explains. "She suffered a great many trials to accumulate the knowledge contained in this book, so that all future Seekers might someday benefit."

"And you've seen this before?" Lita directs the question at me. Though she's quick to correct herself when she adds, "What I meant was, you're *familiar* with this?"

"I'm *familiar* with it *and* I've seen it." I grin. "And while I may not be able to see the actual pages, I *can* read its energy."

"And what is its energy telling you now?" Paloma slides the ancient leather-bound book across the table until it's resting before me.

I lift my palms so they're hovering just a few inches above it.

My attention instantly claimed by a very strong impression I'm reluctant to share.

It can't be.

It's impossible.

And what if I dare say it out loud and it turns out that I'm wrong?

"What do you see?" Paloma urges, her tone leaving no question that she's onto me, knows that I'm not being entirely forthcoming.

"Yeah, tell us what you see," Lita says. "Don't hold back on my account."

I take a deep breath, clear my throat, and say, "The prophecy has changed."

"How?" Paloma moves her chair closer to mine.

"You were right about Cade. He's the one who filled the sky with fire. He did it to force the prophecy. He was impatient. Convinced that if he could just get it going, then he could hasten the day that he'd rise up and rule. But some things cannot be forced, and now the prophecy is . . . dormant . . . for lack of a better word."

Paloma's energy deflates as she sinks deeper into her seat. "I'm afraid you're right," she says. "The night Daire went missing, Chay stood right here beside me as we watched the words lift from the page. I didn't mention it to you until now because I wasn't sure what to make of it. But I'm sure your impressions are correct. Cade is immature, impatient, and so he forced the signs before their time. And though I check the book daily, the space where the prophecy stood remains stubbornly blank."

"Have you checked today?" I venture, unsure if I should voice this incredible sensation I'm getting.

"I checked this morning. It's the first thing I do."

"Check again," I say. "You know, just to see." I strive to keep my voice light, as though I'm merely hoping to be humored. Afraid of giving too much away, planting a seed of hope, when there's a chance I might have it all wrong.

I hold my breath as she slides the book toward her. My cheeks bubbled with air as the cover sounds a dull thud against the table-top, and the worn vellum pages turn one by one. That same rush of air whistling from my lips when she and Lita both gasp, the sound alone confirming the very thing that I sensed. Those ancient, yellowing pages are now shimmering with the promise of new text, where just a few moments earlier it stood blank.

"What does it say?" Lita asks.

"I don't know." Paloma's voice is uncertain but more enthusiastic than I've heard in days. "The symbols are hazy, out of focus . . ."

I'm about to lean toward it, wanting to see if I can maybe intuit something, when I sense a subtle shift of wind. The slightest alteration in the atmosphere that might've gone completely unnoticed if it weren't for the bright flashes of color, the surge of warmth, and the celestial chorus that accompanies it.

It's a chorus I've heard once before.

The tempo lilting, lifting, until it rises into a crescendo so glorious, I can no longer contain it. I leap from my chair and cry, "Somebody needs to go open the gate." Making sure I have their full attention before I add, "Somebody needs to go open the gate and let Daire in—she's home!"

ten

Daire

I pause in the doorway with my eyes closed. Savoring the aroma of mesquite logs burning in the fireplace and ginger tea seeping into the air. Along with the sweet smell of cardamom cupcakes, lavender oil, vanilla perfume, and peppermint soap—the scent of home, family, and friends.

"*Nieta!*" Paloma crushes me to her chest so tightly I can feel her bones jutting from her shoulders in a way I don't remember. "*Nieta,* what happened? Where have you been?" She draws away, runs the back of a hand across my brow and presses both palms to my cheeks. Staring at me with wide, unblinking eyes, as though she can't bear to have me out of her sight for one second more.

"It's a long story," I say, eager to brush it aside in order to get to more urgent topics, like Dace. Just about to ask where he is, when I'm distracted by the deep lines of worry now permanently etched around her wise brown eyes, and the stark streaks of silver in her long dark braid that weren't there before. Her face is drawn. Her body frail. Clearly my disappearance has taken a toll.

I switch my focus to my friends, noting the way they hover on the sidelines, too tentative to approach. Xotichl with her light brown hair, soft gray eyes, and beautiful heart-shaped face—and

Lita with her gorgeous dark eyes, and long dark hair with ends that were recently dyed to look as though they were dipped in red paint. For someone who's not used to having friends, I'm amazed by how much I've missed them. Still, I rushed back for a reason, and I need to confirm that Dace is okay.

"Where's Dace?" I glance between the three of them. "I really need to see him—let him know I'm okay," I say, only to have Xotichl's voice overlap with mine when she raises a hand toward the scar marking my chest.

"You're injured!" she cries, face creased with worry. "I can sense it from here."

"Oh my God!" Lita slaps a hand over her mouth. "Who did that to you?"

"Cade." I shrug, allowing Paloma to guide me to the couch where she settles a blanket over my shoulders, lowers the slim straps of my dress, and examines the wound. "He killed me," I say, amazed at how easily the words just roll off my tongue. "And then Axel saved me."

Axel.

I close my eyes at the memory, but I'm quick to open them again. There's no time for guilt. No room for remorse. I did what I had to. He left me with no other choice.

"Axel? Nobody mentioned an Axel." Lita glances between Xotichl and Paloma. She hates to be out of the loop.

"Axel is . . ." I shake my head, having no idea how to explain him.

Axel is my savior.

Axel is my captor.

Last I saw, Axel was sprawled in an unconscious heap on the floor.

"Axel lives in the Upperworld," I say, figuring it's best to stick to the facts as I know them. "He's the one who stitched the wound closed. He's the one who stopped Cade from stealing my soul."

"What did he look like—was he cute?"

Lita leans forward, eyes wide, as Xotichl shakes her head and says, "Lita—honestly! I can't believe you sometimes." She mumbles something unintelligible under her breath and tucks a lock of light brown hair behind her ear.

"Well, was he?" Lita insists, ignoring Xotichl as she returns her focus to me. "I mean, since there's no cute boys here, I was thinking maybe . . ."

"You were thinking what? That you're going to move to the Upperworld so you can check out the hotties?" Xotichl groans, feigning complete exasperation that doesn't hold for very long before it turns into a grin.

"Well, when you put it like that . . ." Lita folds her arms across her chest and frowns, as the two of them go at it like an old married couple. Their ease with each other making me wonder just how long I was gone, how much I might've missed.

"To answer your question, he had platinum hair, fair skin, and lavender eyes."

"Seriously?" Lita squints as her lips twist to the side, presumably trying to assemble those pieces in her mind.

"You met your spirit guide?" The folds around Paloma's eyes deepen.

"I'm not sure. He never did say. He referred to himself as a Mystic. That's the most I ever got out of him. Though he failed to explain what that is."

Paloma assumes a thoughtful expression. "The Upperworld is populated by Mystics," she says. "Spirit guides and Mystics—and sometimes they're one and the same. Though Mystics are thought to be even more powerful than guides. The tales of their magick are legendary." She reaches toward the buckskin pouch and key at my chest, determined to remove them in order to better examine me, but I clasp my hand over hers before she can get very far.

"Please leave them," I say. "I've been too long without them."

She tips her head in assent and arranges the cords so the talismans hang down my back. "The wound is serious," she murmurs, along with a few choice words in Spanish I can't understand.

"You should see what he did to my insides," I quip. "He sliced my heart nearly in two. I truly was on the verge of death, when Axel restored my breath, took me to the Upperworld, and used some of that legendary magick to sew me back together again." I glance at my friends, noting the way Xotichl leans toward me, as Lita looks on in horrified fascination. Unable to discern what they find more disturbing—my disfiguring scar or the detached way in which I relay the events.

"I will make a poultice," Paloma says. "Something to help the wound fade."

She struggles to her feet, about to head for her office, when I say, "There's really no need. I prefer to keep the scar."

She looks at me. They all look at me. Three sets of eyes bearing the same shade of concern.

"Trust me, you definitely want it to fade," Lita says. "Take it from someone who has the memory of Cade branded on my brain. If I could erase it, I would."

"I prefer to remember," I say. "If nothing else, it'll remind me to never leave myself vulnerable around a Richter again."

"You seriously think you need to be reminded of that? After all that you've been through?" Xotichl tilts her chin in my direction.

"Okay, then I'll use it to remind me of my success," I say, convinced there's no way to argue with that. "It'll remind me of how despite what Cade did, I still managed to avert the prophecy and save Dace's life."

The second the words leave my lips they fall silent. Each of them carefully averting their gaze to look just about anywhere but at me. Lita examines her hands, as Xotichl tucks her chin to her chest and fools with the hem of her sweater. While Paloma, after a few moments of silence, looks upon me with deep grieving eyes.

"What is it?" I say, voice rising with suspicion. "What's going on? Somebody tell me what happened—where's Dace?"

"*Nieta*—" Paloma starts.

But Xotichl cuts in, saying, "Daire, that wasn't the prophecy."

"Of course it was!" I look at them like they've all gone mad. "I know exactly how the prophecy went. I memorized it word for word! *The other side of midnight's hour strikes a herald thrice rung—Seer, Shadow, Sun—together they come—Sixteen winters hence—the light shall be eclipsed—leaving darkness to ascend beneath a sky bleeding fire!*" I recite the prediction so quickly the words all blend together. "If that wasn't the prophecy, I don't know what is! Me, Dace, and Cade—we were all born on the same day, just after midnight, sixteen years ago. Seer, Shadow, and Sun—that's code for the three of us. The sky bled fire during our sixteenth winter, on Christmas Eve. And, in the end, Cade killed me. Only he didn't. He just thinks that he did." I pause, needing a moment to replenish my breath before I go on to say, "The sky was bleeding fire! I know you all saw it—there was no way you could've possibly missed it!"

"While we definitely saw it," Xotichl says. "Thing is—it wasn't a natural event."

My gaze darts between them, having no idea what that means.

"The timing was right," Paloma says in a cool, calm, authoritative voice. "But Cade was too impatient to allow it to unfold on its own, so he forced it into being. Cade made the sky burn."

"I . . . I don't understand." My voice is distant, as though it belongs to someone else. "I don't get it," I repeat, though the truth is, I'm beginning to.

A forgotten space in my memory has now cleared, revealing something Cade said just after confronting me in the Lower-world. Just after I taunted him for being stupid enough to virtually firebomb his own town.

"*It's the prophecy, Daire . . . It just needed a little push to get started.*"

"Cade forced the prophecy so he could put his plan into motion."

Paloma fights to keep her expression steady, but the grim look in her eyes betrays her worst fears.

"Maybe so," I say, desperate to hang on to what I once thought was true. "But I was there, and I'm telling you it played out just like it read."

"*Nieta,* the night you disappeared, the night the snow began to fall, the prophecy vanished from the Codex. Chay and I watched as the words lifted right off the page."

"And now that you're back, they've returned!" Lita jabs a thumb toward the office where Paloma keeps the ancient tome, wearing the excited, clued-in look of someone newly admitted to a clandestine club denied them too long. Clearly Paloma and Xotichl have filled her in on some of Enchantment's more mystical secrets.

"And, what does it say?" I ask, voice weary, head spinning, trying to make sense of everything I've just learned.

"It's . . ." Lita pauses, bites down on her lip, looks to Paloma and Xotichl to say what she's unwilling to.

"It's in transition," Xotichl says. "Blurry and unclear. Which makes me think it's malleable—possibly up to you to decide."

I stare at them, speechless. All too aware that if what they say is true, if that wasn't really the prophecy, then it's quite possible that my perceived death didn't actually serve to avert anything.

Which means . . .

"Where's Dace?" My gaze moves among them—suddenly realizing that up until now, they've successfully avoided answering that very question. "*Where's Dace?*" I leap from the couch, finding no comfort in the three sets of grief-stricken faces that meet mine. Voice shaking, I say, "Somebody better answer me quick, because I'm assuming the worst." I look frantically between them. And it's only a moment later when Paloma is beside me, lowering me back to the couch, and to my surprise, I allow it.

"No one has seen him, *nieta.*" Paloma clasps my hand between both of hers.

"No one? What about Chepi, Leftfoot, Chay?" I ask, knowing how stupid that sounds, I'm sure the elders have been in touch daily.

"No one has seen him since the night you disappeared." Paloma's voice is as gentle as her touch.

"And how long has that been? How long have I been gone?"

"A few days. You disappeared on Christmas Eve," Xotichl says.

A few days. Not as long as I feared, but still longer than I'd hoped.

"And Cade?" My heart stops, refusing to beat until someone answers me. "Please tell me someone has seen him! The twins are connected, if Cade dies, Dace dies. But only if Cade is in human form. If he's in demon form, then Dace can die without him—" The words sound jumbled, making sense only to me.

"Actually . . . someone might've seen him," Lita says, causing Xotichl and Paloma to whirl on her in shock. "And, if it's true, then apparently he's spreading a rumor that Dace is dead."

"Dace is *not* dead!" I say. "He *can't* be!" But just after it's out, I realize my gut instinct is my only real proof to back up my words. I pray it hasn't failed me.

Xotichl whirls on Lita, looking as furious as she's capable of being. "And you're just now telling us this, because . . ."

Lita lifts her shoulders, blows her long, angled bangs out of her eyes. "It's not like I'm the one who saw him. But I overhead Phyre talking about it at the Rabbit Hole. I didn't mention it because I assumed she was just making it up to sound important, and I saw no use in upsetting you and Auden over what I was sure was just a rumor. Anyway, from what I could hear, she claims she ran into Cade a few days ago, and that's what he told her. She said it's the reason he's been laying low. Despite the fact that he and Dace were never close, he's surprised by how devastated he is over the loss. Says it must be something to do with the strange connection twins share . . . blah, blah, blah. Oh, and the whole time she was telling the story, she really played it up big. Doing her best to appear heartbroken, but I'm telling you right now it was a total fake out." She shakes her head and scowls. Then seeing the way Paloma and Xotichl react to her words, she says, "What? I don't see the point in beating around the bush. Daire's the Seeker . . . a bit of a banged-up Seeker, but she's still our only hope left. Lying to her is not going to benefit anyone. And the thing is, with Cade and Phyre both claiming that Dace is dead, doesn't it make you wonder if they might be working together?"

"I don't believe Dace is dead," Xotichl says. "I don't care what they say. I think I would've felt it."

"I know *I* would've felt it," I say, struggling to rise once again.

"*Nieta,* please." Paloma tries to force me back onto the cushions as Lita shoots a dubious look toward my dress.

Oh, right. The dress.

With a firm but loving hand placed on each of my shoulders, Paloma looks at me and says, "*Nieta,* listen—I understand you're upset, and you have every reason to feel the way you do. But the problem is, you're acting on pure emotion and fear, and that will never lead to anything good. If you want to find Dace, if you want to *help* Dace, you'll need to set your emotions aside long enough to take the proper steps to come up with a plan."

"And what would those proper steps be?" I ask, surprised by the soothing effect of her touch, her voice, the undeniable wisdom she speaks.

"First you will use the time it takes me to prepare a proper poultice and a light meal, to rest your weary body and calm your frantic mind. Then, after you've eaten and I've tended to your wound, I will prepare some things for your trip."

"My trip?" I look at her, having no idea what she's referring to.

"If you want to find Dace, you'll have to return to the last place you saw him. Am I correct in assuming that would be the Lowerworld?" At the slightest tip of my head, she says, "I will drive you to the vortex. But first things first."

Paloma turns away, makes for her office, as Xotichl says, "I'm going with you."

"Me too!" Lita echoes. "I'll start by digging the Jeep out of the snow." Before anyone can stop her, she races for the door. Shooting me a look over her shoulder, she adds, "And speaking of, when you get a chance, can you please make it stop snowing? Now that you're back, it seems a little redundant."

eleven

Daire

Paloma's old white Jeep bucks and jumps over the poorly lit, deeply rutted dirt roads as she cuts through the reservation and heads for the grove of wildly twisted juniper trees marking the vortex.

"It's not too late to bail." I swivel toward my friends huddled into the small space in back, deciding to give them one last chance to opt out. "And trust me, if you're smart, you will."

"I'm not smart." Xotichl turns to Lita.

"Nope, me neither," Lita echoes, busily inspecting the ends of her hair. "Dumb as a doorknob, in fact."

I glance at Paloma, and seeing her nod of approval, I say, "Okay, but just to be clear, the journey is extremely unpleasant. And Xotichl, you'll have to leave your cane since it involves tunneling through deep layers of dirt. And while it doesn't actually take all that long, the first time feels like forever. You can't breathe, can't see . . . oh, and did I mention the worms?"

Xotichl shrugs, flips her ponytail over her shoulder, and says, "Bring it."

As Lita steadies her gaze on mine, and replies, "I'm not exactly the princess you take me for. I don't mind getting a little dirty now and then."

Paloma parks just shy of the trees, turns to me, and says, "I will wait here until you return."

I try to protest, telling her I have no idea how long it will take, and how worried I am by her weakened appearance, but she's not having it.

"Do not worry for me, *nieta*. Keep your focus on the task at hand. The Lowerworld is not as you left it. Though much like Xotichl, you don't need to rely on your vision to see." She hugs me tightly to her chest, and despite her frail state, her touch fills me with enough strength to lead my friends toward the trees with more confidence than I feel.

"Just follow me, and do what I do," I tell them. "And no matter how tempted you might be, do *not* try to stop the fall, or worse, claw your way up. It never works, and it'll just make the trip take that much longer. Allow the fall to happen naturally, without resistance. And the second you sense the first hint of light at the end of the tunnel, try to curl your body into as tight a ball as you can. It really helps to cushion the landing, which can be a little rough."

I glance behind me, and seeing they're not the least bit inhibited by my warnings, I launch myself forward. Aware of them falling behind, one by one, as we're swallowed deep into the earth, before landing in a hard bank of snow with Lita flailing beside me in a crazy tangle of limbs, as Xotichl exits last, rolling to a stop just as I coached.

"You really weren't kidding about the dirt." Lita brushes her hands against her knees and begins plucking pebbles and twigs and assorted debris from her hair.

"Or the worms." Xotichl straightens her coat as I help her to her feet. "I felt one skim right past my cheek. Luckily it was gone before I had a chance to properly freak."

I squint against the glare and take a good look around, unable to determine just where we've landed since all of the usual landmarks are covered with a heavy dusting of snow, with more accumulating each passing minute. Paloma was right about it not looking at all like I left it. Hopefully the snow-stopping ritual I worked just before leaving her house will begin to kick in without too much delay.

"So, this is the Lowerworld." I glance at my friends. "What do you think?"

Lita places her hands on her hips and takes a good look around. "Well, I'm sure it's really nice. But at the moment, there's so much snow, it looks a lot like Enchantment."

"Trust me, underneath the snow it's far more beautiful than Enchantment." I shove my hands under my armpits in an effort to warm them, and continue to survey the area. Dismayed to find it absent of spirit animals, including Raven who's usually waiting to greet my arrival.

Have the animals been forced into hibernation because of the snow?

"Is it always like this?" Xotichl asks.

"No." I frown, not liking what I see. "While I've never visited in the dead of winter, I'm sure this place doesn't change seasons. Before Cade corrupted it, it pretty much existed in a state of eternal spring. The flowers were forever in bloom, the grass was lush and green. Like golf course grass, only better." I sigh at the memory. "But despite Cade turning it into a wasteland, last I saw, just before I left, it was definitely returning to its usual springlike state once again."

"Since this is where our spirit animals live, do you think we might meet them?" Xotichl's face is lit with the possibility of meeting Bat who's been guiding her since the day she was born, and I hate to disappoint her.

"I was hoping they'd be waiting for us. They usually are," I tell her. "But with all of this cold and snow, I can only assume that they're hibernating."

And since they can't guide us if they're sleeping, that can't be a good thing.

Though I'm careful to keep my concerns to myself. No use worrying my friends when I'm merely speculating without any proof.

"So normally I would see Opossum down here?" Lita twirls a long chunk of hair around a mitten-covered finger.

I nod, but the truth is, I'm so distracted with trying to determine which way to go, the question barely registers.

"So, if Opossum were here, I could actually meet him and he wouldn't even try to bite me?" she asks, as though she can hardly imagine such a thing.

"Yes, Lita. You and your red-eyed Opossum would frolic through the forest just like they do in Disney movies." Xotichl laughs.

"That is not at all charming." Lita frowns. "I mean, why can't I have a cuter spirit animal? Something adorable and cuddly, like a bunny? Or even something cool, like a fox?" Then realizing what she just said, she looks around and in a raised voice says, "Just kidding! No offense! Love you, Opossum!"

I move ahead of my friends. Hoping to hide my confusion about which direction to take when nothing appears as I left it. I cup my hand to my brow and glance all around, as Xotichl and Lita chatter behind me in a way so distracting I'm just about to say something I'll no doubt live to regret, when I force myself to choke back the words and see the situation from their point of view.

Everyone has their own way of handling stress. Some go inward, like me. Some reach outward, like them. And despite the dire circumstances we face, they must feel pretty excited to transcend the known world for one that most people don't even realize exists. It's the enormity of the task that's making me grumpy, not them. Not to mention how the abundance of snow and cold is starting to grate.

Did I really cause all of this? Was my dying wish fulfilled to a ridiculous degree?

"Even though the nonstop snow-a-thon is kind of annoying, it does offer a sort of stark, quiet beauty, doesn't it?" Xotichl's voice drifts from behind me, and it's enough to knock me right out of my thoughts.

Lita and I whirl toward her, our voices overlapping as we cry, "Xotichl—can you *see* it?"

Her beautiful heart-shaped face lifts into a grin.

"For real?" Lita stands wide-eyed before her.

"Don't get too excited." Xotichl laughs, pushing Lita lightly on the arm, until she's moving again. "I can't see it in the same way you can. But I can make out all of the lines and curves and shapes and shadows in a way I've never been able to before. Usually all I can see are the colorful energy patterns that people and objects emit. But this—well, this is something else entirely."

"Good to know this place has managed to hang onto its magick," I say, exchanging a look of astonishment with Lita as I trudge a few steps ahead, and Lita begins to grill Xotichl. Insisting she describe everything she sees in great detail.

When I stop to get my bearings, Lita comes up alongside me and says, "I hope you're not upset because we're talking so much when we should be looking for Dace." Her large brown eyes droop at the sides. "It's just—it's so exciting with Xotichl being able to see and all . . ."

I shake my head and look all around.

"Then what is it?" she asks. "Are we here?"

I clamp my lips together and swallow a sigh. Not wanting my friends to know just how lost we really are.

"Do we even know where *here* is?" She shoots me a hopeful look.

"We're headed for the last place I saw him—the Enchanted Spring."

"And what do we do when we get there?" Xotichl asks.

Trying to drum up more confidence than I feel, I turn to them, and say, "I'm hoping one of us will be able to intuit something from the energy left over from the event."

"I'm not sure I understand." Lita wears a skeptical look.

"Everything is energy," Xotichl says. "Paloma taught me that, but you'll also learn it in science class. And energy is eternal. It can never be destroyed."

"But it can be transformed." I look at them. "That's how I made it snow. Simple alchemy—the transference of energy." I start walking again, veering slightly to the left and hoping it works.

"Simple, huh?" Lita trudges behind me. "Maybe for you guys, but not for someone like me."

"Don't be so sure," Xotichl says. "It's not as hard as it seems, you just have to grasp the concept. Anyway, since energy never dies, theoretically speaking, the same should hold true for the energy of events."

"And Paloma taught you this?"

"She's taught me all kinds of things. But most importantly, she taught me how to read the energetic vibration of both inanimate objects and all living things."

"So, all this time you could see my energy?" Lita asks, and it's clear from her tone she's not sure how to feel about that.

"Yes. And in case you're wondering, it's a sight to behold." Xotichl laughs.

"Anyway," I say, eager to get back on track. "The idea is that every act leaves a permanent imprint upon the space in which it took place. Though acts that were committed with a lot of emotion—fraught with anger, fear, sadness, or even love—leave the strongest impressions behind. So, surely an act like Cade killing me and whatever happened afterward should bear a strong imprint as well."

"But how exactly will we see it?" Lita asks, running up alongside me. "Will we watch it play out before us like a giant hologram or something?"

"Maybe." I shrug. "I can't say for sure since I've never done it before. All I know is that if the ancient Mystics and modern-day scientists are right, the event should still be here, repeating itself."

"Different people *see* in different ways," Xotichl says. "And some will never see it at all."

"But just exactly what are the different ways of seeing?" Lita asks.

"It might appear in actual images or colors representing those images." Xotichl shrugs. "It might be in voices and sounds. The important thing is to rid yourself of preconceived ideas and self-doubt, and just let it unfold."

"But even if you do see something, how can you tell if it's real? I mean, how do you determine that you're watching an actual event reenacting itself, and not some crazy hallucination or mirage or illusion? Isn't it possible to get so caught up in remembering what went down, that you start seeing stuff that's not really there?"

"It's a good question," Xotichl starts.

"But you have an answer for that as well?" Lita laughs.

"I do indeed." Xotichl grins. "A mirage is the result of refracted light—or the bending of light. A hallucination is when you see things that aren't really there. While an illusion is like a magic trick—a deceptive appearance."

"But, according to that definition, none of those things are really there."

"Most people never actually see what's really there. They only see the obvious—they never look beyond the veil." Xotichl shrugs.

"If you don't look, you can't see," I say, tossing in my two cents.

"Are you guys purposely trying to confuse me?"

Xotichl laughs. "Anyway, if that doesn't work, Paloma's been working with me on psychometry, so I can try that as well."

"And that is?"

"The ability to read the energy imprints left on objects. It can be pretty intense. So, I don't know, maybe I can touch a rock or something, and see what I get."

Lita shakes her head. Looking at me when she says, "Can you do that too?"

I stop before a grove of trees with stark trunks and barren branches—their formation the only thing that's familiar. "The most important thing Paloma ever taught me is that a Seeker must learn to see in the dark, trusting what she knows in her heart."

Lita squints, places a hand on her hip. "So basically what you're saying is that although you pack a heavy arsenal of mad magick skills, in the end, you go with your gut?"

"Never steers me wrong." I lift my shoulders and rise up on my toes in an effort to see what lies beyond.

"If you're saying that to make me feel better, it worked. You two can be a little intimidating, what with all of your big-time mystical gifts."

"Everyone has mystical gifts," Xotichl says. "You just have to believe in them, trust them, and hone them."

Lita starts to reply, but I cut her off when I say, "I think this is it."

I race before them. The treads of my boots leaving deep tracks in the snow as I duck through the trees and into the clearing with my friends right behind me. Xotichl gets right to work. Rubbing her hands together as she stoops toward the ground in a search for pebbles, rocks, something to get a read from, as Lita stands shivering beside me.

"Where exactly did it happen?" Xotichl places a rock in the center of her palm, and rolls it from side to side before discarding it for another.

I move to the place where Cade shoved the athame into my heart and spread my arms wide. "Somewhere around here." I close my eyes in an attempt to get a better feel for the space. And that's when I realize for the first time since I arrived that it's not just Raven who's absent. The air is so still it seems my element Wind has abandoned me too.

Yet the Enchanted Spring is still there. Its waters cooled by the snow, but hopefully its magick still holds. I kneel down beside it and immerse both my hands, filling my palms with water I use to cleanse the wound at my chest. My friends' murmuring voices

fading into the background as I silently state my intentions. Reminded of what Paloma said about it being magick's most important ingredient.

I intend to heal and empower myself.

I intend to uncover the truth of what happened here after I left.

I intend for that truth to lead me to Dace.

*And once Dace is safe, I intend to confront Cade—and this time, I
intend to kill him.*

My reverie broken by Xotichl calling to me, "Daire—I think
you better come see this."

twelve

Daire

Xotichl stands before me, the hilt of a bloody knife grasped in both hands.

My blood.

My knife.

The one Cade used against me.

Her hands begin to tremble, and soon after, the rest of her follows. The sight of her head lolling from side to side, prompting Lita to shriek, "Is she okay? Should we do something to help her?" Her eyes search mine, desperate for guidance.

"Don't touch her," I warn, slowly creeping toward Xotichl as Lita scrambles out of the way. "She'll be okay. She's just *seeing*, that's all." I clamp my lips together and hope that it's true.

Xotichl's breath grows increasingly agitated. Her body violently shudders. And I'm just about to intervene when the knife slips from her fingers and lands in a thud at our feet.

Lita squeals.

Xotichl lifts her face to mine and in a steady voice says, "It's all there. I could tell you if you want, but I think you should see it for yourself."

I hold my open palm above the athame and focus hard on the

hilt, but the knife remains stubbornly in place. Guess the days
spent in the sickbed have left my telekinesis a bit rusty. With no
other choice, I retrieve it the old-fashioned way, by kneeling and
closing my fingers around it. The contact of flesh on wood is enough
to instantly trigger a cache of stored images to storm through my
head.

My battle with Cade, fading into the moment Dace appeared.
Only he wasn't the same. His eyes no longer glinting, no longer
reflecting, they looked just like Cade's—a dull, fathomless abyss,
absorbing instead of reflecting.

It's temporary, Dace claimed. *Not to worry.*

He did it for us—did it to save me.

To save *me.*

When all of this time it was me who was meant to save *him.*

Like most souls, mine is comprised of both light and dark,
while Dace's is preternaturally pure.

It was his light that was destined to die.

I rub my lips together, tighten my grip, and ready myself for
the part that comes next. The moment it all falls apart. With Cade
in demon form, and Coyote doubled in size, Dace and I were outmatched.

Only this time, when Axel whisks me high into the sky, I'm
able to watch what I couldn't before.

Raven flying after us, trailing for a very long distance, until he
came across some kind of barrier and was forced to turn back.

Dace slamming the athame into himself without hesitation.
Willing to pay the ultimate price in order to keep his twin from
destroying the world.

It's not until Lita's hands clasp tightly over mine, and Xotichl
yells, "Don't let her drop it! There's still more to see!" that I realized I screamed.

And now with Lita and me both holding the knife, she's able to
see what I see.

Dace and Cade collapsed in a heap, their souls newly released.

Only to have Coyote catch Cade's in his snout and force it back into him, while allowing Dace's to drift free.

Cade wakes with a sputter and instantly turns on his brother. "Get him out of here," he commands Coyote. "Take him to the darkest recess of the Middleworld where no one will find him. He's of no use to me now."

Lita curses under her breath as we watch Coyote grab Dace by the collar and drag him away, while Cade, still gravely wounded but breathing, inches his body toward the Enchanted Spring, where he rolls into the water and emerges renewed.

Lita drops her hands, leaving me to hold the knife on my own. Her voice small, overwhelmed, she says, "What now? Where do we go from here?"

I open my eyes and lower the athame to my side. "First we find Dace. Then we restore his soul. And once that's done, I'll find a way to deal with Cade, once and for all."

thirteen

Daire

On our return to Enchantment, I'm surprised to find the sun is already up and Paloma is still there, only this time with company. All of the elders: Chay, Chepi, Leftfoot, and Cree, Leftfoot's apprentice, are all waiting for us. Their assorted trucks, Jeeps, and horses circling the site, as they huddle against the cold and keep a steady vigil.

Paloma calls to me the second she sees me emerge from the trees, but it's Dace's mother, Chepi, who gets to me first. Her eyes red-rimmed, her face pale and drawn, she looks as though she's aged twenty years in the short time I've been gone.

"You found him! Please tell me you found him!" She grasps my shoulders too tightly, refusing to loosen her grip until Leftfoot places his hands over hers and gently pries her away.

"Give the girl a moment." He slides a supportive arm around her. Attempting to comfort and keep her contained.

"It's okay," I tell him. Turning my attention to Chepi, I say, "I'm sorry but we didn't quite find him. Not yet, anyway." Forcing myself to hold her gaze, despite the accusation I read on her face.

She holds me responsible. Or at least partially. It's all right there in the hardened glint in her stare. Her belief that her son was never in danger until I came to town and this whole mess began. And while it's true that my arrival got the ball rolling, the truth is, with his connection to Cade, Dace has been in danger since the day he was born.

She steps closer, leaving only a breath of space spanning between us. "What do you mean when you say, *not yet*?"

"I know he's in the Middleworld. In a dimension other than this one. I just don't know where. But he's alive. I know for a fact he's alive."

Her shoulders sink in relief, and I know what she's thinking: *Where there's life, there's hope.* It's the same thought I cling to.

"But you should also know that he's soulless." I rub my lips together, hating to be the one to tell her, but she deserves to know the truth. "I need to locate him quickly." I turn my attention to Leftfoot, Cree, Paloma, and Chay, their faces displaying equal alarm at what I've revealed. "And then, once that's done, I need to locate his soul."

"He'll die if you don't get to him soon!" Chepi cries. "Look what happened to Paloma when her soul was lost! Why are you just standing here? Why aren't you out there searching for him?"

"He won't die," I say, aware that it's a promise one should never make to a grief-stricken mother. The delicate balance between life and death is always tricky at best. Still, it's a promise I make to us both. "This is nothing like what happened to Paloma. From what I saw, he's gravely wounded, which means he'll be physically weakened, for sure. But the twins are connected, and as long as Cade lives, Dace lives. As long as Cade breathes, Dace breathes, no matter how labored." I pause, allowing her to digest the words until they make sense. Until they become solid enough for her to hold on to. "But that also means, and you all need to hear this—" I make a point to glance at each of them before I continue. "The Cade Richter kill order is suspended until further notice. No one makes a move on him until I get this thing sorted." My tone bears the burden of that horrible truth. "While I never thought I'd say this, we need to do whatever it takes to keep Cade alive. Controlled and contained, but alive. Once Dace is taken care of, and only then, I have every intention of eliminating Cade, not to worry. But no sooner."

A low whistle escapes Chay's lips, as Leftfoot says, "Any idea where to look?"

"Coyote dumped him somewhere deep in the Middleworld—somewhere dark, bleak, and ominous where there's no risk of anyone finding him. No one but me, anyway."

"And me!" Xotichl says. And not to be outdone, Lita chimes in as well.

I turn to my friends, tempted to say *thanks but no thanks.* Remind them that it's not their battle to win. But the fact is, it's everyone's battle. Everyone here has something at stake. I may be the only Seeker, I may be the only one with the actual skills to see this thing through, but that doesn't mean I can't accept a little help now and then.

"You can start by hanging with me at the Rabbit Hole tonight," I tell them, hoping to appease Chepi's look of disdain when I add, "There's an entrance that leads to a much deeper dimension of the Middleworld, and I'll need someone to cover so I can get to it. But first, I need to go home, get some provisions, and come up with a plan. After all, you can't hit a target you can't even see, right?" I start to grin, until I realize I just quoted Axel and a shiver slips over my skin.

fourteen

Xotichl

I bounce my knee against the door of Lita's car, debating how best to phrase what I'm about to ask. Deciding I may as well state it like it is, I say, "I know this may sound crazy—" Not getting very far before Lita cuts in.

"Doubtful," she says. "After what I've seen, *crazy* just got a whole new definition. I had no idea there was all this insanity happening right under my nose. And to think of all that time I wasted on Cade . . ."

"Lita—" I'm quick to interrupt before she can go any further. "You have to let it go. Seriously. It's finished. O-V-E-R. And it wasn't your fault. You were literally under his spell."

"You telling me to move on?" Her tone is amused.

"No, the fact that you left him means you already moved on. I'm telling you to take all of that energy you waste in chastising yourself, and channel it toward more useful endeavors."

"I would." She breathes an exaggerated sigh. "But Daire said we can't kill Cade. Or at least not yet, anyway."

We burst into laughter, both of us buoyed by the assurance that the very worst is behind us. Daire is back. Dace is alive. Whatever comes next can only pale in comparison.

"Still," I venture. "I have an idea . . ."

"I'm listening . . ."

"Okay, this is the crazy part, but—you know that church, the one where Phyre's dad preaches?"

"I'll tell you right now I don't like where this is going." Her energy alters, becoming increasingly agitated, as she fidgets in her seat. And since the magick of the Lowerworld is still with me, it appears as a bundle of frenetic, Lita-shaped curves and shadows that repeatedly contract and expand. But I keep that bit to myself. Wanting to see if it lasts before I share the news with my friends.

"Just hear me out." I face the side window, watching as a series of light boxy forms stream past, which I assume are the adobe-style homes most of us live in. "While I get that you don't like the idea, I think we should go there."

She slows into a turn. "You're joking, right?" When I fail to respond, she says, "You actually want to go to that cardboard pulpit he calls a church?" She shakes her head in a way that emits a stream of energy so chaotic and streaky, I have to bite back a laugh. "Why would you ask me to do that? What reason could you possibly have? Do you secretly hate me? Is this your revenge for all of those years when I acted like a total bitch even though, as I recently discovered, it wasn't my fault? Because I thought you were above that sort of thing, Xotichl. I really did." She pauses for breath and I'm just about to speak, when she starts up again. "I mean, we're talking Suriel Youngblood—the snake-wrangling zealot. The same crazy freak who was always preaching about the Apocalypse, or Armageddon, or the Last Days or whatever he calls them, back when we were kids. He scared the crap out of me the day he barged into the hair salon and started screaming about vanity being one of the seven sins and setting fire to all of the fashion magazines. What was supposed to be a special mother/daughter day of bonding, ended up giving me nightmares for years. Even as the cops were hauling him away, he kept right on preaching. That's how big of a lunatic he is. And just so we're clear, all of this is a very long-winded way of saying, sorry, but no. No way. Hell no. He's a freak and he gives me the heebs."

"Okay." I sigh as though I've already moved on. "I was just thinking, maybe . . . but no . . . never mind . . ."

"What—you were just thinking *what?*"

"Well, I was just thinking that the whole thing might be connected. You know, Phyre showing up when she did. Just days before the whole thing with Daire, Dace, and Cade went down. And her father's crazy obsession . . ."

Lita fidgets with the steering wheel. "You don't think that was a coincidence?"

"I don't even believe in coincidence. There's a connection, I'm sure of it. And while I can't get a read on her, which is strange enough in and of itself, I am one hundred and one percent certain there's something very odd about that girl. And wasn't it just last night when you went on and on about how you don't trust her, and how Daire never trusted her, and how you were committed to getting to the bottom of it . . ."

"So I did. And while I meant every word of it, I cannot even begin to imagine how attending one of her dad's scary sermons is going to help."

"I don't even know if he'll be having a sermon. I just thought if we could head over there now, and—"

"Now?" Lita gasps. "This is even worse than I thought! We're filthy. We haven't slept. What could be the point of this?"

"I just thought we could get a read on the place. Find out just exactly what it is that he's preaching about."

"He's preaching about the same crazy crap he's always preached about. The Apocalypse, Armageddon, the Last Days, the End Times, I already told you."

"But is he *still* obsessed with those things? And if so, what are the specifics? I need details—names, places, dates. How exactly does he figure the world is going to end?"

"You think he's working with the Richters?"

I shake my head. "No. I think he works only for himself. He's as vain and egocentric as they come. But I've no doubt there's something very weird going on with him and his daughter, and I think it involves Dace and Cade."

"Okay, so why me? Why don't I drop you off at Auden's and the two of you can enjoy a nice romantic date at Suriel Young-blood's House of Crazy?"

"Because you're here and Auden is probably still sleeping."

"So it's true, I am a consolation prize."

"Also, because everyone in this town knows you. And if Suriel is preaching, I figure he'll be so thrilled to see you in the pews he'll do his best to impress you and really amp up the message, maybe even reveal more than he intends to."

"Oh, how you flatter me, Xotichl Gorman." She huffs under her breath, wanting me to know how unhappy she is with this turn of events. "So if I did decide to go through with this—and I'm not saying I have—but if I did, then what's in it for me?"

"You mean aside from helping Dace and Daire and possibly stopping Cade from destroying Enchantment and maybe the world?"

"Yeah, aside from the obvious." She twists her fingers against the steering wheel. "Oh, forget it." She heaves a frustrated breath. "Seriously, forget I just said that. I'll go. I'll do it. But I just want to make it crystal clear that what you're asking of me is bigger than you think. It's like asking someone with agoraphobia to leave the house, or someone with arachnophobia to make nice with a spider. I've said it before and I'll say it again, Suriel Young-blood freaks me out."

"Only one way to overcome your fears and that's by confront-ing them," I tell her. "And, if you live through it, I might be able to help you with a little problem of yours."

"At the moment, the only problem I can think of is going to Suriel's. Care to enlighten me?"

"Yes, but only if you live through this. Which remains to be seen."

"And to think you look *so* innocent. Who would guess the devious mind that inhabits your cute little head?" Lita laughs and taps the wheel lightly.

"Almost no one," I quip. "Now, instead of making a left, I need you to turn right."

"How'd you know I was gonna go left?"

"By the way your hand shifted when you hit the blinker."

"Seriously?"

I shrug.

"Sheesh. You're more observant than most sighted people." Her car judders in protest as the road grows progressively worse. "Definitely not the affluent side of town, is it?" She groans. "Not that we have an affluent side of town. Other than the Richters' compound."

"What's it like? I assume you've been inside?"

"More than once." Lita makes a small sound of displeasure. "It's like getting a glimpse inside a secret society. Only the chosen few get an invite. I felt so cool and privileged at the time, but in retrospect, it was creepy. Aside from all the opulence and excess, it's a strange mix of eclectic, modern, and tribal, with a sizable stash of priceless antiques. And now that I know what I know, I can't help but wonder if all of those ancient artifacts were used in the family's dark rituals."

"Did you see them perform any dark rituals?"

"None that I know of. But they are sorcerers, so I'm assuming pretty much everything they do is a ritual of some kind. I'm just lucky they didn't use me as a sacrifice."

"I think you were safe. They usually need virgins for that sort of thing."

"Xotichl!" Lita gasps.

"Speaking of—"

"Speaking of virgin sacrifice?"

"Speaking of dark rituals . . . if my senses are correct, the church we're looking for should be right up ahead. I'm picking up on some weird energy." *Along with some dense, dark, and shadowy forms*—I keep the thought to myself.

"Should I drive right up to it, or should I be more covert?"

"Hard to be covert in the middle of nowhere. Besides, better to be obvious about our interest; if we act sneaky, he'll get suspicious."

Lita brakes hard, sending the car lurching forward and back, before cranking the wheel in a series of turns, until she's positioned just where she wants it.

"Now we can make a quick getaway. I plan to leave the engine running as well. You can thank me later," she says, as we climb out of the car and move toward the church, which to me appears as a small, lurching form draped in a heavy cloak of black. But I'm curious how it might look to her, so I ask her to describe it in detail. "Well, it's adobe. Actually, make that crumbling adobe which probably comes as a total shock, seeing that this is Enchantment and all." The laugh that follows is sharp and sarcastic. "Okay, what else . . . it's small, but that's only because no sane person would ever choose to come here, so it's not like he needs a lot of room for overpacked pews. Overall, I'd say it's pretty dilapidated. But then again, you know what they say—zero parishioners equals zero tithing. And yet . . ." I veer closer. She's come to the part I'm interested in. "For being so old and crumbly, it's surprisingly well-maintained. Which I know sounds completely contradictory, but what I mean is that it's wearing a fresh coat of whitewash, there's a freshly shoveled path that leads to the door, and the plants are in decent shape, despite all the snow."

"Oleander, right?" I tip my nose high and inhale deeply.

"Um, yeah. I think so. I'm just wondering where he keeps all the snakes."

"I keep the snakes in their aquariums," a voice says from behind us.

Suriel's sudden and unexpected appearance causes me to jump as Lita squeals and grabs my arm in a tourniquet grip.

"I didn't know you were here . . . we were just . . ." Lita trembles beside me, as I loosen her fingers. Only vaguely aware of my arm tingling from my elbow to my fingertips as I take in the shadowy figure that hosts some of the worst energy I've ever seen.

Other than demons.

And Richters.

Especially Cade.

"If you're interested in the snakes, you've come at an opportune time. I'm just about to feed one." He dangles something before him—something that's squealing and clambering like hell to get free. "Not everyday you get to see a sight like this. Perhaps you'd like to come inside and watch?" His voice is jovial enough, but the words themselves emit a deep greasy yellow that keeps me rooted firmly in place. This man is a dangerous combination of paranoia, lies, and delusions of grandeur. Coming here is probably the worst mistake I've ever made.

"That's a rat!" Lita cries, taking a step back, and pulling me along with her.

"That's what rattlers eat," Suriel says. "You have nothing to fear. When you're filled with divine light, no creature can harm you. But you wouldn't know about that. Your soul is filled with darkness, which is why you're steeped in dread."

Says the man swirling in a cloud of dark, sludgy murk.

"Oh, um, maybe," Lita says, doing her best to play along as she slowly backs away.

"And who's your friend, Lita?"

"You know me?" She gasps, effectively nailing the high notes.

"'Course I do. You're associated with that young Richter fellow. What's his name, Cade?" He speaks the name as though he's merely hazarding a guess, but the greasy, yellow sludge dripping off his tongue betrays his deception.

"No," Lita says, eager to dismiss any perceived notion of her alliance with the Richters. "Not anymore. Not for a while now. I have nothing to do with him."

"Still, you've been touched by his darkness. I can see it in you. I'm sure your little friend here sees it too." He turns in a way that instantly blocks the morning sun at his back, casting me in his long and ominous shadow. "You're not nearly as blind as you pretend, are you, little one?"

Inside I balk, but outwardly I keep cool. A paranoid, delusional, self-righteous freak with insight—he's even more dangerous than I guessed.

The rat, still dangling from Suriel's fingers, squeals in loud protest. Causing Suriel to laugh as he says, "Time to feed." He tries to appear jaunty but doesn't come close to succeeding. "If you girls aren't interested in watching, then it's best you move on. This is a house of salvation, not a tourist attraction. Though you might want to memorize the location. Won't be long before you'll be begging to seek sanctuary here. Never too late to repent."

"What's that supposed to mean?" Lita calls after his retreating back.

"The Last Days are upon us. The Shining Days of Glory will follow. I will bring about the New World by ending this one, and neither of you are ready. Clock's ticking!"

The door slams shut behind him, as Lita grips my sleeve and hauls me back to her car where she hits the accelerator so hard I lift off my seat and slam my head into the roof.

"Sorry about that," she says about five minutes later, after she's laid down some serious tracks. "So is he as creepy as I said, or what?"

"Creepier." I hug myself tightly, wishing I could erase what just happened.

"Wonder if that rat was really for his snake. Seemed like he might be planning to eat it himself."

We burst into fits of laughter, eager to relieve ourselves of the tension.

"Still, I'm glad we went," I say, surprised by my words.

"Why? What did you get out of that other than he's a delusional doomsday fanatic who believes this New Year's Eve will be our last?"

"I don't know," I say. "It's just good to gather as many pieces as possible. You never know where they'll fit. Anyway, can you drop me at Auden's? I sent him a text that I'm on my way."

The rest of the ride is spent mostly in silence until Lita says, "Okay, so what's the prize? I mean, now that I survived the creepy encounter with Suriel, it's time to collect. So tell me, what did I win?"

It takes me a moment to make sense of it. I guess I'd been so focused on trying to find a connection between Suriel's Apocalypse and the situation between Daire, Dace, and Cade, I'd almost forgotten the promise I made. "Well, you know how you're always worried about being a third wheel? I think I've found a way to fix it."

"You setting me up with Auden?" She laughs, which to me appears as a river of golden bubbles streaming from her lips.

"Never!" I grin. "But how about the next best thing?"

"Auden has a clone?"

"Auden has a band. A band with bandmates who all just happen to be boys. One of whom also happens to be recently single, and, from what I hear, he's really cute."

"So, let me get this straight—you're making me visit the preacher who gave me nightmares as a kid, and my prize is one of Auden's recently dumped band members?"

"You really know how to put a positive spin on things."

"Yeah, well, in case you didn't hear me before, my dating days are over. I've kissed practically every boy in our school, including, embarrassingly enough, a few of the scrawnier freshmen, and once again, for the record, every single one of them was found lacking."

"Still, you haven't kissed Greyson. And didn't you recently say that Enchantment was in need of some new recruits? While Greyson isn't exactly new, or a resident for that matter, he is new to you."

Lita sighs. "So, just out of curiosity which one is he?"

"The drummer."

She shifts in her seat. "Are you talking about the cute one whose bangs are always flopping into his eyes?"

"So they tell me."

"For real?"

"If you're up for it, I know for a fact that he's up for it."

She turns away, taps her fingers against the steering wheel. "Maybe. I need some time to think about it. But no promises."

"He'll be at the Rabbit Hole tonight. You can talk, hang out, and see what you think." I gather my stuff and climb out of her car just as Auden comes out to greet me.

"Xotichl—" Lita calls after me. Hesitating before she goes on to say, "You know how when we were down in the Lowerworld and you said you could kind of see shapes and shadows and things?"

I swallow hard, but otherwise keep very still.

"Well, can you still see those things?"

I shake my head, unable to give voice to the lie.

"That's too bad. Guess it was just the magick of the place."

"Guess so." I bite back a grin and turn away, barreling straight into the arms of the beautiful, shaggy-haired shadow rushing toward me.

fifteen

Daire

"I need cigarettes, tobacco, whatever you got!" I shuck off the filthy sweater I passed out in not long after I got home, and replace it with a clean one. "I'm sure there will be no shortage of demons down there and it's the demon snack of choice. Also—"

"*Nieta.*"

I turn to Paloma.

"Don't overexert yourself. You've just returned from a horrible ordeal. You're still healing, you're still weak!"

"I slept twelve hours—how can I be weak? Besides do I look weak?" I raise my hands to my sides, allowing her to get a good look before I turn away and change into a clean pair of jeans.

"What happened to your scar?" She stares at the V-neck of my sweater, the place that bears the mark of Cade's wrath. "It seems to be shrinking, fading. The ointment I used has never worked so quickly."

"I bathed it with the healing waters of the Enchanted Spring. I should bottle some and bring it back for you to use on your clients. It's amazing—heals everything." *Including Cade.* Though I fail to mention that part. No need to worry her any more than she already is.

A ghost of a grin crosses her face, vanishing almost as quickly as it came. "I've tried that on many occasions, it doesn't work. While the effects of its magick can survive the return to the Middleworld, the healing transformation happens only there. Once the water leaves the Lowerworld, it's just water. There's nothing special about it."

"Well, it's healing me," I say. "I feel fine. Strong. Ready to do what I need to."

"That may be so, *nieta*. But don't forget you are thinner, paler, and I have no way of knowing if your friend Axel—"

"He's not my friend," I snap, but Paloma proceeds undeterred.

"I have no idea if he healed your heart properly. I have no idea how long his healing will hold."

"I don't know either." I make a concerted effort to soften my tone. "But I can't let that stop me. It was truly a miracle he was able to save me at all. I have no idea who he is, how he did it, or why he did it. All I know is that so far it's worked, and it's all I have to go on. That, and a whole lot of faith that between the combined efforts of you, Axel, and the spring, the healing will continue."

One look at her face, the way she holds herself so stiffly, tells me she remains unsure.

"Look, I know you're worried about losing me again just one day after I returned, but we both know the score. We both know the inherited dangers of being a Seeker."

"It wasn't quite as dangerous in my day." Her fingers twist nervously at the row of small shell buttons lining the front of her cardigan.

"Somehow I doubt that." I head for my closet, searching for my old green army jacket, but I can't seem to find it. "There were Richters then, just as there are now." I place my hands on my hips and frown.

"Aw, but Cade is a whole new breed of Richter," Paloma says, and as much as I'd like to refute it, we both know it's true. "Still, I fear you are running on adrenaline. And while you may feel strong now, it won't last. That sort of thing never does. You're bound to crash at some point, and then what?"

"You're right." I drop my hands, trading the search for my jacket for a search for shoes. "You usually are. But the thing is, adrenaline is all that I've got, so it's just going to have to suffice. I'm stronger than you think, *abuela*." I lean against the wall, and slide my feet into a pair of old sneakers. The cool black boots Jennika bought me for Christmas got lost along with the rest of the clothes that I died in. "And despite the scar on my chest, I'm not nearly as frail as I look. Besides, I'm the only one who can do this. I was born to do this."

"But your training—"

"My training was hastened, I know. But you've taught me a lot, and you've taught me well. It'll have to suffice. There's only one thing . . ." I reach into my bag and retrieve the bloody athame. "Cade used this to kill me. And Dace used this to kill Cade. And I'm wondering how all of this could've happened, when we sanctified it with Valentina's essence. Wasn't that supposed to protect me?"

"It did protect you. You're still here. And Dace is too."

"Axel saved me. And Coyote saved Dace by default."

"Who knows what forces are at work," she says, taking the knife from me. Her gaze firm as she says, "I will take care of this, if you take care of three things before you leave."

I wait, having no idea what they'll be.

"First, call your mother."

I drop my head in my hands, horrified I had to be reminded to do that. Jennika must be totally freaking. Not to mention how she'll never forgive me for waiting so long to phone her.

"And second, if you're looking for your jacket, it's in my room. I know it's a favorite of yours so I took the liberty of patching it up."

I grin in appreciation. "And third?" My gaze meets hers.

"Meet me in my bedroom when you're ready. There's one last ritual still left to perform."

Paloma swipes two oversized decorative pillows from her bed and places them just a few feet apart on the colorful handwoven rug. Its border surrounded by a thick layer of salt and white tapered candles placed a few inches apart. "Your mother must be very relieved," she says.

"Relieved I'm alive. Angry I didn't call her the second I returned. Bursting into tears every time I spoke, telling me that she feared she'd never hear my voice again, while in the next breath insisting she knew deep down inside I was alive. You know, typical Jennika." I grin at the memory. Vowing to visit her in L.A. just as soon as this whole mess is over. "Oh, and just so you know, she also threatened to board the first plane that's headed this way."

Paloma's eyes flash in alarm, which is something I rarely get to see. But then, just the mere thought of Jennika often has that effect on people.

"I tried to dissuade her. Told her I wouldn't be around much. That as of tonight, I'm heading into another dimension and I have no idea how long I'll be gone. And she took it surprisingly well. Suspiciously well. Which means you can probably expect to find her on your doorstep within the next four to five hours. Anyway, what's this about?" I motion toward the pillows.

"We don't have time for a sweat lodge, and I'm not sure I could bear the heat. This is the best I could do under the circumstances. I only hope that it works." The words are spoken with an undercurrent of urgency that sets me on edge. She motions for me to take the pillow closest to me, as she claims the opposite one. The two of us facing each other, legs crossed, hands resting on our knees, she says, "I'm not sure if this will work, but I have to try." She speaks in a tone so tense, I'm not sure what to make of it.

"Paloma, what's going on here? What is this?" I ask.

"I'm going to attempt a lineage transmission where I pass on to you all of the teachings that were passed on to me from my mother who acted as the Seeker before me. Only for me, the teach-ings were passed down verbally. The same way I would've taught Django had he survived. The same way I'd hoped to teach you, but I'm afraid we're running out of time."

I study her closely, desperate to know what's really going on. Why everything she says results in an ominous chill that runs down my spine. "Paloma, is there something you want to tell me? Are you not feeling well? You worry about me looking pale and thin, but I could say the same thing for you."

"I spent the last few days fasting and praying for your return, that is all, *nieta*. I will regain my strength now that you're back so do not waste your energy worrying for me. I only meant that now, with everything occurring so quickly, there's no time to in-struct you with the same methods in which I was taught. That is all." She nods firmly, as though that's the end of it, but the words leave me unsettled. "I've never conducted a lineage transmission this way. Nor have I taken part in one that was done in this manner. Still, I intend for it to work, and it's the intention that matters the most."

"So what's my part?" I'm eager to be a good student and do whatever I can to help this along. "What do you need me to do?"

"First I need you to sit with your eyes closed and the back of your hands resting against your knees with your palms open so that they're facing the ceiling." Once I'm appropriately settled she goes on to say, "Now open your mind and clear it of thought as best you can."

"That's not nearly as easy as it sounds." I sneak an eye open. "A stylist on one of the movies Jennika once worked on tried to teach me how to meditate, but it was a failure. I couldn't get my mind to shut up."

"Not to worry. Thoughts are natural. They're going to pop up out of habit, if nothing else. But the majority of thoughts are mean-ingless, repetitive, and of no real value or benefit to you. So, when a thought like that appears, all you need to do is acknowledge its presence then be quick to let it go on its way. If you refuse to pay it any real notice, it will vanish on its own. You can begin any time."

"That's it? I just sit here and dispose of random thoughts?"

"No, *nieta*." She leans toward me and presses a cool, dry palm to my forehead. "You just sit there and receive. I do the rest."

While I'm not exactly sure what she means, we're not long into it before a stream of images flows into my head. At first, I'm a little overvigilant. Eager to excel as a receiver, I'm quick to push the images away. Until I realize they're actually Paloma's images that she's sending to me—a series of ancient Seeker teachings that have been passed down through the centuries.

I watch in fascination as incredible stories from previous Seekers, including Paloma's own training rituals when she was my age, unfold in my head. And I can't help but marvel at how youthful she was, how determined, strong, and eager to accept her destiny—a far cry from the way I initially tried to ditch mine.

But, as it turns out, regretful thoughts are of no real value or benefit. So I'm quick to acknowledge them and send them away. Needing to clear as much room as possible for the endless reel of ancient rituals, healing practices, and mystical arts that stream through my head. I even get a glimpse into Paloma's own vision quest. Watching as Wolf devoured her only to rebuild her again, much like Raven did with me.

I observe her battles with Leandro, and while he's not nearly as evil or ambitious as his favored son Cade, he's a force to be reckoned with all the same. But what really strikes me is the way Paloma accepted her role without complaint. Dedicating herself to a life of great personal sacrifice in order to keep others safe, to keep the damage wreaked by Leandro contained. Her life story is a testament to her strength, assurance, and humility, and her reverence for her birthright is something I immediately vow to imitate.

Her life continues to unspool, including the moment she learns her husband, my grandfather, the Brazilian Jaguar shaman, Alejandro, died in a plane crash. A tragedy she accepts with her usual blend of dignity and grace, all too aware that the Richters were responsible. Ultimately succeeding at taking her husband, her son, and, for a while anyway, me. Which only strengthens my vow to stop them. To do whatever it takes to see that it's done—even if it means slaying every last one.

When the images fade, she removes her hand from my forehead and places the blood-crusted athame onto my lap. "Now that you are imbued with this knowledge, I want you to keep your eyes closed as you silently call upon the Seekers who preceded you. When, and only when, you feel their presence, you will open your eyes and slowly pass this blade through the nearest flame until the blood is cleansed. Then you will extinguish the candles using only intent."

I rub my lips together, straighten my spine, and do as she says. And when I'm fully imbued with the power of my ancestors' presence, I grip the hilt tightly and cut through the flame. Watching as the blood bubbles and sizzles until it's reduced to a single droplet that emits a curl of black smoke that rises before me. Its writhing, undulating form expanding and contracting to represent all of the spirit animals of the long line of Seekers preceding me, while allowing a fleeting glimpse of how they were all felled by Coyote.

All of them.

Every single one ultimately losing the battle.

Despite small moments of triumph, in the end, Coyote always won.

When Raven appears before me, I can barely keep hold of the athame for fear of what I might see.

"Raven is always with you," Paloma says. "Just because you can't always see him, does not mean he's abandoned you."

Soon after, Coyote appears, and I watch as the two square off.

"The same goes for your ancestors, and, someday, me." Paloma's voice provides the only source of comfort in a room reduced to one ominous point.

Raven moves toward Coyote, looking small and defenseless, no match for the enemy.

"You must never forget that, *nieta*. Someday you will need to call on all of us in a way you never have before. But you will do so without fear, assured that we will all be there."

The battle begins with Raven spreading his wings wide and Coyote crouching. The two launching toward each other, caught in midflight, when the droplet evaporates, the curl of smoke vanishes, and I drop the athame on my knee, feeling shaky and weak.

"*Abuela*—" I start, only vaguely aware of the heat of the blade scorching my jeans.

But she's quick to shush me. "Extinguish the candles, *nieta*. I know you can do it."

Not only do I snuff out the candles, but I evaporate the ring of salt as well. But despite the success, it's a far cry from the kind of skills I'll need in order to defeat the enemy.

"Although some of the images may have disturbed you, they were intended to empower you and remind you of the seriousness of the task you now face. While it's easy to hate Coyote, it's best not to be led by your hate. It always leads to impulsiveness and regret. No matter what happens from this point on, you must never give in to your baser instincts. Leave the hating to them. If you want to overcome Coyote, you have to become bigger, better, and stronger than they're capable of being."

"But how? You saw the same thing I saw—I'm destined to lose—all of us are!"

"That is not what I saw."

I look at her in confusion.

"Your story is malleable. It is up for you to decide."

"But if all of my ancestors before me failed, how will I be any different?"

"It's all in the perspective, *nieta*. You can look at your predecessors as failures, or you can view them as multiple generations of

Seekers who were able to keep the Richters from waging complete and total destruction."

I take a moment to consider her words. They make sense, but they don't really comfort. "Still, in the end, the Richters always got the best of them. Why will it be any different for me?"

"Because your light will lead the way."

"And theirs didn't?"

"That's not for you to worry about. Aside from the skills that I shared with you, all you need to know is that darkness can never overcome darkness—only light can do that. Use your light, *nieta*. Learn to trust it. It's the most reliable tool that you have."

A grin sneaks onto my face. "So, I can leave the athame behind?" I ask, desperate for a little light in a mood that's turned gloomy.

"No, take the athame." Paloma grins, playing along. "It never hurts to have a good backup."

When I gaze down at the blade, a barrage of concerns resurfaces again. "You sure it's okay?" I ask, remembering how it failed me the last time.

"When you question its abilities, you question your own abilities," Paloma says as though reading my mind. "Never allow yourself to fall into that trap."

I rise to my feet and hug her tightly to me. Choking back a sob as I say, "I'm so proud of you. I only hope that someday I can live up to the example you set."

"You already have," she says, but while she means well, I know it's not true. Or at least not yet, anyway.

"I should go." I swallow hard and pull away. Watching as Paloma heads for the chest of drawers where she retrieves my old green army jacket.

"I'm afraid my fingers aren't quite as nimble as they once were, but I know this is a favorite of yours, so I did my best to repair it."

I run a finger over the fresh lines of stitching mending the holes Cade Richter put there. Much like Axel mended the hole Cade ripped in my heart. If only everything could be stitched up so easily.

I avert my gaze until the threat of tears passes as she helps me into my jacket. Her slim fingers straightening the collar, she says, "I would join you, but—"

I meet her gaze and grin. "Now why would you want to do that? The music's too loud, the drinks are overpriced, and the food is bland."

The joke lasting only a moment before her expression grows grim. "Be careful, *nieta*."

"Always," I say, heading for the door, hoping she believes it.

"Be smart as well. And never forget that to become powerful is to allow a great power to work through you. No one walks alone."

I meet her gaze and nod, then I make my way toward Lita's waiting car.

sixteen

Daire

"For a weeknight, it's a lot busier than I would've expected," I say, approaching the Rabbit Hole entrance alongside my friends. "Still, busy is good. The bigger the crowd, the harder it will be for Cade to spot me. If he's here, that is."

Lita readjusts the strap of her purse and fluffs her hair so that it spills over her shoulders in long, shimmering waves. "It's been packed like this every night."

"People in this town have short memories. The sky rains fire, chaos ensues, people disappear, and they still come back for more." Xotichl weaves her cane so carelessly before her, I can't help but wonder if some of the Lowerworld magick managed to stick, but I dismiss it just as quickly. Surely she'd tell us if it did.

"Either that or their perception's been altered." Lita frowns. "Take it from someone who's been there." She stands before the bouncer, refusing his demand to check her ID. She places her hands on either side of his podium and leans perilously close to his face. "You've known me my whole life," she says. "This is nothing more than a ridiculous charade, not to mention a huge waste of time. And don't even think about marking me with your stupid, freaking stamp. Last thing I need is a red ink coyote emblazoned on my hand." She draws away, shooting him a defiant glare as she folds her arms across her chest.

"What's with the attitude, Lita? You got a problem with Coyote?" He cocks his head to the side and studies her through narrowed eyes. His tone purposely sinister, meant to intimidate, he makes a show of flexing his oversized muscles, as he says, "Maybe it has something to do with the company you keep?" His gaze purposely switches to me. "Maybe you should go back to your old crowd?"

"And maybe you should hear me when I say that I'm through with Coyote. Forever." She turns on her heel and makes for the club's entrance.

"Famous last words." He laughs. "Coyote is a hard habit to quit. Just ask Marliz." His gaze slews toward me, ensuring I heard. "She's back to waiting tables. I'm sure you'll see her inside."

I keep my face neutral, refusing him the satisfaction of knowing he shocked me. Last I heard, Marliz was settled in L.A. after leaving her creepy, abusive fiancé, Cade's cousin Gabe. Jennika got her a job, helped her find a place to live. I wonder if Jennika's even aware that she left.

His sinister laugh chases us all the way into the club where it's soon replaced with blaring music coming from the band on stage.

"Well that was . . ." Lita flattens her lips and narrows her eyes, searching for just the right word.

"Weird. Strange. Bizarre. Ominous. Take your pick." Xotichl sighs.

"And can you believe Marliz is back? Do you think they altered her perception all the way from L.A.?"

"Doubtful," Xotichl says. "I don't think it works long distance. Besides." She turns to me. "Paloma and the elders have been working some kind of new protection spell in order to block it."

"Well, I hate to break it to you," Lita says. "But it's not working. I mean, look at this place—more than half of Enchantment is here!"

My gaze cuts through the crowd, desperately seeking the one person I'm most interested in seeing. "The magick only works for as long as people want to be protected," I say. "When you live in a town like this, it's easier not to see the truth." I turn to my friends.

"Well, that's depressing." Lita frowns.

"And speaking of depressing . . ." Xotichl nods to the far side of the room where Lita's former BFFs, Crickett and Jacy, are hanging on Phyre's every word.

"You can see that?" Lita asks, beating me to it.

"I can *sense* it," Xotichl says. But her lips tug at the side, leaving me to think, yet again, that she's purposely hiding something.

"Whatever." Lita shrugs in dismissal. "It's about time they found someone new to emulate. You have no idea what a relief it is to hang with people who *don't* try to copy your every move. Not to mention how they were always stealing my style. At least you guys never do that."

"Yes, at least we have that in our favor." Xotichl laughs.

"Okay, so what's the plan?" Lita eyeballs my overstuffed bag. "And just how long are you planning on being away? Your purse looks like it's ready to burst."

"As long as it takes," I say, addressing Xotichl when I ask, "Is Cade here? Can you sense his energy?"

She lifts her chin, slowly scanning the room. "I can feel his presence. He's definitely in the building, but not in this room. The energy's dim."

"So he's already out clubbing?" Lita scowls. "Figures. So much for mourning the loss of his twin." She rolls her eyes and shakes her head in disgust.

"Listen." I keep my voice low and lean close. "I was originally planning to hang for a bit before making my way to the vortex. But since I'm pretty sure the bouncer's already alerted Cade that I'm here, there's no point in pretending. I'm just gonna go for it, and hope for the best."

"And what about us? What should we do?" Lita looks at me, hoping for a juicy assignment.

"Just be your usual charming self. Socialize, eavesdrop, observe. And if Cade approaches you, do *not* antagonize him." I shoot her a serious look. "We'll deal with him later, I promise. Same goes for Phyre, if you run into her, play nice. After what you told me about her father, I can't help but think that the more we can learn about her, the better."

"Keep your friends close but your enemies closer?" Lita cocks a meticulously groomed brow.

"Something like that. But seriously, just keep your cool. I can't be worried about you starting trouble when I need to focus on locating Dace."

"Fine." She frowns. "I solemnly swear that, for the time being anyway, I will refrain from going medieval on Cade. But just so you know, when the time comes, I plan to be right by your side, taking him down."

I start to turn away when Xotichl calls after me.

"Just . . . be careful," she says.

I nod.

"Also, if you don't return soon, we're going after you. So no long reunions when you find him, okay?"

I flash a tight grin and make for the hall. Unwilling to tell them the truth—that Dace has changed so much there's no saying what I might find, or if I'll be able to help him.

But I have to try.

If it's the last thing I do, I have to at least try.

seventeen

Daire

Despite the original plan being to charge straight for the vortex without any pretense, by the time I reach the bathroom I change my mind. Thinking a little caution never hurt anyone, I steal a moment to lean against the wall and fumble aimlessly through my bag, all the while scanning for Richters. Any Richter. They're all working against me.

As soon as I've ensured the all-clear, I make for the long hall that leads to the vortex. Covering only a handful of feet, when a familiar voice calls out from behind me.

"Daire. Daire Santos."

I respond with a lowered chin and a quickened pace.

"Don't pretend you didn't hear me when we both know you did. I will chase you down if that's what it takes."

For a brief moment I consider letting her make good on her word. But since there's no point in making this any worse than it already is, I stop in my tracks.

"When'd you get back?" Her spiked heels snag the carpet as she approaches.

"When'd *you* get back?" I turn just in time to find her heavily made-up eyes hooded with suspicion and fixed hard on mine.

"You never learn, do you?" She tucks a lock of bleached-blond hair behind her ear and fiddles with her large silver hoop earring with a hand that seems to sag under the weight of the massive rock that she wears. A large, square-cut, brilliant blue tourmaline on a platinum band, flanked by slightly smaller blue tourmalines, that, if I had to guess, came straight from Cade's mine.

"Seems we have that in common." I motion toward her new engagement ring, nearly triple in size to the one she wore before. Caught by the way she lifts her hand high and flutters her fingers. Eyes widening in admiration, and . . . something more . . . something I can't quite determine.

Her gaze dreamy, she says, "For the record, I appreciate everything your mom did for me. She really helped me. Went above and beyond."

"Jennika's a good person. She's always willing to help those in need."

Marliz returns her hand to her side as her irises clear once again. "Still, don't get the wrong idea. I've no plans to return the favor."

"Jennika's set. She's not really in need of your help," I say. Convinced by the edge in her tone, and the strange look on her face, that this is no random conversation. Marliz has an agenda. All Richters—and, in her case, soon-to-be-Richters—do.

"She may not need my help, but you do." Marliz continues to study me. Looking as though the sight of me pains her. "Go home, Daire. Go back to where you came from." She drops her gaze to her feet, digging the toe of her boot into the dirty gray carpet.

"You've been saying that to me since the first night we met," I reply, noticing how her voice went from vengeful to wistful in a handful of seconds. Her moods changing so quickly it's hard to keep track.

"Maybe it's time you listened. It's the best advice I can give you." She centers the pointed toe of her boot on a wadded-up gum wrapper and kicks it out of her way.

"And why should I listen to you, when you can't even manage to stay away?"

"I have my reasons." She glances down at the rock on her finger, eyes wide and luminous.

"Let me guess—you're back with Gabe?"

She continues to gaze at the ring, nodding ever so slightly.

"So, you're willing to trade your happiness for a handful of shiny minerals?"

Her gaze hardens into something dark, feral. Dropping whatever hint of pretense remained. "You've got ten seconds to return to your friends and take your party elsewhere," she says.

I square my shoulders and tighten my grip on my bag, poised for pretty much anything. "I think we both know that's not going to happen."

She looks me over for a long moment, then snakes her fingers into the front pocket of her denim miniskirt, retrieves her cell phone, and says, "I'm sorry to hear that."

"Don't be. From what I can see, you have far more problems than me." I start to turn, troubled by the encounter, but not for the reasons she thinks.

"I'm not kidding, Daire! I'll tell them what you're up to!"

"You have no idea what I'm up to," I mumble, eager to put some distance between us.

"You leave me with no choice!" she shouts.

"There's always a choice!" I glance over my shoulder long enough to see her tapping on her cell phone, bringing it to her ear, then I break into a run. Racing down a hall that, while not technically booby-trapped, may as well be.

Leandro's office lies just before me, with the door ajar and a phone ringing.

I rush past the opening, barely reaching the door's other side when a familiar voice barks, "What is it—I'm busy." Followed by, "What? The Seeker? You sure? Cade swore she was dead!"

Leandro's muffled curse soon followed by a hand crashing hard against a desk, and the squeak and protest of a body launching from a stiff leather chair, as I storm the hall at full speed.

My insides sear with a pain that's white hot. My lungs threaten to explode in my chest. Still I push past the agony and sprint for the vortex. Ignoring Leandro's voice calling out from behind me, commanding me to stop, I slip my hand in my purse, retrieve the cigarettes Paloma gave me, and dive in headfirst.

Shoving through the wall that isn't really a wall, I burst free to the other side, only to be met by a sinister voice saying, "Hello, Daire. Last I saw you, you were dead."

eighteen

Daire

The heels of my sneakers screech and slide across the tin floor until I'm standing flushed and breathless before Cade.

With a long black scarf wrapped loosely around his neck, and a black knit cap pushed back on his head, he looks cozy, relaxed, healthy, and fit. Having planted himself at the entry of the large tin pipe that acts as a passageway to the cave and the second vortex beyond, he lounges in his overstuffed, antique chair like a spoiled young king at his throne. Bearing not a single sign of having bled out from a gaping hole in his gut just a few days earlier.

I steady my breath, regain my footing, and say, "And last I saw you, you were dead too." I move toward him, wanting him to know that while he may have succeeded in surprising me, it's not the same as scaring me. "But that was before your faithful Coyote restored you."

Cade tilts his chair back. Assesses me through narrowed eyes. The corner of his mouth tugging in amusement, he motions toward the stash of cigarettes in my hand, and says, "Seriously, Daire—three packs?" He makes a disapproving cluck of his tongue. "You really should reconsider. Smoking is a dreadful, nasty habit that's been proven to hasten your mortality. And I think we both know that, as a Seeker, it's a risk you can't afford. Your kind tends to die young."

I move toward the edge of his chair, shooting him a bored look as I sing, "Been there, done that." I settle before him. "Actually, I brought these for your friends. Last few times I was here they really seemed to enjoy them."

Cade crosses his legs and drapes his hands over the armrests in a way that allows me to see the blue tourmaline ring I don't remember him wearing before. "Very thoughtful, Seeker. But, as you can see, my *friends,* as you call them, aren't here at the moment. In anticipation of your visit, I gave them the night off. Sent them to a dimension far, far away where they can keep an eye on my brother."

His eyes meet mine as though daring me to react, but other than a quick intake of breath, I keep my face neutral, refuse to show the slightest trace of concern. Refuse to let on how the mere thought of his demons sniffing around Dace sends my heart racing. Dealing with Cade is like a never-ending poker game. With stakes this high, I can't afford a single mistake.

"It's a shame about that whole Echo business, isn't it?" He tilts his head to the side and impersonates a thoughtful expression. "Guess that's something Leandro didn't anticipate when he was conjuring us." His lips pull into a frown as he breathes a staged sigh. "Leandro certainly has his faults, and sometimes I can't help but think he's a burden. Though I'm sure you feel the same way about Jennika and Paloma. It's such a drain trying to humor their outdated ideas while we forge much greater destinies of our own. Still, what are we to do?" His gaze drifts along with his voice, musing on the idea for much longer than it warrants, before returning to me almost as an afterthought. "Anyway, you really should forget about Dace. Trust me, it's for the best. Last I saw, he wasn't looking so good. Which left me with no choice but to hide him in a place where no one will ever find him."

"Guess that remains to be seen," I say, with far more confidence than I feel. Rejecting the picture his words form in my mind. Unable to bear the thought of Dace injured and suffering, left to rot in a demon-filled land.

His face hardens into a series of sharp angles and edges, as he uncrosses his legs and leans forward. Technically, he may be Dace's identical twin, but Dace is incapable of looking like this. Or at least he used to be.

"I hate to break it to you, Santos, but this is as far as you'll get." He grips the armrests so tightly, it seems he's struggling to contain himself, trying hard not to shift. "You're trespassing, and I just won't allow it."

"I'm not sure you have a choice." I stand my ground, aware of the nagging tug of foreboding swirling inside me.

"Tough words coming from someone who, not long ago, was lying spread-eagled beneath me."

I start to go at him, if for no other reason than to permanently erase the smirk from his lips. But then I remember all of the reasons I can't kill him, or at least not yet anyway. And I force myself to settle for glaring instead.

"Too bad Dace interrupted us when he did. I could tell you were really starting to enjoy it."

He's baiting me. Wants me to react, lose my cool, but I refuse to bite.

"And yet, now that you're back . . . well, I'm beginning to think I liked you a whole lot more when you were dead. Turns out, the memory of you is much more appealing than the reality."

"Sorry to disappoint." My shoulders rise and fall as I stare at a point beyond his shoulder and calculate my next move.

Two dozen steps from here to the cave? Two and a half?

"Oh, you've disappointed me so many times I've lost count." He drums his fingers against the armrests, the metal band of his ring clinking hard against the dark wood echoing all around me.

I crick my neck from side to side, and heave a bored sigh. "So tell me," I say. "Are we done here?"

He lifts his chin and stares down the length of his nose.

"Are we finished with the banter? Is the repartee portion of the evening over? 'Cause if so, I'd really like to get going. I have places to be."

"This is as far as you go, Seeker." His irises glow a deep burning red, but only for an instant before turning icy-blue and opaque once again. "Your little adventure ends here. Now."

"As if you could stop me." I take another step forward, stopping when my knee nearly meets his.

"What're you going to do Seeker, kiss me or kill me?" He squints in amusement.

"I'm going to kill you," I say, my tone straightforward, just stating the facts as I know them. "But not yet. Though someday, I promise you, I will. "

"Sounds like a date." He wiggles his brow, runs his tongue around the rim of his mouth.

"Best one you'll ever have."

I slip around the side of his chair and break into a run. Taking the tunnel at full speed, pushing myself harder, forcing my strides to be longer, when the crash of my shoes slamming hard against the tin floor is soon joined by his.

If I am operating on pure adrenaline as Paloma claimed, I hope it holds long enough for me to escape him.

The sound of the chase blares in my head. A screaming, deafening crescendo of bodies pounding tin that causes my ears to ring, my eyes to tear, until the next step lands on softer ground— propelling me out of the tunnel and into the cave.

A far cry from the spartan cave of my Santos ancestors, the Richters' cave is one of carefully curated luxury. Plush. Luxurious. Loaded with fine antique furniture and art-covered walls. Ill-gotten gains.

I swerve around the couch. Nearly clearing the den, when Cade rushes up from behind me, moving with unfathomable speed.

He gropes at my shoulder. Yanks hard on my hair. Slowing me

just enough to grab hold of my bag and jerk hard on the strap. The sudden reversal flinging me backward until I smack into his chest.

He absorbs the blow easily, lifts his free arm, and secures it tightly against my neck. "It's too late for you, Seeker," he hisses, his breath surprisingly hot in such a cold space. "You should've never left the Upperworld. That is where the glowing one took you, isn't it?" He loosens his grip just enough for me to confirm it, but when I gasp a lungful of air instead, he tightens his chokehold again. "This town already mourned you. Their collective grief lasted less than a day. Seems you didn't make much of an impact during your brief stay in Enchantment. Even Paloma, as ineffective as she is, boasts a better record than you. Guess that makes you the *Sorriest Excuse for a Seeker That Ever Was.*" He laughs a crude laugh as he hauls me up tighter against him. Repositioning his arm so it's pushing hard on my larynx. "This feels a little redundant, doesn't it? I resent having to kill you again. I have better things to do with my time."

"But it was so much fun the first time," I croak, the words garbled, unintelligible.

He presses down on my windpipe, severely cutting my oxygen supply. Using his other hand to lift the edge of my sweater, he says, "I want to see your wound, Seeker. I want to see how the little glowing man fixed you. Why do you think he did that—hmm? Why do you think he would come all the way down from the cozy trappings of the Upperworld to save *you*? You got a thing for Mystics? You been two-timing my twin?"

He throws his head back and laughs, and I use the distraction to jab my elbow hard against my side in a desperate attempt to keep myself covered and hang onto my bag. I can't afford to lose any of the tools Paloma stashed in there.

But my head is growing dizzy. My vision faint. And Cade is so unfeasibly strong, he merely rips the bag from my shoulder and chucks it clear across the room in one seamless move.

"Oops!" He clucks in a way that reverberates hard against my eardrum. "Seems you're flat out of luck. You're completely un-armed and outmatched, Santos." His breath is hot, fetid, as his tongue runs a leisurely lap around the shell of my ear. "How will you ever defend yourself now?"

It's a good question. One I'm not sure how to answer. Still, I shore my resolve. Tell myself I can do this. I cannot let him win.

But with my neck tissues collapsing, and the flow of oxygen reduced to a trickle, I have only a handful of seconds at best be-fore I fall completely unconscious.

Ignoring the fiery pain seizing my chest, I raise my leg high, center my foot, and brutally slam it into Cade's knee. And while it doesn't take him down like I hoped, it's enough for him to loosen his grip so I can break free.

I stagger toward my bag, coughing and wheezing as I gulp down great mouthfuls of air. Having just grabbed hold of the strap when Cade appears beside me and circles my arm in a viselike grip.

"You're done, Seeker." He spins me until I'm staring into his unfathomable eyes.

Just like looking into Dace's eyes the last time I saw him.

Which is why I have to survive. I have to reach Dace, restore his soul, and reverse whatever horrible thing he did to make him-self resemble his brother.

"That's what you said last time, and look, I'm still here," I croak, my voice hoarse, damaged, still I manage to jerk free and put a few more steps between us. Though it's not until I'm stand-ing triumphantly before him with my hands curled into fists, when I realize he freed me too easily.

For Cade, this is no more than a game.

This is how he enjoys himself. This is why he was gripping the armrests, trying to hold on for whatever treat he's planned next.

I didn't break free.

I'm exactly where he wants me.

No sooner have I realized the truth, when he launches his body hard into mine. The impact of his weight knocking me to the ground so brutal, I'm amazed my head didn't explode on contact. And before I have time to react, he's waling on me.

He fights for real. Fights dirty. Fights to the death. His fists pounding into my flesh until it's all I can do to deflect.

"You're no good to me now, Seeker!" he shouts, his knuckles repeatedly driving into my skin. "The prophecy has begun. I am the darkness ascending. Whatever strength I drew from the love you shared with my brother, is no longer needed. I have risen. I have transformed. I have become what I was created to be. You and your kind are no match for me."

He drones on and on. Ranting about his greatness, his power, his birthright to rule all. The tiresome diatribe eventually mutating into some ancient, tribal dialect I've heard him use before. And not long after that, his hands are back on my throat.

I buck wildly beneath him. Thrashing, kicking, biting, hair pulling, scratching at his hands, trying to loosen their grip, but it's no use. Whatever I do barely penetrates.

It's true what he said. He has transcended. Bearing the strength in human form that was once reserved for his demon form.

And it's not long before my limbs tire, growing useless and weak, as my sight begins to dim from the edges in. Shrinking my vision to one point of light.

One point of light that dances, leaps, wiggles, and twists.

One point of light emanating from the lit torch on the wall nearest me.

"Use your light, nieta. *Learn to trust it. It's the most reliable tool that you have,"* Paloma said to me. And while it's not technically *my* light I see flickering before me, for the moment, it's all that I've got.

I reach for the buckskin pouch at my neck and fold my fingers around it.

"Your dying breath and you waste it on that?" Cade sneers. "You deserve to die, Seeker. Haven't you figured it out by now? It's superstitious nonsense! If it worked, then why has your life been reduced to this? Why did your dad croak at sixteen? Why is your entire family, with the exception of Paloma, who barely counts she's so useless—why are all of them dead? Ever stop to think about *that*? You fell for the whole pack of lies, Santos. When the truth is, any magick worth its salt doesn't live where you seek it. It's not in the elements. It's not in the earth. Magick, true magick, only thrives in the darkest of men—the worthy few. All the rest are mere fodder, existing to sustain us. Lazy, apathetic losers, content to live small meaningless lives, who willingly leave their souls at risk for people like me to control. Still, it's nice of you to entertain me with your foolish beliefs—as if killing you wasn't pleasure enough."

He throws his head back and lets out a roar so loud, so primal, so Coyote-like, the surrounding walls tremble. And just when I'm sure he's going to change into his demon form, he surprises me by staying the same. Only harder, fiercer—as though the two versions of him have merged into one.

His fingers lace tighter, as his thumbs press hard on my windpipe. "Funny how the harder I squeeze, the bigger your eyes grow, yet the less you can see." He leans closer, his face looming directly above me. "Look at me, Santos!" he cries. "Look. At. Me! I want to be the last thing you see before you die. This time, just like the last time. I want you to remember the way I looked when I killed you for the second time!"

With my vision reduced to a pinprick, I continue to stare past his shoulder, focusing on the small beam of flame.

"Look at me! I command you to *see me!*" He screams, but I maintain my focus, allowing the Fire Song to stream through my brain.

> *At the whim of the wind*
> *I can smolder or singe*
> *Comforting as easily as I harm*
> *A single lick of my flame begets irrevocable change*
> *Be like me when you seek to transform*

"Damn it, Seeker—do what I say! Look at me!"

The light grows brighter. So bright I can no longer bear it.

I shutter my eyes against the flame.

"Open your eyes, Seeker! Don't make me—"

The flame flickers and flares against the back of my lids, but it's too late.

Outraged by my refusal to obey, Cade squeezes so tightly my whole world goes black.

Only this time, unlike the last time, there is no one to save me.

My limbs are the first to go. Turning into numb, deadened stumps.

My torso goes next.

And then—

A horrible scream fills the air, as I'm flung to the far side of the room where I roll to my side, gasping and wheezing, as the burning, demon version of Cade twirls and dances before me.

I scramble to my feet, my fingers softly exploring the damage he's wrought on my throat, as Cade flails about the room. Screaming in agony, searching for something in which to put himself out.

Would've been far more effective to stop, drop, and roll, but it's not my place to interfere.

I stagger toward the hall. All too aware that while I may have survived this one, I'm in such bad shape I have no idea how I'll go on. A trip to the Enchanted Spring is out of the question. There's no time to waste. Now that the Richters are on to me, I need to get deeper into the Middleworld as fast as I can and find Dace.

I've just barely made it to the back wall when a sudden surge of warmth rushes up from behind me, as the final line of the Fire Song repeats in my head.

Be like me when you seek to transform.

The fire beckons. Curling and twisting, inviting me to join it.

Be like me when you seek to transform.

I look past it to where Cade, still overtaken by flames, continues his hysterical dance.

Be like me when you seek to transform.

This is no ordinary fire. This is my Fire Song—my magick at work.

Be like me when you seek to transform.

Without hesitation, without fear, I move toward the inferno until I'm fully engulfed in its flames. Trusting they will restore me, transform me, heal me, just like the song promised. Its warm loving fingers coaxing me through, urging me safely toward its other side where I emerge completely renewed.

I steal one last glance at Cade, seeing him already beating the flame. Without a second to spare, I plunge through the wall, landing in the first of many dimensions of the Middleworld.

nineteen

Dace

Another visitor.

Since Suriel left there've been many—most of them demons working for Cade.

Even Coyote stopped by long enough to jerk his snout against my cheek to ensure I'm still breathing before he moved on.

But no matter how much I plead, not a single one of them was willing to put me out of my misery. So why should this time be any different?

I roll onto my stomach, bury my face in the dirt. Muttering, "Go away!" But still it draws closer. "If you're not going to help, then feel free to scram. I've no use for gawkers, so get the hell out. You can tell Cade I'm still breathing, still existing, just like he planned."

"Now why would I do that?"

A brilliant veil of light swoops down from above—its warming rays permeating my flesh. Thawing the places long turned cold.

"You're a mess," the voice says. "But I'm here to help. I can heal you. Erase your wounds like they never existed."

"Not exactly the kind of help I'm after, so push on." I burrow deeper into the dirt. "It's not light that I seek, but rather its opposite."

"I don't understand." The voice bears kindness, a trace of confusion. Probably paired with a face to match. Still I stay right as I am and refuse to acknowledge it. Though that doesn't keep it from asking, "If you're not looking to heal, what is it you want?"

"Salvation. Atonement. Daire," I reply, my lips grinding into the dirt. "Think you can manage that?" My tone is purposely gruff and sarcastic, and my request is met with silence, just as I thought. "Go on. Shove off," I growl, the words a harsh rasp, but the meaning is clear.

"Dace, I—"

"Beat it!"

It's only when the light retreats that I raise my head and chance a quick peek.

Platinum hair. White tunic. Pale skin. And he glows.

Go figure.

It's amazing the things you see way out here.

twenty

Daire

The air is acrid and dry. Instantly parching my throat, chapping my lips, but still I push on through the bleak, barren land that stands as a gateway between one world and the next.

Unlike my previous trips, this time, instead of trekking toward the massive dune that drops into the Lowerworld, I go the opposite way in search of the Middleworld dimension where Coyote left Dace.

According to Paloma, each of the three worlds contains numerous realms. And from the orders Cade gave to Coyote, to *"drag Dace to the darkest recess of the Middleworld where no one will find him,"* I take him at his word and head for the deepest, dreariest plane.

While the Upperworld is populated by benevolent human guides (*Axel included?*), and the Lowerworld with benevolent animal guides, the Middleworld is the only one populated by both humans and demons alike. Though it's not always easy to tell them apart. Coyote wears many disguises.

Unfortunately, everything here looks the same. Endless miles of dull yellow, snow-flecked sand, offering no natural markers of any kind—no shred of vegetation, not a single sign of life. It's a dead, dried-up land. Making it impossible to tell if I'm on the right path.

A dead, dried-up land.

Land.

That's it!

It's been a while since I last called upon the Earth element, which is why it takes a few moments to remember the melody. But as soon as the tune pops into my head, the lyrics to the Earth Song instantly follow.

> *I am constant and strong*
> *Eternal—everlasting*
> *A provider of shelter and solace*
> *Strength and perspective*
> *Look to me when you're lost—and I'll give you direction*

I'm three verses in when a path clears before me and I hit the trail at a full run. Cutting and curving through the valley of sand toward a bleary horizon I soon recognize as the first of many portals into the Middleworld's many dimensions.

In the Lowerworld, transcending dimensions is all about descent. And, from what I saw, the Upperworld runs just the opposite. But here, the portals are laid out like dominoes. Some placed closely together, others occurring miles apart. Though it doesn't take long to detect a surprising amount of order amidst all the chaos. Despite each passing veil leading to an entirely different landscape—some carpeted with sand, some with dirt, others with sharp-edged rocks—each successive portal leads to a land that's progressively bleaker than the one that came before.

Still, it's not until I've passed through several layers inhabited by strange, shadowy figures, when I come upon one overrun with a preponderance of small, run-down huts.

Instinctively, I reach for my athame, as my eyes continue to survey the land, and my feet keep a steady pace toward the next veil. My relief at having made it through unscathed, ending the second I see the dimension beyond is markedly worse.

Markedly worse and inhabited by demons.

Lots and lots of demons.

And unlike the demons in the previous dimensions, these ones are not shy.

These are Cade's demons.

Despite having the advantage of seeing them first, it's only a matter of seconds before they surround me like a carousel of massive, scaly, hulking bodies with oversized heads, flame-colored eyes, twisted snouts, and lipless, gaping holes standing in for their mouths.

I wave my athame before me, turning slow circles as I search for the leader, the one who poses the biggest threat. Determined to go after him first, if for no other reason than to send a warning to the rest that despite my appearance, I am not one to be trifled with.

The largest among them is the first to step forward. With a horrible snarl shrieking from his abyss of a mouth, he roars with such force the ground trembles beneath me.

The move meant to intimidate, but it falls appallingly short.

All it takes is a determined swing of my athame to cut him off at the knees. Then I kneel down beside him and slice off his head, just to ensure he truly is dead.

That's the thing with demons. When it comes time to fight, the stupid ones always man the front line, while the smart ones hang back to evaluate. And more often than not, the leader looks nothing like you'd expect.

I kick the beast's leg stumps out of the way, and have a go at the rest of them. My blade cleaving into thick scaly torsos, gouging out eyes, slicing through well-muscled necks until the ground all around me is littered with oversized, misshapen heads, and only the smallest demon is standing.

The leader's eyes meet mine, and I give a little wave of my hand, urging him to join me.

But this one's smarter than the rest, and after taking a moment to consider, he turns on his heel and disappears. Leaving me to move toward the next veil where I pause on its other side, struck to see that the path has ended and Dace is nowhere in sight.

Has the energy become so murky and stagnant that Earth can no longer guide me?

Or, is it now up to me to call on what I know in order to find him?

I go quiet and still, alert to the smallest shift in the atmosphere, any sort of sign that he's here.

A shuffle of dirt.

Could be a strange animal, or yet another tribe of demons, but it's worth checking out.

A softly murmured voice.

I can't make out the words, but it sounds like English.

With no more to go on, I race toward it—my certainty growing with each passing step.

He's here.

Living.

Breathing.

Which means it's not too late to save him.

Driven by the promise of being reunited with Dace, I crash straight into a scene that stops me dead in my tracks.

twenty-one

Daire

Breathless and horrified I watch as he stands before an old dead tree with his back turned toward me. Grasping either side of the hollowed-out trunk with a set of palms that emanate a stream of energy so dark, it's only a second later when the tree is annihilated as though it never existed.

Before he can turn that same dark magick on me, I creep up behind him, press the athame to his neck, and say, "Tell me where he is."

He doesn't so much as flinch. Doesn't so much as glance back at me. Doesn't react in any notable way.

Maybe because he recognizes me just as easily as I did him.

"Tell me where he is, Axel. Tell me what you've done with him, or so help me God, I will . . ." I leave the threat unspoken, allowing the sharp tip of my blade pressing into his neck to fill in the blanks as I keep a close watch on his hands. Magickal hands. Lethal hands. And I can only pray he didn't use them on Dace.

"Drop the knife," he says, his voice soft and coaxing, betraying no hint of fear. "There's no need for violence. In case you haven't noticed, physical threats may slow me, but they'll never stop me." He lowers his hands before him and stares at his palms in dismay.

Seeming not to notice or care that I continue to press the blade to his neck.

"I know he's here," I say. "And if you don't take me to him right now, so help me, I will cut you." I jam the tip into his flesh, just enough to show that I'm serious.

"I have no doubt you'll make good on your word. Still, you've already tried to kill me once. What makes you think a second attempt will end any better?"

"Because I'm stronger." I glare. "And because this is no longer just about me. There's much more at stake."

He drops his hands to his sides as though they're of no use to him. "If you truly care about Dace, if you really want to help him, you'll put the knife away and go home. This is no place for you. Trust me on that."

I lift onto my toes, curl my arm around his neck, and press the blade hard against the hollow of his throat. Last time I found myself in a similar situation, I hesitated and it ended up costing me greatly. It's a mistake I won't make again.

"You've got less than a second to tell me where he is," I warn, taken by surprise when instead of resisting me, instead of answering me, he drops his head back and freely offers his neck. His deep purple eyes rolling skyward to meet mine, bearing no trace of the soft lavender gaze I remember.

"Do it," he says. "If it pleases you, I won't move to stop you."

At his urging, I shove the knife in. Slicing through a soft layer of smooth, ivory skin—only to gasp in disbelief as a stream of golden fluid seeps from the wound.

That's why he glows. It comes from inside!

"What are you?" I whisper, watching as the fluid coagulates, then dissipates, as the gash seals shut, leaving no sign it ever existed.

"I already told you." He straightens his spine, cricking his neck from side to side as he turns to face me for the first time since I arrived.

"I know what you told me, but you're more than a Mystic. That much is clear." My gaze rakes over him, trying to get my bearings, trying to make sense of his being here.

"Am I?" He shrugs. "I'm not sure what I am anymore."

Our eyes meet, and for the first time since I got here, I'm no longer sure what to do. He's not acting at all like I expected him to.

"Why are you following me?" I snap, in desperate need of some answers. "Why are you here? There's no way you can ever convince me to go back if that's what you're thinking!" The athame wavers before me, though it's no use where he's concerned.

"I don't even know if I can return. I wouldn't dream of taking you." His dark gaze appraises me, and for the first time ever he looks weary, broken, and as lost as I currently feel. "Besides, you're fully healed now from what I can see. Exactly how long have you felt better, Daire?"

I stare at him without blinking.

"Much longer than you let on, I presume."

I stand mute before him, staring at the place on his forehead where the chair landed. Noting how, just like his neck, it bears no trace of trauma.

"I'm not interested in apologies," he says. "If that's what you're worried about."

"What are you interested in?" My gut clenches. "I demand to know the truth."

"Why do you think I'm here?"

"Because you're following me—stalking me! You think that just because you saved me you can claim me!"

He shutters his eyes, mumbles something unintelligible under his breath.

"You held me in a locked room—bolted from the outside—with no way to escape! You held me hostage against my will—and tried to keep me weak, so I wouldn't be able to leave!"

"Is that what you think?" His face clouds with pain.

"That's what I know! Now where the hell is Dace?" I start to push past him, only to have him grab hold of my arm and pull me tightly against him.

"Don't," he says, his gaze fixed on mine. "Trust me, you're not ready for that. It's worse than you can imagine."

I try to jerk free, but it takes a few attempts to succeed.

"You won't like what you see," Axel warns, but I dismiss it with a wave of my hand. Following the set of tracks that lead to my broken, bloodied, but still breathing boyfriend.

twenty-two

Dace

I wake from the dream with bleary eyes, a foggy brain, and the memory of Daire's sweet scent clinging in a way so insistent, so real, I instinctively roll onto my back and thrust a hand before me in a foolish and desperate attempt to make contact. Trying not to picture myself as I really am—a tortured mind, a wretched body, with five stupid fingers grasping at air—refusing the truth my heart knows too well.

She's not there.

Never will be.

This is a place of deep fetid darkness and gloom. Home to demons, those who hunt them, and the soulless, like me.

A light as bright as Daire's has no place here.

Even that strange glowing man was quickly overcome. Took only a matter of minutes to see his radiance permanently snuffed and diminished.

Still, my longing to gaze into her glittering emerald eyes and taste her sweet lips manages to persist. My need far too fervent to be tempered by something as simple as truth, I continue to grasp and pull and yearn until I wear myself out, burrow deeper into the earth, and wait for the dreamstate to claim me again.

twenty-three

Daire

I drop beside the crumpled form, my fingers frantically digging through layers of earth. Clearing his back of debris, I grab hold of his shoulder and try to roll him onto his side, only to have him mumble something incoherent and push me away.

"Dace—please, it's *me!*" I cry, trying to make him face me again, but he's quick to deny me.

"He's gravely injured and severely traumatized." Axel's voice drifts from behind. "He's been down here too long to believe it's really you." His tone is straightforward, containing no hint of smugness, and yet the words manage to grate to no end.

Determined to ignore him, I lean closer, press my lips to Dace's ear, and urge him to open his eyes and see that it's me. Only to have my heart sink in despair when he shrinks from my touch and squeezes his eyes tightly shut.

"Either end me or leave me!" he croaks in a voice so damaged, I barely recognize it as his.

"I will *never* end you. And I have no intention of leaving without you," I say, managing to force him onto his side until his face is just inches from mine. "Dace, please!" I beg, reaching for the key at my neck and holding it up before him. "You must remember this, I'm sure that you do. I wear it as a symbol of our love and I gave you one to match." I slip a hand under his bloodstained sweater, hoping his key is still there, that he didn't lose it on his hellish journey here. Breathing a sigh of relief when I curl my fingers around it and bring it to his face. "Tell me you remember. Tell me you haven't forgotten the time we spent together." I press the keys together until they're perfectly matched, then I lower my lips to his and kiss him until he finally relents and kisses me back.

His lids flutter open. His eyes meet mine. And when I see the emptiness inside, my heart collapses in my chest.

Soulless.

It really is true.

But when he brings a hand to my face, and cups his palm to my cheek, I know that some semblance of Dace has managed to stick.

"I've dreamed you so many times," he says. "How do I know I'm not dreaming now?"

"Because I'm here. This is real. And I would've been here earlier but—"

"So I am dead." His face floods with inexplicable relief. "I finally managed it, and now we can be together for eternity."

"No!" I shake my head, desperate to refute it. "No one's dead. We're both alive. And now I'm going to get you out of here."

But before I can finish, he's already turning away. Closing his eyes in denial, he says, "You died. I saw you die. I watched the whole thing."

"Not the *whole* thing!" I cry, my throat parched and constricted, but I force the words past. "So much more happened, but we'll go over it later. For now, I need you to trust me enough to help you get out of here. Okay? Dace?"

He slips from my grip. His consciousness fading, voice drifting, he says, "I'm soulless . . . no good to you now . . ."

I try to prop him up, heave him onto my shoulder. But in his unconscious state, it's like lifting an unwieldy lump of dead weight.

I glance over my shoulder, glaring at Axel as I struggle with Dace. "The least you could do is help," I say, only to stare incredulously as he remains resolutely in place. "If you had an ounce of decency in you, you would—"

Before I can finish, he says, "It's not my job to help him." I sputter in outrage, about to comment on his unbelievable selfishness, when he goes on to say, "I shouldn't even be here. It's my job to *guide* him, no more. But now I'm afraid I've overstepped some of my most sacred boundaries." He shoots me an uncertain look, rakes a hand through his platinum curls, and though I have no idea what he's getting at, I'm far from amused.

"Listen, Axel," I say. "Here's the thing: You either help me lift Dace, or you get the hell out of my way. I have no time for word games, and absolutely no interest in your existential dilemma. With or without you, Dace and I are out of here."

I pull on Dace's jacket again, finally getting some traction, when Axel heaves a deep sigh and comes around to Dace's other side. Easily propping him onto his shoulder, he looks at me and says, "I should probably explain. I'm Dace's spirit guide."

twenty-four

Daire

"You?" I stare. The disbelief in my tone is nothing compared to the disbelief I wear on my face. "You're Dace's spirit guide?"

Axel nods in almost imperceptible assent. His stride quick and purposeful, his gaze fixed straight ahead.

"And why did you fail to mention this earlier? Why did you save me and not him?" I glare hard at him, but no matter how long I hold the look I can't get him to return it. "You left him for dead. Left him abandoned and soulless in the dreariest dimension of the Middleworld. You haven't done a single thing to protect him. So excuse me for being suspicious."

"My oath was to guide him, *not* to protect him. There's a difference."

I gaze at him wide-eyed. Every word he speaks just makes it worse. "That's it?" I cry, my hands curling to fists, blood rippling to my cheeks in a combination of anger and frustration. "That's your defense? You're going to argue semantics? Is that the best you can do?"

He ignores the outburst and carries on without a word. And when we pass through the vortex, I steel myself for the onslaught of demons, only to watch in disbelief when the few remaining ones take one look at Axel and flee.

"If you are Dace's spirit guide like you claim," I say, after we've traveled quite a ways, "then why'd you choose me over him?"

For the longest time, he refuses to engage. Remaining stubbornly silent through a succession of veils before he says, "I chose you over Dace, as you put it, because I knew that you were the key to ultimately saving him."

I stare at his profile for a long time, before I say, "That doesn't make any sense."

He nods in acknowledgment, but steadfastly refuses my gaze. "On the surface, it probably doesn't," he says. "But the fact is, Dace loves you and you love Dace. You are fated for each other."

I continue to stare. My interest now piqued.

"As Dace's spirit guide, it's my job to guide him. Much like Horse does, only I do so in different ways."

I switch my gaze to Dace's battered, unconscious form. Barely able to keep my anger in check when I say, "Well, you've done a really bang-up job there, haven't you, Axel?" I scowl. "Really. Stellar work. Way to go."

He ignores the slight and goes on to say, "While I am always attuned to him, and my influence is strong, it is only to the degree that Dace is willing to allow it, or acknowledge it. I am the nagging tug he feels in his gut. I am the gentle push toward a particular choice. I'm the intuition he doesn't always choose to act on. I'm there to guide and influence only. It is not my place to interfere with his choices. There is such a thing as free will, and I have to say that Dace Whitefeather has never failed to exercise his."

I weigh his words in my head, but remain unconvinced.

"Think of life as a classroom. You humans arrive here in order to learn and grow. And most of that learning and growing comes from the mistakes that you make. It's just the nature of things. Humans would never learn anything if their guides were always interfering, or trying to protect them."

"But you *did* interfere! You just said that you saved me to save Dace. I was already dead, I took my last breath, when you gave me the kiss of life!"

Axel's lips flatten. His face grows conflicted.

And in that moment, I know that I'm right. His expression providing all the proof that I need, to know that his feelings for me go far deeper than he's willing to admit. Far deeper than they rightfully should.

He pauses a long, thoughtful moment, before he turns to me with a regretful gaze. "By allowing you to live, by restoring your breath, I'm afraid I've broken my most sacred oath."

His expression is broken. He's speaking the truth.

A truth that reveals just how much I've misjudged him.

Axel wasn't hiding me because he's secretly in love with me.

He was hiding me because he wasn't supposed to save me.

"It's true," he says, having eavesdropped on my thoughts. The look that follows assuring me there's no need for embarrassment. "Dace was meant to die, not you. That's why I was there—it was time to guide him home. But instead of Dace, I ended up taking you."

"So it really was the prophecy, then?" I gaze off into the distance. The entire foundation of what I knew about life feels suddenly tenuous.

"Cade's forcing it was a little premature, but only a little. It was going to happen anyway. But now, because of what he did, everything's changed."

"Because I died instead?"

"Partly."

"And the other part?"

Axel looks at Dace.

"So, let me get this straight, you were there to whisk Dace to the Upperworld because it was his turn to die?"

He nods.

"But then everything got messed up, and I died instead?"

He inhales deeply, lifting his shoulders and dropping them again.

"And so, somewhere between the Lowerworld and the Upperworld you decided to save me, even though it went against your most solemn oath. And you did so in order to ultimately save Dace." I stare hard at him, but he doesn't respond. "And then you proceeded to hold me hostage so no one in the Upperworld would discover what you did, while everyone in Enchantment assumed I was dead."

He turns away.

"So all of this time you were basically protecting yourself?"

He closes his eyes.

"What kind of a Mystic are you, anyway?"

"According to you, not a very good one."

He shifts Dace higher onto his shoulder, and if nothing else, the gentle way in which he handles him tells me he truly does care for his charge. Still, there are too many unanswered questions for me to even think about lowering my guard.

"Why can't you heal him like you did me?"

"I'm not sure. It's either because the energy here is too dark and heavy. Or . . ." He pauses for a moment, before he's able to continue. "Or I've been down here too long and too often, and now it's influencing me in ways it never has before. Or, I've been stripped of my magick as punishment for what I've done. This is all new to me. I can't say for sure."

"I saw you annihilate that tree. That's pretty much the opposite of healing energy."

"Energy never dies, it just transforms. The magick's still with me, it's just that it's so much easier to destroy than create."

"Do you know what happened to Dace's soul?"

"I know it's not here."

"Does that mean you do know where it is and you won't tell me?"

He looks away. "Daire, please."

"Axel—if you're purposely holding back much-needed information for some messed-up reason, you're only delaying the inevitable because I will find it!"

"I have no doubt you will."

"So why not save me the time, and tell me now?"

"Because I don't know where it is. But I've told you enough already, more than I should."

I scowl, shoot him a dirty look, curse him under my breath, but he's like Teflon, none of it penetrates.

He just continues to haul Dace through the veils, as I race alongside him. Glancing over his shoulder to say, "I guess you'll just have to try to trust me—like I once tried to trust you."

twenty-five

Xotichl

"So where is lover boy Greyson anyway?" Lita taps her square-tipped nails hard against the table, resulting in an incessant clinking that's magnified by a lull in the music.

"Don't be nervous. He'll be here," I say, trying to keep my rubbernecking in check. I've never seen the Rabbit Hole in the way I can now. And though I can't see it clearly, it's even spookier than I thought it would be. Still, I need to get it under control, be more discreet. I'm not quite ready for anyone to know I can almost, kinda see.

"Nervous? Over a boy?" Lita's voice rises in outrage. "Please." She continues with the nail drumming, as I focus on her energy sparking and flaring—a definite sign of nerves if I've ever seen one. "He's the one who should be nervous. It's his job to impress me, not the other way around." Her head bobs, her nails tap, and it's not long before her leg joins in, swinging back and forth. And I know I need to change the subject before she rockets right off her stool.

"So tell me, what do you see?" I ask, eager to see if it matches the shadowy visions before me.

She ducks her head, takes a sip of her soda, as I watch the

swish of her energy, the tilt of her straw. "Okay, well . . . the band is taking a break, and I hope it's a long one because they totally blow. I mean, where's Epitaph when you need them? Especially the drummer?"

"For the last time, he'll be here." I groan, wondering what I was thinking when I agreed to set her up on a date. "And, for the record, I already know about the band. I'm blind, not deaf, you know."

"Oh, right. Sorry. So let's see . . . Phyre is still holding court, but she keeps looking over here. Though every time I catch her looking over here she pretends she wasn't actually looking over here but rather at a spot just slightly to the right of over here."

"Next time she looks, call her over."

Lita leans in and lowers her voice to a furious whisper. "You've got to be kidding. Daire gave specific instructions to eavesdrop. She never said anything about getting chatty with the enemy."

"Daire told you to be your normal charming self—and that includes small talk."

"I don't think I remember how to be charming. It's been so long since I tried."

"I'm not sure you ever knew how." I raise a grin to soften the blow. "People were mostly afraid of you. But you can use that too. Just, turn it up like you used to."

Lita grumbles a string of mostly unintelligible words, though it's not long before she perks up again. Sliding her elbows across the table, she grabs hold of my arm, and squeals, "Oh my gosh— Cade's here! He just walked up to Phyre and gave her a hug . . . um, actually, I think it's more like she's giving him a hug. She seems a little *lingering*. Like she has no plans to live in a world where she's not hugging Cade. But, from the looks of it, he's not all that into her. He extricates more or less gracefully, but not before she runs a finger down the length of his cheek, and looks at him all starstruck and dreamy . . . Gag. Consider yourself lucky you can't see this. It's straight out of the Come Hither playbook. So forced it's embarrassing to watch. Anyway, better her than me. That's what I say."

I peer across the room, seeing far more than I let on. Still, it's not quite as clear as Lita's version, so I'm quick to press for more. "What's Cade doing now? Are you sure he's not into it? I mean, she is really pretty, right?"

"If you're into tall, slim, perfectly proportioned, exotic-looking girls with smooth skin, full lips, perfect noses, and cat's eyes—then yeah, I guess she's okay," Lita says, her voice clearly sour.

"You're not jealous, are you?"

"Please." She straightens her spine, fluffs her hair so that it falls softly over her shoulders, and tugs on her sweater to put a bit more cleavage on display. "Anyway, Cade's always been hard to read, but one thing is sure—he loves the attention. He *lives* for attention. But whether his interest is truly reciprocated is anyone's guess. What about you—are you getting a read on his energy?"

I shake my head and continue to peer toward the far side of the room.

"Okay, so back to Phyre—she's acting really flirty. Like seriously, seductive and flirty. Her body language alone is like some over-the-top, animalistic, mating dance. But despite the fact that she's going all-out, they're mostly just talking, and he seems kind of distant and uninterested . . . and . . . oh great . . . oh crap! He just caught me looking and he just smiled, and now . . . oh crap, crap, triple crap . . ." Lita slumps down in her seat and leans toward me. "Pretend I'm not here."

"How am I supposed to do that when he already saw you?" I say, aware of Cade's frenetic, dark energy drifting our way.

"I don't know—I just—what do I do? What do I say?" Her voice is frantic, her energy panicked.

"Just play it cool. And whatever you do, *do not* kill him. Daire gave strict orders to hold off for now."

I've barely uttered the words when a shadowy figure fills the space next to Lita and moves in to hug her, though she's quick to bat him away.

"Dream on, Richter." She shoves a hand hard against his chest. "That show's been canceled, and there's no scheduled reruns."

He laughs in a way that's meant to be intimate, but it comes off as creepy. "I can't believe you're saying that when we've shared so many good times. Don't tell me you've forgotten already?"

"Trust me, I'm drawing a blank."

"I'd be more than happy to remind you." He leans toward her again, prompting her to lean so far back she's about to topple right off her stool.

"Back off, Coyote." She keeps a firm distance between them. "You smell like smoke, evil, and demons. Must be the scent of your soul."

Cade throws his head back as a loud, raucous roar fills the space. "Coyote?" He lowers his chin, swipes a hand through his hair. "Where'd you get that?" He switches his focus to me. "Little blind girl telling you stories?" He keeps his tone light, but his energy betrays him. It's dark, menacing, meant to intimidate.

Lita tips forward, angling her hand as though readying to slap him. "You little—" she starts, her words suddenly stalled when he catches her wrist in his fist.

"I always liked it when you got feisty." He tightens his grip and pulls her so close I'm not sure if he's going to kiss her or bite her. "If you're looking to reminisce, darlin', I can take you somewhere much more private than this."

She yanks her wrist free, jerks out of his reach. "Time for you to *vamanos*," she says in a tone that leaves no doubt she means every word. "You overstayed your visit from halfway across the room. So why don't you go back to pretending to mourn over your brother?"

"I'm done mourning," he says. "It's like the say, life is for the living, right? Besides, no matter how cool you try to play it, I saw you watching me, Lita. I saw the way you looked at me. I figured you were ready to apologize."

I concentrate hard on her energy, trying to subdue it with mine. Paloma's only just taught me this trick, but if there was ever a time to use it, it's now. Cade's tossing her a hook thick with bait, and Lita can't afford even a taste.

"I was staring at Phyre, not you." Lita's energy settles, stifled by mine.

"Phyre?" Cade's lips quirk with amusement. "What's the matter, Lita? Can't replace me so you thought you'd give girls a try?" He bursts into laughter, acting as though he said something funny. "Or perhaps you're upset to watch her claim your place so easily?"

Lita responds with a sigh and a groan.

"Your pride is wounded. It's perfectly understandable. Still, I gotta admit, that was the quickest popularity coup I've ever seen. That kind of thing never would've happened when you were with me. And I'm afraid you got used to it, took it for granted. Didn't realize just how good you had it when you were protected by the entire Richter clan. But now, out here on your own, you have no idea just how vulnerable you've become."

His words chill. Just as he intended. And for the first time since he's joined us, Lita's guard falls, and I watch as she grows increasingly nervous and twitchy.

Cade notices too, seizing the moment to say, "While I'm willing to forgive your transgressions, don't take too long to decide. If you insist on keeping this sort of company"—he quirks a brow at me—"well, I'm afraid there won't be much I can do to protect you."

"I don't need your protection!" she snaps, practically spitting the words. But she's agitated, uncertain, and Cade senses it as clearly as I do.

"Clock's ticking, Lita. Your days of grace are about to run out."

"The days of you and me have definitely run out. So why don't you go hook up with Phyre? I'm sure she's more than willing to ignore your putrid Coyote breath."

He grins, tipping a hand to his brow as though to salute her. "As you wish. Just don't be too upset when you see us together. Remember—it could've been you."

He starts to move away, appearing as a glob of gray making for the other side of the room, when he dramatically smacks his palm against his forehead, makes a hasty U-turn, and decides to rejoin us. A feigned move if I've ever seen one.

"Almost forgot, I have something for you." He reaches into his pocket, and offers Lita something small, dark, and ominous. "It's a tourmaline," he says, urging her to take it from him.

"And why would I want a tourmaline from you?" She shifts uncomfortably on her stool, keeps her hands in her lap, unwilling to claim it.

"Because it's a rare blue stone and it's extremely valuable. I was meaning to give it to you before you dumped me. Yes, I said it. You dumped me, and you left me completely heartbroken. See how much I've grown? I'm able to admit that it was you who walked away and left me devastated by the loss. And while I know you won't believe it, it's important for me to remind you that not every moment with me was as bad as you're determined to believe. I'm hoping this stone, given to you with no strings attached, might help to remind you of that."

"I know where you got this," she says.

"I've no doubt you do." He shifts toward me, clucking his tongue against the roof of his mouth. Turning to her with a lowered voice, he says, "Don't be a fool. Don't let your pride get in the way of common sense. If nothing else, the stone is extremely valuable. You can sell it if you want. But I hope you'll decide to keep it. It would really mean a lot to me."

"All the more reason to flush it," she says, watching as he places it on the table before her.

"Up to you." He shrugs. "Though I hope you'll reconsider."

He makes to leave as Lita raises her arm, aiming the stone at the back of his head. But I stop her before she can release it, and force her arm back to her side.

"What're you—crazy? I don't care how much he claims it's worth. You think I actually want this thing?"

"No. But Paloma might." I keep my voice purposely low.

"Why? What do you *see*?" She leans toward me.

"You go first," I say. "I don't want to taint your impression with mine. Describe it exactly as you see it."

She places it back on the table and rolls it from side to side. "It's surprisingly large. Probably worth a fortune, like he said. It's shiny, and perfectly polished and cut. It appears to be flawless, but I can't say for sure. Oh, and the color is a really deep blue. It's kind of mesmerizing. Or at least it would be if I didn't know where it came from."

"Is that all?"

"In a nutshell, yeah. Why—what do you see?"

"To me it looks just the opposite. Like a dark, murky, and ominous blob."

She jerks backward. "Well, now I really don't want it!" she says, watching as I scoop it right up. "And I don't want you to have it either. I think we should ditch it. I don't think it's safe."

"Not to worry," I tell her. "The Richters can't touch me. Besides, I don't plan to keep it. I'm thinking we can drop it by Paloma's as soon as we're out of here and see what she makes of it."

"Well, shouldn't we go now?"

I shake my head and say, "Not when Greyson just got here."

twenty-six

Daire

A soon as we reach the vortex, I look at Axel and say, "This is the part where you become less of a solution and more of a problem."

He stares blankly. "I'm not sure I get what you mean."

"Well, for one thing, are you even allowed to cross into the Middleworld for extended periods?" I ask, reminded of the time Paloma's Wolf made the trip to the Middleworld to help restore her soul. He grew increasingly weak the longer his visit dragged on, forcing Leftfoot to rush him back to the Lowerworld as soon as the task was completed. And I can't take the chance that the same thing will happen here. I can't be expected to race Axel back to the Upperworld when I barely escaped from there myself.

"I'm not an animal," he says, tuning in to my thoughts.

"Right, you're a Mystic. A Mystic who reads minds."

He shrugs, clearly having no concept of just how annoying, not to mention invasive, his mental eavesdropping is. "And your other concern?"

"I have no idea how to explain you."

"I'm not sure an explanation is necessary."

I groan in frustration, wishing I could've handled this alone. I hate being in Axel's debt, and I can't wait for our involvement to end.

"The only entry I know of is via the Rabbit Hole, and it's usually packed. Or at least it was when I left. Which is not only incredibly risky and dangerous for Dace—I can't afford for the Richters to see him in his current state—but also, to the outside world, you're a bit odd. They'll see you as a deathly pale guy with unusual eyes who's wearing a dress. You won't exactly blend in."

"I'll handle it," he says. Responding to my doubtful expression, he adds, "Really. Consider it already handled. Just lead the way."

"This is the way." I motion toward the filmy veil before us. The last in a very long succession of them. He nods, motions for me to go first, but I refuse to so much as consider it. "Oh no," I say. "No way am I turning my back on you."

"Seems like something I should say to you, no?" He cocks a brow, challenges me with a sharp purple gaze. Still, he falls into place, stepping through the vortex with Dace braced against him as I move to join them.

"It's late," Axel says, the first to reach the hallway. "Or early, depending on your perspective. Either way, the place is vacant."

"Maybe so, but it's packed with surveillance cameras," I tell him, remembering my first visit here, how I found my way into Leandro's office in search of my cell phone, only to find Cade vigilantly watching the wall of TVs projecting the goings-on inside the club.

"They can't see me. Not to worry."

"And you know this because . . ."

"Because I cannot be seen by most."

I study him, not one bit convinced.

"It's the way the light bends around me. I can only be seen by those who are meant to see me."

I frown. "But your magick isn't working, remember?"

"It's not magick—it's just, *me*. It's the way that I'm made."

"Cade saw you," I press, unwilling to give in so easily.

"And while I have no explanation for that other than it was a special circumstance, if I come across him again, I'm sure he'll look right through me." Responding to my look of distrust, he adds, "Ninety-nine percent sure."

With no other option but to gamble the odds, we make our way through the club. Suddenly faced with a new set of worries when I realize there's no way to exit without setting off an alarm.

I've got to find a new vortex! It's not the first time I've thought it.

"The Richters control the town and the people within it," Axel says. "I'm sure they see no need for that kind of security."

He makes a good point. Still, I refuse to exhale until he swings the door open and proves good on his word.

Making our way across the lot, we're halfway to Dace's truck (Axel swears he doesn't need the key to start it), when I spot Auden's old, beat-up wagon parked a few spaces away. And I'm flooded with relief to find my friends have ignored my advice and decided to wait for me.

I rap my knuckles against the driver's side window and peer inside. Auden and Xotichl are up front talking to Lita and a boy who looks vaguely familiar who are sitting in back.

Lita sees us first. Swinging the door open, she leaps from the car. Her dark eyes flashing, cheeks widening into a grin when she sees Dace. Until she notices his wounded, weakened state, and she turns to me in distress. "What happened? Is he okay?"

"He will be. But I need to get home to Paloma's, and quickly." I cast a wary gaze toward her friend in the back. Unwilling to say anything more until I know who he is, and maybe not even then.

"Oh, that's Greyson." Lita jabs a thumb in his direction as she focuses hard to my right. "And you are?'"

I glare at Axel accusingly. So much for light bending.

Before either of us can reply, Auden and Xotichl are out of the car and rushing toward Dace. Seemingly unaware that Axel is supporting him, they barrel into his space. Causing Axel to jump away in surprise, as Dace lists precariously to the side.

"Is this the friend you were waiting for? Looks like he's had one too many," Greyson says, coming to stand beside Lita.

In Dace's current, unconscious state—he really does appear to be suffering from a hard night of excess.

"He's fine," I say, stepping in to take Axel's place. I clutch Dace tightly to me. The sharp edge in my tone warning my friends to say nothing more while Greyson is here. "But we need a ride home." I shoot Auden a pointed look, and the next thing I know, he's slipped behind the wheel with Xotichl beside him, as Greyson says an awkward good-bye to Lita. Clearly longing to kiss her, but settling for a handshake instead.

Dace and I settle into the large space in back, as Lita claims the space beside Axel in the row just before us and greets him by name.

I balk, Axel goes paler than I've ever seen him, as Xotichl tilts her head toward us, and Auden squints in the rearview mirror, trying to discern who she's talking to.

"Am I missing something?" he asks, as Xotichl shifts until she's fully facing them.

"Nope." I sigh. "There really is an invisible man back here. I can see him, Dace can see him, and, apparently, Lita can too."

"Kind of hard to miss a guy with platinum hair, pale skin, and purply eyes. I knew right away it was you." She pokes a finger at his shoulder. "You're exactly like Daire described you." She studies him in a way that's a little too appreciative for my comfort.

And I'm just about to say something, anything, to distract her, when I notice the glimmer in Axel's eyes when he returns Lita's look.

twenty-seven

Daire

After calling Paloma to give her a recap and tell her we're on our way, I turn to my friends and say, "So, any news? Any sign of Cade?" I keep a close watch on Dace, alarmed by his irregular breath, the way his skin remains clammy, despite my attempts to warm him.

"Oh, we saw him. We talked to him too." Lita glances at me. "He was acting all flirty. Trying to convince me to take him back. As if." She peeks at Axel sitting beside her, her lips sneaking into a grin. And I don't know what bothers me more—Cade's attempt to win her back or the way Lita leverages it to get Axel's attention.

"He hit on you in front of your *date*?" I ask, the question undeniably pointed. "That's pretty aggressive, even for Cade."

"Greyson stopped by later." Lita switches her focus between Axel and me. "Besides, it wasn't a date. Or at least not on my part—"

Before she can go any further, Xotichl interrupts. "None of that's newsworthy," she says. "But this might be." She drops something into Lita's hand and urges her to pass it to me. "It's a tourmaline," she explains, as I stare at the shiny blue stone on my palm. "What do you think? Are you getting anything?"

I focus on the stone, trying to glean from it all that I can. Noting how it feels disturbingly warm. But that might be because it was in her purse, or because I've grown used to Dace's icy-cold touch. The only thing I know for sure it that it came from Cade's ill-fated mine.

"I'm not sure what to think." I rub my lips together and continue to study it. Unable to detect anything out of the ordinary. Or at least not on the surface. I've no doubt there's more to this thing than meets the eye. Cade's not known for being altruistic. A gift from Coyote always comes at a price. "Did he say *why* he gave this to you?" I curl my fingers around it, close my eyes, and strive for a deeper impression, but come up empty.

"I guess he misses me. Can't envision a future without me." Lita sneaks another peek at Axel. "So he's determined to win me back, and he thought a priceless gem might help. As if I could be bought so easily. Please."

Worked for Marliz. The image of Marliz gazing at the new tourmaline engagement ring Gabe gave her blazes in my mind.

"The stone has a strange and troubling energy," Xotichl says, cutting into my thoughts. "And while I can't get a clear read on it, I figured we could give it to Paloma and see what she says."

I continue to flip the stone in my hand. "It feels warm," I say. "That's all I've got. Then again, I'm not as good with the energy reading as you are."

"Can I see it?" Axel reaches for it. His lips pressed and grim, he assumes a thoughtful expression as he makes careful study of it. "You said it feels warm, but for me, it's just the opposite. Almost like it's been refrigerated or something."

"That's how it felt to me too." Lita grins, eyes flashing flirtatiously. "It felt as cold as Cade Richter's heart. Yet another reason I was eager to ditch it."

I snatch the stone from Axel and drop it into my bag. "I'll show it to Paloma and see what she thinks," I say, already swinging the car door open the second I spy Paloma's blue gate, well before Auden's had a chance to properly stop.

Paloma meets us at the door with a darkened gaze and grave face. Casting a concerned look at Dace's wounded, unconscious state, she hurries us into her office where we get him settled on the padded table she saves for more serious cases. Then we quickly edge out of the way and give her enough space to work.

"Where'd you find him?" she asks. Having assessed his energy, she wipes her hands on the sides of her housedress, and busies herself with her numerous jars of potions and herbs.

The grim expression she wears causing my voice to shake when I say, "Found him just where I expected—in the deepest, darkest recesses of the Middleworld. Have you been?"

With a curt nod of her head, she gets to filling a bowl with purified water, while instructing me to retrieve a clean cloth from the top drawer near the sink, so I can use it to cleanse Dace's skin.

It's busywork. Meant to help quell my nerves, distract me from my growing list of concerns. Still, I'm grateful for something to do, so I'm quick to obey.

"He's remained unconscious the whole trip," I tell her, softly running the damp cloth over Dace's forehead and curving around the slope of his cheek, removing a thick, stubborn crust of blood and debris. "Which was for the best, believe me. Though, if he does wake up and starts acting strange, don't be alarmed. He's deeply traumatized. Convinced that he's dreaming." My voice catches, reminded of the haunted look on his face when I first found him, unable to imagine the kind of horrors he's seen.

"Yet you were able to carry him all the way back here on your own?" Paloma lifts a brow, shoots me a questioning look.

I shake my head. Dip the cloth into the bowl. Watching as the water instantly darkens to a deep, brownish red. "Axel was there. I couldn't have done it without him." The words leave a bitter taste on my tongue, as I jab my thumb in Axel's direction, illustrating his place by the wall. Watching dumbfounded when Paloma looks over her shoulder and squints into the distance. "You can't see him, can you?" I say, stunned into silence when she shakes her head to confirm it.

Paloma can't see him, but Lita can?

"No matter," she says. "I don't need to see him to utilize his healing abilities."

I sneak a glance at Axel and frown. "His magick isn't working," I say. "If anything, it bears the opposite effect."

No way is he laying hands on Dace. Not after what he did to that tree!

But Paloma ignores me, summoning Axel to her side as she covers Dace's wounds with a thick, herbal poultice.

"He is here?" She motions to her right, sensing the moment Axel claims the space just beside her.

"Yes, but, *abuela,* you have to know, his magick—"

"I don't need his magick." She's quick to put an end to my argument. "I need his intent. It is our spirit guides that allow us to perform healings. I don't make the magick, *nieta.* I merely serve as a channel for their benevolent energy. You and Axel both love Dace. That much is clear. And since Love is the strongest force in the universe, I need you both to concentrate on that Love, while I proceed to transfer that healing energy to Dace's wounds." Then looking at me, she adds, "A Seeker always has something to work with, *nieta.* Even in the bleakest of times. Sometimes intent is all that's required."

"Sometimes? You mean like this time, right?"

My voice is screechy, overly anxious, begging for the sort of assurance she just can't provide. Instead, she motions for me to take Axel's hand, and at first, I can't help but hesitate. The twins are connected in mystical ways, which means the act of energizing Dace will also benefit Cade. But with a stern nod from Paloma, it's not long before I grip Axel's fingers in mine, squinch my eyes shut, and project all of the Love I hold in my heart into Dace's inert form.

twenty-eight

Dace

A welcoming wave of warmth ripples from the top of my skull all the way down to the soles of my feet. Enveloping my outsides as thoroughly as it consumes my insides.

I struggle to lift my head, needing to see the source of the heat. Counting two sets of hands hovering over my flesh. The larger ones bearing illuminated palms.

"Almost there . . . hold on . . ." a familiar voice says as an electric jolt surges through me. The current so forceful, so gripping, my head thrashes from side to side, my hands curl to fists, as my body goes rigid with a heat so intense, I'm not sure I can bear it.

Though no sooner have I thought it, when my body falls cool and limp, the hands move away, and a tentative voice says, "Dace? You okay?"

A delicate finger trails down my cheek, and I open my eyes to see a beautiful girl with brilliant green eyes chewing hard on her lip.

The vision alone enough for me to leap off the table and fold her into my arms. I hug her tightly to me. Needing to fill my senses with her. Needing the assurance that she really is here. That I'm not just dreaming her.

I cup my hand to the back of her head, filling my fingers with her soft silken strands. I've yearned for her for so long. Feared our reunion would never come. But now, with her face nestled into my neck, inhaling her soft, sweet scent, there's no mistaking that she really is here. Clinging to me just as desperately as I cling to her.

Our love equally earnest—equally deep.

Or is that just a memory embedded in me?

As though sensing the change, Daire's the first to pull away. And from the moment she looks into my eyes, the truth can no longer be denied.

I'm still soulless.

And without the soul, I can't fully grasp the experience.

I can see her. Feel her. But it's as though it's happening to someone else.

Like I'm observing it from a distance.

As though there's an invisible barrier wavering between us.

Like I'm going through a checklist of the emotions I should feel, rather than actually experiencing them for real.

Her gaze is dark and probing. Seeking a substance that's no longer there.

The place where my soul once resided is now a vast, empty void.

Still, my heart continues to beat. And, just like before, it beats only for her.

For now, it's all that I've got.

It'll have to suffice.

"How do you feel?" She blinks back the grief and brings a tentative hand to my cheek.

"Healed." I force a grin to my cheeks in an effort to prove it.

She meets it with an encouraging look of her own. Her lips parting, about to say something more, when there's a commotion at the front door and Chepi bursts up the ramp and into the room, followed by the rest of the elders.

My mother comes at me in a flurry of shrieks and tears. Burying me deep into the folds of her arms as she murmurs a string of soft words, spoken in our native tongue.

I smooth my hands down her back, shocked by the way her shoulder blades jut from her flesh. Angel wings she used to call them. Every time I fell ill as a child, she'd fast and pray and slowly waste away until I recovered.

"Mama, please. There's no reason to cry," I whisper, "I'm back. I'm safe. I'm healed. And it's just a matter of time before my soul is restored."

At the mention of my missing soul, she's quick to jerk away and stare deep into my eyes. Confirming what I've just told her, she whirls on Daire and says, "You promised you'd get his soul back!"

I start to intervene, but to Daire's credit, she receives the blow gracefully, doesn't so much as flinch. "I promised to find him, which I did. Restoring his soul is next on the list."

Chepi is flustered and angry, mumbling words that don't make any sense. "I'm taking you home." She pulls at my waist. "You've had a long journey, you need to rest."

I uncurl her fingers and fold my hands over hers. Holding her before me and absorbing her anger until her expression softens, her shoulders droop, and she's calm enough to hear me when I say, "Mama, please. I don't need to rest. My body is healed, strong. I can take care of myself. I've been languishing too long as it is. First, I need to get my soul back. And then I need to deal with Cade. Only then will I be able to fully rest again."

"You say you're strong now, but how long will it last?" Chepi looks to Paloma, seemingly unable to see Axel standing beside her.

"With a little help from a divine source, Dace's wounds are healed." Paloma allows a faint smile as she trains her focus on me. "I closed your wounds and gave you a very intense healing infusion. I'm sure you feel the heat swirling within you?"

I nod. It's intense, but nothing I can't handle.

She nods in approval. "Let your temperature be your gauge," she says. "You'll know it's time for another infusion when you begin to feel cool. If you wait too long and grow cold . . . well, I'm afraid you'll be right back where you started." She fixes me with a hardened stare, eager to impart the seriousness of her words.

"So, that's it?" I crack a half-grin. "When the engine runs cold it's time for a tune-up?" I translate her warning into the kind of grease-monkey language I understand best.

"How long will it last?" Daire asks. Her bottom lip receding into her mouth, dragged along by her teeth.

"It was a pretty strong dose." Axel looks between Daire and me. "But there's no way of knowing for sure."

"Whatever it is, it'll have to suffice," I say, eager to get going. To use the strength while I have it. But Axel remains unconvinced, looking at me with a pinched and troubled face.

"Who are you talking to?" Chepi casts a squinted gaze around the room.

"Axel. Dace's spirit guide is here," Daire says, but the words fail to comfort.

"But they only appear when someone is meant to die!" She cries, clutching at me once again.

"Yes. I was meant to die," I tell her, instantly regretting the blunt tone of my words when I see the look of pain that crosses her face. Still, there's no point in lying. She deserves to hear the truth. "Only I didn't die. For whatever reason, I managed to live. So now I'm going to make sure I use my life in a way that matters." I look at Daire as I add, "Starting now."

"I understand your impatience to get started," Leftfoot says, his eyes sending me a silent message I'm slow to understand. "But it's the middle of the night and you've already suffered quite an ordeal. Why not take Chepi's advice? A few hours of rest won't make much of a difference."

I narrow my gaze on the old medicine man. It's a rare occasion when I don't follow his advice.

This is one of those occasions.

"There's no time—I have to use the energy while I have it!" I say, already moving away.

"Do you even know where to look?" he asks, his voice neither taunting nor superior, merely matter-of-fact.

My reply of silence is proof that I don't.

"Better not to waste your energy by floundering around. Let me do some of the groundwork first, so you can go in when it counts. Come on, Dace." He slips an arm around me, pats me on the back. "Come back to the reservation with us. You and Daire can head out at daybreak."

Typical Leftfoot. Always trying to separate me from Daire. Making me wonder if he suspected all along that the love Daire and I share serves to strengthen my freak of a brother. Still, I look upon him with a deep-rooted fondness. He's taught me everything I know—always been like a father to me.

"You all go ahead," Chay says, taking Leftfoot's side. "I'll stay here. Paloma and I can do some work through the night while Daire gets some sleep." He smiles at me with a face so benevolent, so sincere, there's nothing I can say to refute it. "Few hours from now, you'll be rested, refreshed, and heading in the right direction. What do you say?"

I turn my focus to Daire, as Chepi and Paloma murmur their approval. "Fine," I say, knowing there's no use prolonging the fight when it's so much easier to give the appearance of going along. The elders are a formidable force, especially when they all band together. Still, sometimes I need to do things in my own time, my own way.

Before anyone can stop me, I move toward Daire and pull her into my arms. And the second her lips meet mine everything fades until all that's left is this kiss.

Her touch is soft and lingering, both of us knowing the moment we break away, the gravity of the situation will descend once again.

One second—her lips move gently with mine.

Two—her breath becomes one with my own.

Three—there is nothing I wouldn't do for this girl.

It's the vow I take with me, as I reluctantly draw away and head for the door.

twenty-nine

Daire

Chay works in the garden out back, collecting fresh herbs and flowers from the long list Paloma gave him, while Paloma and I work on cleaning her office, moving around each other with practiced efficiency.

After a prolonged silence, she turns to me and says, "*Nieta*, what's wrong? Dace is back, his wounds are healed, and yet, you seem rather blue."

"Not blue." I sigh, ashamed by my small, petty mood in the midst of all the good she just mentioned. "More like . . . lavender." I return the bowl to the cupboard and face her.

"This is about Axel." She wipes her hands on a towel and folds it back neatly. Paloma's always been able to read me.

"He wasn't supposed to save me," I tell her. "Dace was meant to die, not me."

"So he interfered with destiny?" Her voice is soft, but her gaze is needle sharp. "And you're unsure of his motives?" She tips onto her toes, straining to put the last jar away. But I'm taller, so I'm quick to swoop in and place it there for her.

"Let's just say that while I may have misinterpreted his motives from the start, now that he's explained it, I'm left with even more misgivings than before. He claims he saved me to save Dace. But he did so at great personal risk, and I'm not sure what to do with that. It makes me feel like I'm weirdly indebted to him."

"So you'd prefer he would've let you die?"

I shoot her a sideways glance. "I told you it was stupid."

Paloma presses toward the sink and turns on the tap. Rinsing the cloth I used to cleanse Dace's face and hands under a hot stream of water. "*Nieta,* what you need to understand is that Axel was created for this. He was created to guide. If he chose to do something that went against his creed, he did so knowingly and willingly."

I study her carefully. Watching as she alternately rinses, twists, and crumples the cloth in her hands until the blood is mostly gone and the remaining water streams clear.

"What do you mean he was created for this?"

"*Nieta,* Axel was never human." She inspects the cloth. Still stained with Dace's blood, she moves to dispose of it.

"But I thought you said the Upperworld was inhabited by benevolent beings who once walked among us and now choose to guide us?"

"It is. As you probably saw for yourself. But there are also those who've never taken corporeal form."

I frown. Needing a moment to process. "But how can you be sure of that when you couldn't actually see him?"

"I don't need to see him to read his energy—his intent. Tell me, what color are his eyes?" she asks. "Are they unearthly?"

I rub my lips together, grudgingly admitting, "They're lavender. The color of my mood." A grin sneaks onto my lips.

"Otherworldly irises. I figured as much. Listen, *nieta,*" she says. "Axel's choices belong to him and him alone. It's the decisions we make at the crossroads of life that define us. Axel just experienced his own defining moment."

"So his true character is that of a rebel angel?"

Paloma grins, but it's faint, and rather short lived.

"Oh, and to top it all off, I think he has a thing for Lita." I don't even try to contain the groan that escapes my lips. "And from what I can tell, it's strongly reciprocated."

Paloma looks at me with a face more alarmed than amused, her features pinched with concern. "Then I shall hope they both come to their senses, and soon. That will never end well."

The words leave me sobered, wondering if I should try to warn Lita, or at least find a way to distract her from him.

"Oh, and speaking of Lita—I almost forgot . . ." I snake my finger into my pocket, retrieving the tourmaline and handing it to Paloma. "Cade gave it to her. But while Lita doesn't want it, Xotichl says its energy is off, and thought you might want to see it. I can't get anything from it, but we figured maybe you could. There's a lot of tourmalines floating around over there," I say, going on to tell her about Marliz's engagement ring.

Paloma folds her fingers around it, testing its heft, its weight. "Maybe they just want to get rid of the inventory," she says, though her expression reveals a deeper concern. "And yet, I think we both know the Richters never give freely. There's always an ulterior motive where they're concerned." She drops the gem into her pocket, and ushers me down the hall. "I'll look into it. But for now, get some rest, *nieta.*" She brushes the back of her fingers over my cheek, tucking a rogue lock of hair behind my ear. "I won't let you sleep long, I promise. I know you're anxious to get to work. But a few hours of rest will do you some good. Chay and I can handle things until then."

I step obediently into my room and pause on the door's other side with my ear pressed hard against the wood. The soft shuffle of Paloma's feet moving down the hall and into the den where her voice mingles with Chay's is all the cue I need to rush toward my window, slide it open, and slip outside into a frigid, cold night.

My shoes slam hard on the gravel, resulting in a loud crunching sound. But after a few moments pass and no one comes to check, I race across the courtyard, sneak around back, and cross the garden, all the way to Kachina's stall.

Judging by the way she whinnies in greeting, lowering her head to nuzzle against me, I figure she must've missed me as much as I missed her.

Which is pretty much the opposite of Cat who arches his back, gives me a good solid hiss, and instantly flees.

"Guess Cat's still Cat." I run my hand down Kachina's neck and over the perfect stripes of her brown-and-white mane. "What do you say we follow his lead and get out of here too? A little late-night ride might do us some good."

Whether or not she understood, I can't say for sure. But when she sees me retrieve her bridal and bit, she definitely perks up with excitement.

Not wanting to waste time with the blanket and saddle, I hop onto her bare back and nudge her out of the stall. Making my way to the reservation where I find Dace waiting for me by the grove of twisted juniper trees.

"I wasn't sure if you'd make it," I say, unable to suppress a grin at the sight of his long, glossy, dark hair spilling over his shoulders, the narrow V of his torso, the perfect fit of his jeans. I force my gaze away. Scold myself to focus. Concentrate. He may look as strong and sexy as ever on the outside, but without the soul, he's just not the same. "Where's Axel?" I squint into the darkness, search for some sign of him.

"Trying to make his way back." Dace offers his hand, helps me slide from Kachina's back. His face creased in distress when he sees the way she now veers away from him when she's never done that before. "Animals know," he says, voice saddened, eyes fathomless.

"She'll adjust," I say with more confidence than I currently feel. "I'll talk to her."

But Dace stops me before I can start. Taking my hands from her reins, he watches her wander a few feet away. "Allow her to honor her instincts. I don't plan to be like this for much longer. I'm sure she'll come around once I'm back to my old self."

I stand silently before him, feeling suddenly shy and uncertain. Though it's not long before my shyness is overcome by the sheer, irresistible pull of him.

I whisper his name, pressing so close I can feel his breath on my cheek. Remembering the kiss we shared in Paloma's office, I long to repeat it. Long to be with him again. But for now, I'll settle for enjoying his nearness.

This isn't the real Dace.

He's soulless.

Incomplete.

Fueled by a temporary infusion of energy.

Who knows how long it will last?

I can't afford to lose sight of that.

No matter how tempting he may look under the glow of the moonlight, I have to stay focused, on track.

Have to use what little time we have left.

"Tell me about Phyre," I say, the words coming out of nowhere, but somehow the question feels right. Lita and Xotichl don't trust her. I don't trust her. And just like Kachina needs to honor her instincts, I need to honor mine. "What's your history? Why is she back? What does she want from you?" I lower myself to the ground, needing to feel something solid beneath me, if I'm to see this conversation through to the end.

I lean against a twisted tree trunk, and Dace does the same. Reaching for my hand, he grasps it for a moment, squeezes our fingers tightly together, then releases just as quickly. His touch leaving a trace of heat I attribute to his energy infusion. Which means I should be able to detect the moment it starts to run cold.

"Our history is we were together a few years back, for a very short time." He exhales deeply, as though the statement required great effort.

"How together? Explain *together?*" The words came out a little more rushed and frantic than I'd planned. Causing my face to grow hot, my stomach to clench. But despite my horror at sounding like a jealous girlfriend, I need details—need to know what they shared.

He rubs a hand over his chin. Squinches his eyes until they're reduced to mere slits. "You know, *together*," he says, voice clearly demonstrating the full measure of his discomfort, which only seals my determination.

"*Together* in the way that we were *together*?"

"No." He turns to me with a clenched jaw and a glacier gaze. "I mean, we slept together, yes, but it was *nothing* like us. Please don't ever say that, Daire. Don't ever *think* that."

"So you remember us?" I ask, the words sounding pathetic, needy, and small.

He leans his head back against the tree and closes his eyes. "I remember all of us." He sighs. "I remember everything. From the very first moment I saw you that day at the gas station, I knew my life was forever changed. You're not just embedded in my soul, Daire. You're part of my DNA. I even remember you from the dreams I had, long before I knew you were real."

My shoulders sink at the mention of the dream that started it all. I had it too. It always started off well enough, with Dace and me enjoying ourselves in the Enchanted Spring, until Cade came along, turned into a demon, and killed Dace while I helplessly looked on. Only in Dace's version, Cade killed me. And I can't help but wonder if Cade made us dream the dream on purpose, or if it sprang up organically.

"As for why Phyre returned, I really don't know," he says, returning to one of my original questions. "Though I'm not sure it was her choice. Her mother's been missing and presumed dead for years, and while her sisters, Ashe and Ember, went to live with an aunt, for some reason Phyre chose to stay with her father."

"Why would she do that when everyone says that he's crazy?"

Dace shrugs. His shoulders rising and falling in a way so languid, so elegant, I force my gaze away. "He is crazy. I used to think she did it because she felt sorry for him. But now I'm no longer sure."

"Meaning?"

He licks his lips, runs a hand through his hair. Clearly hating every moment of this, but determined to appease me, he says, "Last time I spoke to her, on Christmas Eve, right before I followed you to the Lowerworld, she was spouting all kinds of nonsense about the Last Days."

"Last Days?"

"Some Apocalyptic diatribe her dad's been preaching for years. According to him, the Last Days are when the sinners all burn, and the righteous will either stay behind to enjoy the Shining Days of Glory or ascend into the clouds to enjoy the festival there . . . or, whatever. The guy's nuts. A total crackpot. Who knows where he gets this stuff?" He brings his knees to his chest, wraps his arms around them. "Anyway, she claimed the burning sky was a sign. Said it was too late for any of us, and begged me to go with her to find her father. Said he'd know what to do. I told her he was crazy. That she should go to the reservation and seek refuge with one of the elders. And when I saw she was too far gone and nothing I'd said made a dent, I went after you. Oh, but before that, she also mentioned something about how she and I wanted the same thing."

"Which is?" I lean toward him. Determined to ignore the enticing sweep of stubble along his jaw. The way his biceps strain against the fabric of his shirt.

"To see Cade dead."

Not quite expecting that, I inhale a sharp, involuntary breath.

"At the time, I didn't take her seriously. I thought it was just another fawning attempt to get back with me again. But now I'm not sure. Especially after her father came to visit me in the Middleworld."

I balk. So many questions forming in my head, I'm not sure

where to begin. "You're actually saying that some self-proclaimed, self-righteous, religious zealot of a freak found you days before I did, and he didn't even try to help you? He didn't even try to bring you back so that you could seek help? And what the heck was he doing all the way out there, anyway? How does he know about it? How did he get there?"

"Which question would you like answered first?" Dace's fathomless eyes meet mine, as his lip tugs into a grin.

I shrug, knowing that soon enough, he'll answer them all.

"Among all of his other accolades, it seems he's a demon hunter."

My eyes widen. Wondering if I'll ever reach a point where I'm no longer fazed by the more surreal aspects of the world we live in.

"He was there to stake me. And he almost succeeded."

I try to imagine a scene like that in my head.

"The wound at my chest? That was him."

"He thought you were a demon?"

"Claims he's known since the day I was born. Thinks I'm the key to the Last Days. He's been planning to kill me for the last sixteen years."

"But you were able to fend him off?"

Dace looks away, shifting uncomfortably, and allowing a lingering silence to droop between us. "Look," he finally says. "If you want to know the truth—I begged him to kill me. I repeatedly thrust myself into his stake."

"But why? Why would you do that?" I grasp hold of his arm, try to make sense of his words.

"Because I thought you were dead. And I was convinced it was due to my failing. I couldn't live with myself. But mostly, I couldn't live without you. I though that maybe if I was dead, I might be able to find you again in whatever dimension you were resting in. I know it probably sounds stupid, but Daire, I was broken. Lost. I guess in a way, I still am."

I open my mouth to speak, but no words will come.

"The reason he didn't kill me is because when he looked into

my eyes, he saw that I was soulless. He said he needed the soul.
That I was useless without it."

I breathe a sigh of relief. If nothing else, at least I know Dace is
safe from the lunatic. Or at least for the time being anyway.

"Wasn't long after that he packed up his kill kit and said he'd
go after Cade. After all, we're one and the same. Funny how he
knew that, isn't it?"

"Hilarious." I shake my head and frown.

"Oh, and there's more."

My gaze meets his.

"He said that Phyre told him she'd killed me. Apparently that
was the task he'd given her. He was pretty upset to find out she'd
lied."

"That's it," I say, having heard all that I need. Driven by an instinct I cannot ignore, I leap to my feet and race toward the place
were Kachina grazes a few feet away.

"What're you doing?" Dace asks, slowly getting up to join me.

"We're going there. Now. We're going to the Youngbloods'
house."

thirty

Daire

After a few failed attempts, Kachina finally relents and allows Dace onto her back. "They're off the reservation," he says, settling behind me. "I have no idea where they live."

"It's a small town. I'm sure we'll be able to find it." I squint into the darkness, trying to determine which way to head.

"What time do you think it is?" Dace's lips push against the shell of my ear, causing tiny pinpricks of pleasure to crawl over my skin.

"I left my cell at Paloma's," I say, striving to stay focused, on task. "But judging by the light, or rather lack of light, I'd say it's close to sunrise."

"Always darkest before the dawn?" His mouth drifts to the side of my neck. And though my back is turned toward him, I can picture him perfectly. Hair spilling over his cheek . . . lips full and inviting . . .

I lean against him, savoring the feel of his arms wrapped snugly around me. He may be soulless, but he's still the boy I dreamed about. Still my fated one.

After a while he asks, "Are we wandering, or do you actually have a plan?" The words are edged with laughter.

"My plan is to follow Wind," I tell him. "Paloma says I'm a daughter of the wind, so I called on it when we first set out. It's rare that it fails me."

"Which means that it has?"

My lips flatten, my eyes continue to seek the horizon. "Not really *failed*—it was more like, *unavailable*," I say, feeling inexplicably defensive of my element. "Not to mention it was under extreme circumstances."

"Such as . . ."

"Such as when Cade stifled my magick in the Lowerworld, just seconds before you arrived on Christmas Eve. Then again during a more recent visit to the Lowerworld. It's like everything is in a state of hibernation down there. It won't stop snowing. Won't warm up enough to give way to spring. And I haven't seen Raven or Horse since that night. I'm beginning to miss them."

"None of that bodes well for those of us up here."

It's a sobering truth, and I meet it by staring silently ahead.

With our bodies swaying to the rhythm of Kachina's gait, I keep a close eye on the tree limbs, trying to determine the direction in which they waver and bend. Every now and then checking the pattern of the dirt swirling under her hooves.

After traveling a good distance, I ask, "Dace, do you still have use of your magick? I'm thinking the more magick we have between us, the better."

"We're about to find out." He lifts his hand until it's centered just inches from my chest. But after a few seconds of nothing, he says, "Apparently not. I was trying to palm your key. Guess the magick really did come from a place deep inside me."

"I'm sure it will return along with your soul," I say, becoming so lost in the thought, I miss the moment Wind stops. But luckily, Dace notices.

He folds his hands over mine and gives a quick tug on the reins. "This is it," he whispers. Nodding toward a depressing, broken-down trailer that looks more abandoned than lived in. "I recognize the junker parked outside. Suriel's never been one for creature comforts. He takes great pride in rejecting all forms of materialism by paring his possessions down to the absolute minimum. Which in his case amounts to two cheap black suits—one worn basically every day, the other reserved for Sundays—two ties, two white shirts, one pair of shoes, two black socks, and one belt. Phyre showed me his closet once just to prove it."

"What, no sweatpants for long days of lounging in front of the TV snacking on chips and salsa?"

"They don't own a TV. Or, as Suriel calls it—the devil's box. You know, idle hands, idle minds, the devil's workshop, and all that."

"But from what I've seen of Phyre, she has more than two sets of clothes. She always looks stylish—wears makeup and everything."

"I know." Dace's shoulders rise and fall against mine. "I always thought it was weird how he indulged her that way. He wasn't like that with her sisters. He was so much stricter with them. Which is probably the reason they chose to live with their aunt. Anyway, now that we're here, what do we do?"

"I'm not sure," I admit, not having really thought past this point. "I guess we lay low and observe. See if we can get some kind of read on what they're up to. How they plan to kill Cade. Which, of course, we can't let them do."

"Funny how just a few weeks ago, Suriel's quest to kill Cade would've made him an ally." Dace's tone is light, but when I crick my neck to face him, his expression is serious.

"And now it makes him a threat." My voice is somber, as my gaze moves over him. "Why do you think Phyre didn't kill you when she had the chance?"

"I don't know." He rubs a hand over his chin, squints into the distance. "I guess no matter how much her father has managed to influence her, deep down inside she's still a good and decent person who knows right from wrong." He looks at me then, shoulders heavy with remorse when he says, "Look, Daire, I know I should be angry at her for putting me in jeopardy, but I can't. Back when I knew her, she was a sweet, normal, kind of sad kid. I guess I feel sorry for her now, just like I did then. She was ostracized, treated cruelly, all because of her father's insanity. The kids at school made a point to avoid her and her sisters. They never had one single friend. Then, when her mother disappeared and her sisters left to live with their aunt . . . well, I guess after being isolated with only Suriel for so long, the world finally broke her until he was able to effectively brainwash her." He wipes a hand across his brow and shakes his head, as though releasing himself from the hold of the past. "Look!" he says, arcing a hand toward the Sangre de Cristo mountain range, as we watch in silent awe as the sun's ascent washes the rugged peaks in a glorious coating of pink.

"Chepi taught me that all of nature—the sun, the moon, those mountains—all of it knows you from the time you were just an idea. That we're all cells with different purposes, yet we are all connected—existing to serve each other as well as the whole. Too bad Suriel never listened to Chepi. He divides the world into the righteous versus the sinners. As if it could ever be so clearly defined. Everyone straddles the balance between light and dark."

Everyone but you. Or at least the former version of you. Before you adopted your brother's worst attribute.

I study his profile as he tracks the sunrise. His features are both soft and sharp, sculptural and beautiful. As long as I avoid looking into his eyes, I can pretend nothing's changed.

"Do you have an element?" I ask, desperate to clear the thought from my head.

"Earth." He grins, his eyes meeting mine. But there's no depth behind them, so I'm quick to look away. "I've felt the connection since I was a boy."

"Do you ever call on it?" I keep watch on the trailer, the broken-down shed, the filthy white car.

"I never learned how. Chepi did her best to shelter me from that kind of thing. Why, you want to teach me?"

I smile softly, and lean against him. "Maybe someday." My breathing slows, keeping tempo with his, as the sky unfolds into a blooming canopy of silvery blues and pinks.

"They'll be up soon. If they're not already," Dace whispers into my ear. "Suriel likes to greet the start of each day."

He slides off Kachina's back and helps me do the same. Then, not wanting her to attract any unwanted attention, I slap her on the rear, and tell her to find a nice place to graze. While Dace and I duck behind the old, broken-down shed just off to the side that's even more dilapidated than the trailer.

A moment later, just like Dace said, a light switches on from inside. Allowing us to make out two shadowy figures moving behind a filmy yellow curtain.

"It'll start with a sermon," Dace says, and, sure enough, Suriel's voice pierces the silence, roaring so loudly it bleeds through the walls of the trailer and into the yard. I stare at Dace, wondering how he knew that. "He's a creature of habit." He grins. "Never deviates from his routine."

Though the words aren't easily discerned, every now and then we're able to catch one of Suriel's favorite catchphrases. *Last Days are here . . . Shining Days of Glory shall commence . . . Suriel is but a humble servant, his daughter a tool of thy will . . .* More Apocalyptic nonsense. The guy is obsessed.

When he reaches the end, he leaves his daughter to dress as he stumbles from the trailer, turns toward the mountains, drops to his knees, and begins once again. Only this time we get to watch it as well. His body listing from side to side, his head rolling back, his tongue lolling free of his mouth.

"Guess you're not the only one connected to the earth," I joke, trying to make light of the scene unfolding before me. Mostly because it's giving me a serious case of the creeps.

"He claims spirit has ahold of him when he does that. Used to freak us out when we were kids."

Poor Phyre. To have to grow up like that . . .

I start to feel sorry for her. Start to feel a flood of compassion for her predicament. I used to think Jennika was embarrassing with her crazy hair colors and piercings and penchant for drama, but compared to Suriel, Jennika looks like a 1950s sitcom mom.

Though the sentiment is short lived. Vanishing the moment Phyre exits the trailer and I remember her goal to kill Dace.

She runs an uncertain hand over her halo of curls. Tugs her black miniskirt to better cover her thighs. Standing straight and rigid beside her father, as though she doesn't dare move. Her features blunted, her face inscrutable, as she watches Suriel shake and sweat and convulse in a frenzy of righteousness.

With spot-on timing, she anticipates the exact moment he wakes from the trance. "I'm headed out," she says. "Thought I'd get an early start."

Suriel gets to his feet. Runs his palms down the front of his suit and straightens his tie. Then he reaches into his pocket and pulls out a small glass vial filled with some sort of cloudy liquid. His voice as stern as his face, he says, "It is time."

Phyre nods. Tilts her head back. Parts her lips.

"This is your final chance to redeem yourself."

She closes her eyes and offers her tongue.

"You know our deal. See that it's done by midnight, Phyre. Any later is too late." He shakes the vial into her mouth, counting the drops until he's satisfied it's enough.

As soon as she's absorbed it, she tucks her chin to her chest and casts her gaze to her feet. Assuming a pose of supplication.

"I think you know what awaits you if you lie to me again . . ." Suriel's voice drifts with implied threat.

Phyre nods. Squeezes her palms tightly together.

"You were begotten in sin and you shall end in sin!" Suriel shouts in a voice so thunderous my body gives way to an involuntary shudder. "It is your role. Your birthright. The destiny you were born for. It is a great honor to be called upon and used in this way. Now leave and do what you must. May the Glory of the Shining Days be upon us!"

In an emotionless voice, Phyre repeats that last part, then turns and heads in our direction. Making straight for the shed as Dace and I freeze with our breaths held in our cheeks.

The door squeals in protest as she forces it open. Emitting another shrill, creaking sound when she exits just as quickly, and heads for Suriel's car.

"What is that?" I whisper, squinting into the distance, trying to make out the rectangular object she hauls into the trunk.

"Looks like an old gas can," Dace says. Still squinting, he turns to me and adds, "What the hell are they up to?" His eyes meet mine.

"I have no idea," I say. "But I'm about to find out. Will you watch over my body and make sure I stay safe?"

His questioning gaze follows mine to the raven that's landed on the roof just above us. Reminding me of one of Paloma's earliest teachings.

While he should not be mistaken for your actual spirit animal—he is still considered a brother, as all ravens are that inhabit the Middleworld. Raven is a messenger of the spirit realm—the things he will show you can shift your life dramatically. He will teach you to venture into the dark in order to bring forth the light . . .

The raven appearing at exactly this time is an omen, not an accident. Of that I am sure.

Dace folds my hand in his, gives it a squeeze of unspoken solidarity. "I would go with you, but . . ." He leaves the sentence unfinished, but we both know how it ends.

Can't soul jump if you're soulless.

"It's better I go alone," I say. "I need you here to watch over me while I'm gone. But if Suriel sees us, or if you start to feel like you're losing your energy, don't hesitate to break the connection and wake me."

Dace pulls me close, presses a brief, sweet kiss on my lips. His softly whispered, "Be careful, Daire," the last thing I hear before my energy merges with the raven's and the two of us become one.

thirty-one

Daire

So far, the raven is turning out to be a very hospitable host. Allowing me to direct him as I please, as we follow the path set by Phyre's car.

She drives fast and with purpose. Pushing the speed limit until the back wheels begin to fishtail—causing big puffs of dirt to spin in her wake. Still, she handles it well, as though she's done this before. Refusing to slow until she pulls onto the private paved road that leads to the Richters' massive, adobe-style compound, where she parks just outside the gate and settles in to wait.

She's going to kill him? Now? Before most people have eaten their breakfast?

I direct the raven to a nearby tree. Choosing a limb that allows me an unobstructed view, I watch via his small beady eyes as Phyre flips down her sun visor and inspects her hair and makeup in the dirty, rectangular mirror. Satisfied with what she sees, she slaps the visor in place, holds an open palm before her, puckers her lips, and spits. Staring at the small pool of saliva with a gaze so transfixed, I can't even begin to guess what she's up to.

Is she bored? Has she completely lost her mind? Is this another method

of scrying where she tries to read a deeper meaning in the formation of
the bubbles, like some people do with tea leaves?

Her reverie broken by the electronic hum of the heavy, rod-iron gates swinging open, as Cade's shiny, black, four-wheel-drive truck barrels out. And I watch as she wipes her hand on her leg, leaps from her car, and, with her arms spread wide, jumps right in front of him.

Cade slams on the brakes. Tires squealing in protest, which is surprising in and of itself. I would've figured he'd run her right over without looking back.

His truck lurches forward, as he lowers his window and cranes his neck out. "What the hell?" he shouts. "What're you—crazy?"

"Maybe." She bats her eyes. Grinning seductively as she makes her way to the open driver's side window. "Only one way to find out." She leans against the door and cocks her head to the side, encouraging a spray of curls to tumble into her eyes.

"I don't have time for crazy," Cade says, not the least bit intrigued. "As you can see, I'm in a bit of a hurry."

"That's too bad." She pouts. "I was hoping you'd make time for me."

"And why would I do that?" His features sharpen, though, if I'm not mistaken, his voice betrays a hint of burgeoning interest.

"Because I feel lonely. Despite all of my friends, I feel like no one truly understands me."

"And I do?" He shucks a hand through his short crop of hair and snorts with amusement, but Phyre remains undeterred.

"We have a connection, Cade. Don't try to deny it. You know there's something between us. And so, I thought that maybe we could hang out. Keep each other company, or something . . ."

His face remains placid, hard to read. But I notice he doesn't turn her away.

"I was on my way to town. But then I thought I'd stop by and see what you're up to." She runs a slow finger along the rim of the door, but despite the attraction, Cade's not playing her game.

"I know you live in that dump of a trailer, Phyre. This is hardly on your way to town. Not to mention it's six in the morning. You in the habit of dropping in on people so early?"

"Not people. Just you." She lifts her chin, smiles through a halo of curls. "I know you like to go for an early morning run. I thought maybe I could join you?"

Cade looks her over, eyes glinting when he says, "You're not exactly dressed for running."

She lifts a shoulder. Tugs on her miniskirt. Remains grinning before him.

"You stalking me, Phyre?" His voice lowers, almost to the point of gruff. But I can't read the tone. Is it desire? Disgust? Will he make her beg for it, because she's coming dang close.

"Not stalking. More like . . . admiring," she says. "There is a difference, you know."

He stares, bobbing his head back and forth as though weighing the pros and cons of a brisk morning run versus a quick roll with a beautiful girl.

"I could show you the difference. If you're up for it . . ." She bites her lip, takes a step back from the car. Holding herself in offering—leaving it to him to decide.

"What're you after?" He works his jaw, rakes her with a deep, probing gaze.

She moves toward him, leans into his open window, and says, "Listen, I don't see the point in playing games, so here it is: I like you."

He nods like a person who's so used to being admired, it would never occur to him to question her word.

"And now that you and Lita have broken up, I thought that maybe—"

"You got a twin fetish? Is that it?" He's quick to cut her off.

She freezes.

"Didn't you used to be with my brother?"

She bites her lip. Casts her gaze to the side.

"Is this your way of keeping his memory alive?"

"No." She returns to him with an open, earnest face. "I know you're nothing like him. I can see the difference in you. You're darker. More dangerous. And it's that very darkness that attracts me to you."

Cade's eyes narrow to slits. His fingers drum against the steering wheel. "Careful what you wish for," he says. "You're venturing into territory you don't understand."

"Don't be so sure." She places a hand on his arm. Her fingertips stroking his flesh, her tongue wetting the rim of her lips.

And as silly as it looks from up here, from the place where Cade sits, it holds a certain appeal.

His features blunt. His gaze clouds. And when I see his lips part, it's clear that he's hooked.

Phyre leans closer. Wets her lips again. Leaving them glossy. Dripping. Wet. Ready for him.

And without knowing why, I get this incredible urge to stop them. Convinced deep in my soul that this is no ordinary kiss.

It's the first step to killing him. She'll seduce him, render him vulnerable, and then finish him off in a way he couldn't foresee, so she can report back to her crazy dad that her task is complete.

If she kills Cade, she kills Dace. And I won't let that happen.

They angle their heads in opposite ways. Veering closer, lips just a short breath away, as the raven spreads his wings wide and swoops down between them.

Phyre screams, bats her hands frantically at her head, then screams even louder when a clump of shiny, black feathers fall to her feet.

As Cade settles back in his seat and directs his attention at me.

"Looks like Raven is against this particular love match," he says, granting me a small wave of his hand, before he slams hard on the gas and leaves Phyre standing alone in the street.

thirty-two

Dace

Daire's softly breathing form lies beside me. Her head in my lap, her long legs stretched out before her. I run a palm over her cheek, whisper soft words she can't hear. For the moment, she's like me. Living, breathing, but soulless. The true force of her energy has taken a journey, and it's up to me to look after her.

I keep to my place on the far side of the shed. Watching as Suriel heads in and out of the trailer. His actions deliberate, purposeful. His body jittery, as though he's downed two too many cups of coffee.

Only Suriel doesn't drink coffee.

He shuns all forms of stimulants.

Shuns anything that creates a false sense of euphoria.

There's only one path to heaven, he claims. And it's clear that the tremor in his hands, the quake in his knees, is a direct result of his delusional beliefs of self-grandeur. His absolute certainty of his exalted place in the world.

He's a psychopath, pure and simple.

He's the very thing he preaches against.

I watch as he exits the trailer, this time carrying a bag I recognize from our meeting in the Middleworld. He drops it on the bottommost step, before taking a seat on the one just above it. Then he dips a hand inside, removes his blood-crusted stake, and holds it before him. Staring at it with the kind of unhinged, crazed admiration that's easy to see from all the way over here.

Returning the stake to its place, he retrieves a glass bottle filled with some kind of clear liquid he anoints himself with—daubing it onto his forehead, his chin.

Holy water.

I'm surprised he doesn't burst into flames.

When he's finished with the ritual, he closes the bag, leaves it on the step, and heads into the shed where he proceeds to make such a racket of creaking hinges, dull dragging sounds, and unearthly, odd shrieks, my curiosity gets the best of me and I creep toward the filthy, square window at the back, clear a space with my fingers, and look in.

At first, it's hard to make out what he's doing. Aided only by the single bare bulb swinging overhead, it takes a while for my vision to adjust. Though it's not long before I'm able to discern Suriel's form, busily putting together a pile of red sticks with digital displays wound tightly around them, which, despite the tricky lighting, can't be mistaken for anything other than the explosives they are.

What the hell is he up to?

I press closer. Clear a wider space to better see.

The squeak of my fingers moving over the glass, alerting Suriel to my presence.

He lifts his head. Centers his gaze right on mine.

And though I know I should bolt, for a few, terrifying moments, I'm frozen in place with legs turned to lead.

He pulls his lips wide, grinning as though my presence on the other side of the window has rendered him indescribably happy. Then he drops the bundle of explosives onto the pile, wipes his palms down the sides of his suit, and reaches for an old, rusted crowbar he uses to pry the lid off a rather large crate. Releasing a wild-eyed beast he's been keeping for some unfathomable reason.

The sight of its snapping snout, its rows of sharklike teeth dripping with bloodlust as it turns its attention to me, reminds me of Axel's warning.

"You have to be vigilant with your thoughts, your actions, yourself."

I turned to him with a questioning gaze.

"Without the soul, you're like an empty vessel. Leaving you vulnerable to demon possession."

I shot him an incredulous look. Sure he was exaggerating.

"Demons are everywhere. They come in all different forms. Able to appear in spirit form as well as their own hideous demon forms—depending on which dimension they're in. But the one thing they all have in common is their desire to materialize and live under the guise of humans. Though in order to do so, they need either a willing body, or a vacant, soulless body. Soulless bodies are always preferred, though obviously harder to come by. They'll be after you, Dace. They'll scent you from miles away, and will stop at nothing to get to you."

"So you're saying I'm walking, talking demon bait?"

Axel's lavender eyes went grim.

"If that's true, then why didn't they want me before? Back when I was in their lair?"

"You were weak and wounded. Ironically, it's the only thing that saved you. But now that you're healed . . ." He heaved a deep sigh as his eyes met mine. "Vigilance, Dace. Until you get your soul back, you can't afford to relax." He was vanishing before me as he said it, his form beginning to dim.

"Where you going?" I asked, not sure what to make of it.

"I have to find my way back. I've already interfered in your life more than I should."

"But what if I need another energy infusion?" I asked, watching as his eyes narrowed with regret.

"Just make sure you locate your soul well before then."

Though the warning was intended for me, I'm not the only soulless body in jeopardy.

The beast hurls itself against the back wall, causing the wood to splinter and crack until it starts to give way. Leaving me only a handful of seconds to decide what to do next.

Do I fight him?

Slay him?

Beat him to a pulp and watch him bleed into the ground?

Or do I try to grab Daire and get the hell out of here?

With her idle body sprawled across the dirt, she appears so defenseless, so vulnerable, there's no question I have to do whatever it takes to get her to safety.

I'll fight the demon if it comes to that.

But only if it comes to that.

The demon continues to beat down the wall. His claw breaking through first, followed by a foot, as Suriel screams and shouts from inside, egging him on.

I lunge for Daire's body, scoop her into my arms, and race for Kachina. Remembering too late that Kachina fears me. There's no guarantee that she'll help.

Though she is inclined to help Daire.

She runs up beside me and lowers her neck, allowing me to drape Daire over her back, just as a loud crash rings out from behind, and the demon lumbers straight for us.

thirty-three

Daire

Long after Cade has left, Phyre remains in her car. Her face hidden in the palms of her hands. Her shoulders spasmodically jerking as though crying.

She drags a deep breath, peers into the rearview mirror, and wipes a careful finger under each eye. Taking a moment to consider the tears she's collected, before drying her hands on her legs and driving away.

With a gentle nudge from me, the raven soars alongside her. Trailing her over a series of gutted dirt roads and random turns, with seemingly no destination in mind. Until she pulls a quick U-turn and speeds toward Native Land.

The reservation?

What could she possibly want there?

If she can't get the twins, will she go after Chepi?

Or is she simply licking her wounds with a visit to her childhood haunts?

The raven grows fidgety, hungry. Irritated by this extended bout of hospitality, he wastes no time in squeezing me out. Leaving me to wake with a start, surprised to find myself draped in Dace's arms as Kachina races furiously beneath us.

"What happened?" With bleary eyes I squint toward the horizon, trying to determine our location. "Where are we? Where are we going?" I gaze up at Dace, noting the look of extreme apprehension masking his face. The way he keeps looking behind us, as though we're being chased.

"I'll fill you in later." He drags hard on the reins, urging Kachina to a much slower pace, though it takes her a while to obey. She's lathered and restless and as spooked as Dace seems to be. "You okay?" He presses his lips to my hair, clutches me tighter against him.

I nod, shift deeper into his arms, and peer past his shoulder. Seeing nothing out of the ordinary. Nothing to worry about. Whatever it was, it seems to have passed.

"What'd you see?" His voice is tight, distracted, as he peers behind us again.

"I watched Phyre try to get with your brother. But I intervened before it could go anywhere."

"Cade was into it?" Dace greets the news with a look I can't read.

Is he surprised? Disappointed? Jealous? Or is that just me, projecting my own conflicting emotions onto him?

"I think he was more amused than anything," I finally say. "It seemed like he was kind of stringing her along. You know how he loves his little games."

Dace flattens his lips in reply.

"Can I ask you something?" I pause, unsure exactly how to proceed. But I need to know, so I force myself to press on. "This'll probably sound weird, but—was Phyre a really wet kisser?"

Just as I expected, Dace shoots me an incredulous look.

"I know it sounds crazy," I say, my voice hurried, eager to explain. "And the only reason I ask is because she kept wetting her lips till they were all gloppy and dripping. And, even before that, I watched her spit on her hand and stare at her own saliva like she was totally transfixed by the sight of it. And I'm wondering if it has something to do with that weird vial she drank from?"

Dace shifts uncomfortably, looks behind him again, even though we both know whatever it was he was worried about is now gone. "A preoccupation with saliva doesn't ring any bells," he finally says, reluctantly voicing the words. "As for the vial—who knows? Knowing Suriel, it's probably holy water—specially blessed by his own crazy, delusional self."

"Okay, so basically she's just a weird girl, then." I lift my shoulders, aware of a slight rush of blood coloring my cheeks.

"I think we've already confirmed that." Dace's bottom lip tugs at the corners, but the mirth is short lived. Next thing I know, he's back to peering behind us, as I take a moment to look all around, trying to get my bearings and figure out where we are.

"Are we anywhere near the reservation?" I ask.

"We can be. Why?"

"Phyre was headed there when I lost contact. It might not mean anything, but I think we should check in, see what she's up to. Make sure Chepi's safe."

"I don't think Phyre would hurt Chepi. She looked to her like a mother after her own mother went missing." Dace speaks with confidence, but I'm not convinced. I wouldn't put anything past her.

"Yeah, well, she also claims to be madly in love with you, and yet, look what happened there. Her father gave her strict orders to kill you, and it's not like she warned you."

That's all it takes to convince him to nudge Kachina toward the reservation. After stopping by Chepi's and learning she's not home, we're on our way to Leftfoot's when I spot Phyre's dirty white car parked just before the grove of twisted juniper trees.

"She knows about the Lowerworld?" I shift my gaze between the vortex and Dace, catching the deeply troubled look on his face, but he just shrugs in reply.

Quick to dismount, he offers a hand and helps me down as well. Then we step between the grove of trees and leap into the vortex that sees us tunneling deep into the earth before landing in a heap. We take a moment to collect ourselves, take a good look around. The surrounding landscape just as frozen as the last time I came here with Lita and Xotichl.

"This isn't natural." Dace's eyes narrow. His lips fall flat and grim. "Of all the years I've been coming to the Lowerworld, I've never seen it like this."

"I'm afraid the snow is my doing." I make a guilty face. "It was my dying wish—only now, it won't seem to stop."

Dace studies me for a moment, then turns to survey the land once again. "And where's Horse? He's always here to greet me."

"My guess is he's hibernating." I rub my palms together in an attempt to keep warm. "I haven't seen Raven either. Not since Christmas Eve. And until this is settled, I don't expect to. But the real question is, where's Phyre? Where do you think she went?" I study Dace's profile, his high, sculpted cheekbones, his wide brow, as he squints against the glare and looks all around.

He shakes his head, runs a hand through his glossy sheet of hair, but it's not exactly the answer I was looking for. I need something more.

I clear my throat, forcing myself to ask the question that leaves me feeling more than a little intrusive. More than a little ashamed. At the risk of sounding like a nosy, jealous girlfriend, I say, "Dace, did you and Phyre ever come here together?" I clamp my lips shut before I can say anything more. My desire to hear his most heart-felt denial, in direct conflict with my need for a good jumping-off point. The Lowerworld is huge. Any hint on where to start looking would be a big help.

"I never came here with her." He leans toward me, takes my hands in his. Squeezing them warmly, he says, "Daire, you need to understand that our relationship—if you can even call it that—was fleeting. We weren't together nearly as long as you think. I had no idea she knew about this place. Just as I have no idea what she might be doing here. But we have one thing in our favor."

I look at him.

"Snow." His eyes glint, crinkling at the sides. "Maybe all of this snow is a good thing. With the spirit animals in hiding, it's remained fairly undisturbed. Which should prove a big help in finding her tracks."

It's a good theory—or at least on the surface. But what he forgets is that the Lowerworld is home to many dimensions. Which means Phyre could've landed just about anywhere. Which also means we could wander for days and never catch sight of either her or her tracks.

Then again, she hasn't been here all that long. So there's still a good chance she hasn't made it beyond this very first level.

Dace laces his fingers with mine, and we set off exploring. Our voices silenced, feet trudging forward, eyes constantly darting, surveying an all-white landscape. Having covered a good distance, before we finally reach a place where the snow's been disturbed.

"Looks like she landed here." Dace moves ahead, circling the area where a bank of snow has been flattened. Shifting his gaze to a trail of small footprints, he says, "And this should lead us to her." He grasps my hand with his much cooler one. And I can't help but wonder if his energy infusion is starting to wane, or if it's a result of this frozen landscape we're in.

"Dace, you feeling okay?" I study him carefully. All too aware that should his strength fail, there's no one around here to help me restore him.

"I'm fine." He pulls me toward the trail. But the way his jaw clenches, the way he averts his gaze, leads me to believe he's anything but.

Still, with no other choice, I trek silently alongside him. Unwilling to put a voice to the long list of questions storming my brain.

Are these Phyre's tracks?

And if so, what do we do once we find her?

Wouldn't our time be better spent searching for Dace's soul?

What if we've fallen way off track—and what if it's all my fault?

What if Phyre really is just sort of tragic and odd, but otherwise has nothing to do with any of this?

What if I'm endangering Dace by leading him on this crazy, nonsensical chase?

Dace squeezes my hand and pulls me to a stop. The alerted look on his face enough to quiet my thoughts.

"Do you hear that?" he whispers, nodding in the direction where a strange sort of chanting and wailing is coming from somewhere deep within the woods.

A chill slips over my skin. One that has less to do with the frigid climate we're in, and more to do with the tone of the song.

It's the sound of sadness and melancholy.

If complete and utter despair had a note, it would chime just like this.

Dace is the first to move toward it, but I'm quick to catch up. With lowered heads and stooped shoulders, we creep quietly forward. Edging up alongside a grove of tall pine trees flecked white with snow, I stare at the scene before me in complete disbelief. Only vaguely aware of Dace's whispered voice in my ear, saying, "Well, that explains it."

thirty-four

Dace

I gape at the spectacle before me. Telling myself it doesn't truly exist. Just a trick of my mind. Not unlike the delusions that plagued me back in that hell dimension of the Middleworld.

Sinking into the comfort of a deeply rooted denial, when Daire drags a startled breath beside me that confirms it's real.

The ice sculpture is elaborate.

Intricate.

Diamond shaped and massive in size, it's been carefully carved by a talented hand. Its surface so shiny and slick, it serves as an easy distraction. Though a closer look reveals a much smaller diamond sculpture suspended inside, containing a radiant sphere that shimmers in a nimbus of light.

I recognize it the instant I see it.

And judging by Daire's horrified gasp, she knows it too.

Though I can't imagine how she managed it, somehow Phyre has captured my soul and encased it in ice.

It's only when I lift my gaze higher that I see the razor-sharp stake she's rigged to hang precariously above it.

It's an ingenious contraption.

One that commands a sort of awed reverence.

One that requires a few hushed moments to take in its full magnitude—to understand how it works.

Its execution deceptively simple—the ice melts, the stake drops, and just like *that* my life force is eternally snuffed.

Taking Cade's life force right along with me.

The first solid step toward fulfilling her father's prophecy.

She always did have a flair for grand gestures—maximum dramatic impact. Still, I'm surprised she found the will to go through with it.

I start to rush toward it, eager to claim it. Until Daire grasps my sleeve and holds me in place. Her troubled gaze directing me to see what she sees.

Phyre, standing off to the side. Her eyes dark and dreamy, watching the stake inch its way toward my soul.

"Isn't it beautiful?" She addresses us while keeping her gaze fixed firmly in place. "You know, it never used to snow down here, so I figured I should at least try to make the most of it and use it to my advantage. It was a real labor of love. Took me days to complete. You don't have to hide." She skews her gaze, looks at us sideways. "I know you're there, Dace." Her cheeks widen, her lips begin a slow curl at the sides. "I always know when you're near." She switches her focus to Daire and her features fall flat. "Just like I know that was you keeping me from Cade. I'm not stupid. I know you joined with that raven. I know who you are."

I chance a cautious step forward, all the while keeping my eyes on the sculpture. Phyre's unstable. Completely unhinged. Best not to make any sudden moves. Best not to startle her.

I'm just about to sneak another step, when she says, "I said you could stop hiding. I didn't say you could come any closer. I want to see you, Dace. I always want to see you. But now, after everything that's happened, I only want to see you from afar."

I choose to obey. Remain rooted in place. Figuring it's better to earn her trust than to force the issue and antagonize her into doing something entirely regrettable.

"I loved you, you know." She swivels on her heels until she's fully facing me. And that's when I see her eyes are red-rimmed, her cheeks are misted with tears. "In fact, I still do. Just because you choose to love the Seeker doesn't change my feelings for you."

Her voice breaks a bit at the end, and thinking it might provide me an entrance, I stretch an arm toward her, and whisper her name. Urging her to take hold of my hand, to stop what she's doing, so we can all talk this over.

But before I can get very far, she lifts an arm in protest, warning me back. And that's when I see the full scope of this hideous tableau that she's set. The mass of dried twigs clutched in one hand, the empty gas can (presumably the same one I watched her place in the trunk of her car) lying empty beside her, and Cade's ubiquitous silver-and-turquoise lighter pinched between two of her fingers.

"It's too late," she says, her face strangely expressionless, her voice matter-of-fact. "Too late for all of us." She shifts her focus to the twigs, and with a flick of her thumb sets the torch ablaze.

"Phyre!" I shout, and though I'm quick to lunge toward her, the move comes too late.

She's already lowered the torch to the snow.

Already ignited the gasoline rainbow encircling the sculpture that plays host to my soul.

The fire erupting in a blinding flash of heat and flames that instantly gets the surface of the outermost sculpture melting at an alarming rate. Causing the stake rigged above it to descend toward my soul.

The sight of it leaving me speechless. Frozen in horror. Watching as Phyre inexplicably directs her breath on the blaze. Every inhale and exhale alternately tempering and stoking the flames.

"I know you don't believe it," she says, allowing the flames to settle. Her tone, light, conversational, picking up right where she left off, as though she hasn't just significantly shortened the life span of my soul. "But the brief time we spent together were the absolute, hands-down, indisputable, best days of my life." She purses her lips, breathes a quick hiss, sending the flames into a mad, sudden fury again. "Those moments were the only piece of beauty I could ever call mine." She turns to me, curious to see how I'll react.

"And yet, you're determined to end me," I say, less interested in her invented version of the past than the events unfolding before me.

The fire rages.

The ice sweats.

The dagger descends.

As the torch she wields in her hand emits a hazy cloud of noxious, hard-to-breathe fumes.

"You shouldn't blame me, Dace. And you shouldn't look at me that way—like I'm some kind of monster." Her lips droop into a pout, as though I've deeply offended her. "None of this is my fault. It's not like I asked for this life. I was chosen. Pure and simple. And now, I'm merely fulfilling my destiny. Doing what I was born to do." She arcs the torch before her and thrusts it into the flames. And I watch as her lips pull back at the sides, face flushing with pleasure the second fire meets fire. "As it turns out, killing you was what I was born to do." She sneaks a peek at me. Ensuring I'm suitably horrified, she lowers the torch to her side and allows the fire to settle. "If it wasn't me standing here, then it would be one of my sisters, Ember or Ashe. It's our family legacy, Dace. It's not like I can change it, or alter it in some way. That's not to say I liked it at first, 'cause believe me, I didn't. But once my father explained the idea, once I made the decision to accept my fate, I began to see things differently. Everyone has a destiny, a purpose. And yet most people just shuffle through the course of their lives, totally clueless. You and me are the lucky ones. We figured it out early on. Besides, I think it's kind of romantic that our fates are entwined. I knew from the moment I met you that there was something bigger between us. Which is why you should take solace in the fact that your end will come from me. I mean, wouldn't you rather exit at the hand of someone who loves you?"

"I prefer not to exit at all." I slew my gaze toward Daire and shoot her a wary look, warning her to stay put.

Phyre's clearly gone crazy. And it's best for Daire to keep a low profile and not interfere. Anything Daire says or does will only provoke her. Besides, I'm the one who tarnished my soul, leaving it vulnerable. I should be the one to negotiate its return.

"You disappoint me, Dace." Phyre heaves an exaggerated sigh. "Death doesn't just happen to other, less fortunate people. It happens to all of us. Just like it will happen to you. We're all going to exit someday. Though I guess I should've figured you'd say that. It's astounding the delusions people willingly cling to." She returns her attention to the fiery blaze. Alternately stoking it and calming it with deep, purposeful breaths—enjoying the tease. "You have no idea what a favor this is. At least this death will be quick and painless. At least you'll be spared the horrors of the Last Days, which, just so you know, truly are upon us. I'm afraid Enchantment won't fare so well. It's a town filled with blasphemous heathens and sinners. So, with that in mind, I think it's best if you consider this as my final gift to you. Two years ago I gave you my virginity, and now I give you an easy exit from a pain-filled world."

She opens her mouth, gathers her breath, and I can't let her do it again. The large sculpture has almost completely given way. And it will only take a few more well-directed breaths to see that the smaller one is history as well, leaving my soul completely exposed. Leaving the dagger to finish its hideous, downward course.

"I don't see it like you do," I say, my mouth so dry, I have to force the words past. "I don't see the world as pain-filled. I see wonder everywhere I look. I see wonder in *you*." I study her closely, pray the words penetrate. But one look at her face tells me it's a total fail.

"You really need to work on your perspective." She frowns. "You need to take off the blinders and see the world as it really is."

I rub my lips together, desperate to get through to her. "Phyre, listen to me, please. This is *not* your destiny." My gaze pleads with hers, but she's quick to turn away in dismissal. "This is *not* destiny, divine law, or anything of the sort. This is your father's madness run amok. You don't have to go through with it. You can walk away from him and I'll make sure you get the help that you need. Put out the fire, release my soul now, and I promise you that Suriel will never be allowed to go near you again. I will see that you are settled somewhere safe where he will never be able to reach."

She tilts her head to the side and swings her torch haphazardly before her, filling the space with a cloud of acrid smoke that burns a path through my throat and makes my eyes sear. "Do you love me, Dace?" She turns, as though she hadn't heard a single word I'd just said.

I rub my lips together, knowing it's a test. Knowing better than to lie.

"Did you ever love me?"

I remain quietly in place.

She laughs a brittle, broken laugh, and lowers the torch to her side. "And yet another reason I love you. You're always honest. Always honorable. More people should be like you. The world would be a better place. There'd be no need for Last Days, that's for sure."

"Phyre, for whatever it's worth, I really did care for you," I say, squinting my eyes, trying not to choke on the fumes.

"I know. Everyone used to tease me and my sisters because of the things my dad said. But you never did. You never judged me for the things that he did. For that, I remain forever grateful."

"I still care about you. I'm also worried about you. The last two years you've been out there on your own, with no one to turn to. I understand. I really do. And because of it, you're under Suriel's influence. But what you're doing now—this isn't you. You're nothing like your father. You're your own person. Able to make your own choices. You have too much to offer to allow yourself to go down this path."

"That may have been true once, but not anymore." She smiles softly, singing the words, as she lifts the torch yet again and moves precariously close to the flames.

She's losing it. Becoming so unstable, so unpredictable, that one false move—one false word—and I'm instantly annihilated as though I never existed.

Such a stark contrast to a few hours before when I was begging for release, and my wish was steadfastly ignored.

Be careful what you wish for, as Chepi always warned.

But now with Daire back in my life, I have everything to live for.

I risk a step forward. One that's meant to go undetected. But then a wave of nausea ripples through me, and I falter, aware of my body tingling, cooling.

The energy infusion that Paloma and Axel gave me is now leaving my body.

In an instant, Daire's by my side, trying to steady me. But I shirk from her touch. Knowing it will only spur Phyre on.

The ice is melting. My energy is waning. And I need to use what little time I have left to convince Phyre to end this madness while I still can.

"What's the matter, Dace? You look a little pale. Is it because of this?" Phyre bites hard on her lip, as she lowers the torch yet again. Giving in to a fit of nervous giggles when the outer sculpture collapses, and the stake drops even lower. Its tip glowing fierce and red.

"I'm good," I say. "Strong. Never been better." It requires all of my effort to straighten my spine, square my shoulders, yet it still fails to convince her.

"Your brother is a natural liar. While you, old friend, are not." She stifles a satisfied smirk, but her flashing eyes give her away.

"Speaking of my brother, I heard you paid him a visit." I move toward her. Just one foot, slipping over the snow, sliding slowly before me. If I play this right, the other will soon follow. And then again. And again. Until I'm close enough to disarm her.

"What can I say?" She shrugs. "I miss you. And he's the perfect stand-in."

"We may look alike, but that's where it ends." I grit my teeth, clench my jaw, and struggle not to look otherwise pained as I bring my left foot forward until it surpasses the right. "Surely you're aware of that?"

"Of course I'm aware. I'm not an idiot. Sheesh." She shakes her head, mutters under her breath, then faces me again. "Cade is dark. You're light. He's yin. You're yang. And just like yin and yang, you're connected. Equal parts of the whole. One can't exist without the other." Seeing my look of surprise, she says, "I know all about it. You're the polar opposites of each other. The positive and the negative charge of the universe. And the way you interact influences the destinies of all living things. Which is why I have to kill you. Still, there is a kind of beauty in such perfect symmetry, don't you think?"

"I never thought about it that way," I say, talking just for the sake of talking. Trying to keep her distracted, unaware of the slow but steady progress I'm making.

She makes a face. "Really, Dace?" She casts her gaze to the ground and sighs. "And here I'd convinced myself you were more introspective than that. Guess I only saw what I wanted to see."

"I only just learned about our connection," I say. "I haven't had a lot of time to process it. How did you learn about it?" I arrange my face to look curious, as though I care about the answer, as I complete another step toward her.

"Suriel told me." She stares at her boots, digs the toe deep into the snow. "He suspected early on. He's much sharper than most people think."

"You seem to have grown very close."

"He's all I have left now, isn't he?" She lifts her gaze to meet mine, and for an instant, I'm reminded of the same sad girl I once shared a few intimate moments with.

"I'm not sure I'd agree." The words require great effort. Every breath requires great effort. But I'm so damn close, I can't give up now.

"Please." She rolls her eyes. "I'm as alone as alone can be. The kids at school aren't really my friends. They don't really know me. Don't actually care about me. The girls just try to steal my style, while the boys try to get in my pants. It's nothing like what I had with you. But now I no longer have you, do I?"

"Of course you do," I say, voice soft and coaxing. "We'll always be friends, Phyre. And I'm here to help you—just say the word."

"Really? Is that why I could never get you to so much as talk to me?" She meets my gaze head-on, and I can't help but flinch. There's no denying it's true. "From the moment I returned to Enchantment you've been bent on brushing me off. Making it all too clear how you couldn't wait to ditch me so that you could be with *her.*"

She glares at Daire. Her face hardening in renewed fury, almost as though she'd forgotten she was there. And I chance a look too, seeing Daire staring straight ahead, her gaze fixed on the rapidly melting sculpture, as though she's planning something big. And though I've no idea what it is, I hope she'll hold off long enough for me to do what I need to.

"Remember the day we made love?" Phyre continues to stare at Daire, but Daire steadfastly ignores her, refuses to engage. "I said, *Do. You. Remember. The. Day. We. Made. Love?* Answer me, Dace!"

My shoulders are sagging, my breath is becoming ragged, still I manage to say, "I do. I do remember." Hoping it'll be enough to appease her. It's all I can do to hold myself up.

"What do you remember most about it? What word, if you had to pick one—and, make no doubt about it, you do—what word would you use to describe it?"

"What word would *you* use?" I ask, my pulse slow and labored, stalling for time.

"No, that's not fair. I asked you first!" she sings, as though this is all a good bit of fun.

"Novel," I say, my head growing dizzy, my vision blurry.

"Novel?" She frowns, kicks hard at the snow. "You mean like a book? Like a scene in a romance novel or something?"

The moment I shake my head I instantly regret it. It increases the dizziness, leaving me woozy, unsteady on my feet. "Novel as in *new*," I say, pushing through a fresh wave of nausea. "And by that I mean, it was all new to me. I'm afraid I had no idea what I was doing."

"But you do now. Is that what you're saying?" She glares at Daire, starts to swing the torch wildly again. Causing the ring of fire to spark and flare, as a noxious cloud of filthy smoke permeates the air.

I shout in protest. Then instantly regret it. It only serves to egg her on. "Phyre—" I try again. "You've put me in a difficult spot, and I don't know what you want me to say. All I know is that it was new . . . and unexpected, and . . ." *Daire, please forgive me.* "Wonderful all at the same time."

Phyre settles the torch by her side, seemingly satisfied. But it's not like it makes any difference. The fire is raging, the ice is liquefying, and the once frozen-solid walls of the small diamond sculpture are well on their way to completely collapsing.

I sneak a peek at Daire, overcome by the regret of her having to listen to this. But she remains as stoic as ever. Concentrating so hard on the stake, I wonder if she's even aware of what Phyre is saying.

"It was wonderful for me too." Phyre grins, dips her head shyly. So lost in her memories, she misses the moment the outer shell shrinks, dissolving into a small pool of water.

But Daire notices. I can sense it in the way she stiffens behind me, as I fight to hang on to what little energy remains. Trying to estimate how long it can possibly hold up, and all I know for sure is, it won't be long until it's gone.

"You know why I instigated it, right?" Phyre asks, seemingly obsessed with this subject. She refuses to quit.

My mouth grows dry. My throat constricts. I can barely breathe, much less respond.

"I mean, we both know I was the aggressor. You were so cute and honorable, if I'd left it to you, nothing ever would've happened. Was he like that with you too?" She turns to Daire with a challenging gaze. But Daire looks right past her. "Anyway, I knew I was leaving soon. But what I didn't tell you, was that I also knew I'd return."

I grunt in reply, it's the best I can do.

"The reason I didn't tell you is because I knew things would never be the same. I knew that someday it would come to this. I knew that sometime during our sixteenth year, I would have to kill you." She pauses, casts a contemplative gaze toward the fire. "You have no idea how awful it was to live with such a truth. And don't think I accepted it easily. I fought with Suriel every day, all day. Or at least until I realized it would be done either way. Then I figured it may as well be done by me." She takes a deep breath and returns to me. "But mostly, I didn't mention it because I didn't want you to feel like you had to make a bunch of false promises you'd be unable to keep. It would've soured everything, and it was important to me to keep the memory in my heart—just like your soul is now—frozen in time—glorious, luminous, perfect, and safe."

"But my soul isn't safe." I nod toward the dissolving diamond, and the quickly melting ice pedestal that supports it. Seeing her look of confusion when she notices, seemingly for the first time, the dire state of the sculptures. It won't be long before the only thing separating me from a quick and decisive death will be the ice-covered rope (now nearly thawed out) that holds the dagger. "You've got a red-hot stake hanging right over it. Any second now, it'll penetrate."

Her body grows anxious, fidgety. Allowing me a small seed of hope that she might not go through with it. That she's plagued by doubt.

But no sooner have I thought it, when she turns to me and says, "Turns out my memory wasn't safe either." She dismisses my life—the state of my soul—with a casual tilt of her shoulders. "It's tarnished by the current reality." The moment she says it, the outer crusting of ice holding the rope in place begins to give way. Prompting the stake to drop until its red-hot tip is dangling a mere foot from the top of the diamond sculpture, a foot and a half from my soul.

"You can't tarnish a memory," I say, speaking the first words that pop into my head. I slide another foot forward, knowing it may well be my last. Won't be long before my knees refuse to hold me. "A memory stands on its own." The words come out mumbled, gruff, but still she meets me with a wistful look.

"I wish that were true. I wish things were different. I wish I didn't have to do this."

"You don't have to. Really, you don't—"

"You're wrong! I do. I mean, sheesh, Dace. We've already been through this! I procrastinated in the beginning, but then, the day I watched your soul drift free—"

"You were there?" I gasp. "That night—on Christmas Eve?" I had no sense of her. Had no idea she was with us. Watching.

She tilts her head toward me, causing a spray of curls to bounce into her eyes in that naturally charismatic and flirtatious way that she has. In another life, with other parents, she would've been a model, a movie star, or maybe even a politician. But instead, she ended up with Suriel, and he turned her into a killer.

"I wasn't there when you lost it. But later, when I saw this glorious orb soaring above me, I knew that very instant it was yours. And the funny thing is, I was down here looking for you. And look, I found you. Or at least the real and true essence of you." She gazes at it admiringly. As though she enjoys seeing it so vulnerable and exposed. "Wanna know how I knew it was yours?" She casts her gaze my way, as though daring me to say *no*.

But I've grown so weak I can no longer speak.

"I knew by the way it shined so bright. It was the brightest thing in the sky. Except for this ugly little dark spot right here." She motions toward it with the torch, and my heart, barely beating, seems to leap into my throat. "That part's kinda blemished, and icky. How'd you get that, anyway?"

I made a soul jump into my brother and took a piece of his darkness as a souvenir.

I try to force another step forward, but end up stooped over with my hands desperately gripping my knees. My head hanging forward, breath panting, coming too fast—like a dog after a very long run, thirsting for a hit of oxygen, a fresh bowl of water.

"Guess you and Cade aren't as polar as I thought. You clearly contain a piece of him. I wonder, does he contain a piece of you too?"

I drop to my knees, swaying precariously toward the cold ground before me. Aware of Daire's agitated presence beside me, and Phyre's increasingly uninterested gaze.

"Well, it'll be interesting to find out," she hums. "So amazing to have this opportunity to get an inside peek at you both. Chance of a lifetime, when you think about it."

She lowers the torch once again, and I use my last surge of strength to say, "Phyre, stop!"

She turns toward me with widened eyes.

"This is not who you are."

"You don't even know me." She turns away.

"You're the girl who found the abandoned nest of baby sparrows and opened the makeshift orphanage in order to house them, raise them—remember?"

Her body goes rigid, she rubs her lips together, and I know that I've managed to reach her.

"You took them in, fed them with an eye dropper. Tried to teach them to fly with the paper airplane I made."

"Two of those birds died."

"But the other two survived."

She licks her lips, loosens her grip on the torch.

"You did that, Phyre. You saved those birds. Because you cared. Because you valued life for the wonderful gift that it is. You still do. You know you do. You haven't changed as much as you pretend to."

Her cheeks glisten with tears, her lips lift at the sides, as her sad glittering eyes meet mine. "You truly believe that?" she asks, her voice soft, her will fading.

"Of course I do," I whisper, dragging myself toward her. "C'mon." I reach a tired hand toward hers. And when she lets me, when she doesn't push me away, I use the last remaining bit of my strength to wrench the torch away. "You don't have to do this." I drop the torch just behind me where it sizzles in protest until it's snuffed out by the snow.

I slip off my jacket and pull it over my head. Prepared to charge through the flames and reclaim my soul, when Phyre catches hold of my arm and with a hardened gaze says, "I was hoping I could give you salvation with a kiss—but you never let me get close enough. So now, I'm left with no choice. Fire is the only way to deliver your doomed and damaged soul."

She fills her lungs with air, and exhales with all that she has. The sheer force of her breath meeting the flames, causes them to explode into a raging inferno that triggers the diamond shell to collapse, as I'm swept off my feet and slammed hard into a snowbank.

My vision tunnels.

Daire screams.

And the stake plunges straight for my soul.

thirty-five

Daire

Dace falls.

The dagger drops.

And I leap over his body and rush toward the blaze, fully intending to breach it like I did in the cave.

But when the toe of my boot smolders and burns, when the hem of my jeans scorches and singes, I realize this particular fire is not mine to control. It'll burn me. Possibly end me. And I can't take the chance.

I whirl toward the stake, overcome with relief when I see the uppermost part of the rope is still frozen, still attached to a barren limb, still hanging on, if only barely.

And of course, there's still Phyre. Crazy Phyre. Seeming not to notice or care that the so-called love of her life has fallen into an unconscious heap. She turns on me, not so much as missing a beat in her continued attempts to hurt me.

"I can't help but be jealous of you." Her gaze is open, direct. I can feel the weight of it nudging my cheek. "But make no mistake, that's not why I'm doing this. It's not a pathetic, *if I can't have him, then nobody can,* kind of moment. There are much bigger things happening here. Do you know about the bigger things?" She pauses, waits for me to reply, and when I don't, she goes on to say, "You probably think you do, being the Seeker and all. But the world is much bigger than you and me. As soon as that stake drops, the twins will be gone, and not long after, I'll be gone too. I used to resent it. Used to fight against it. But now I've learned to accept it."

She leans forward, forces a smile to her lips. And I know this is it. One more exhale, that rope will snap, and Dace and Cade are history.

While I'm nearly ready for her, nearly ready to put the plan I've been working on this whole time into action, I need a few moments more. So I do what I can to distract her.

"I have a similar situation," I say, chancing only the briefest glance her way, enough to make sure I've successfully stalled her, if only temporarily. "I was furious when I first learned I was the Seeker. I even tried to run away. Though clearly, I didn't get very far."

"It's not the same." She scowls, rolls her eyes, and gets into position again.

"Not the same, but similar. You have to admit that it's similar." My voice rings too frantic, too desperate, I seriously need to tone it down. Still, it does seem to bear some effect. As witnessed by the way Phyre leans back ever so slightly, closes her lips, twists her mouth to the side. "Like you, I also have a destiny." I swallow hard. Remind myself I can do this. Try not to think about how many times it's recently failed. "But unlike you, my destiny is for the greater good . . ." I rub my lips together. Start counting down in my head.

One . . . I slowly lift my hand.

Two . . . I flatten my palm, turn it toward the dagger.

Three . . . I beg a silent plea to the universe: *Please, don't let this fail me!*

"And mine?" Her voice is snappy, impatient.

"And yours . . ." I grit my teeth, spread my fingers, and prepare for what's next.

"Speak, Seeker!" she screams. Her voice reverberating so loudly, it causes the flames to surge, the tree limbs to shake, and the dagger to drop even farther, dangling precariously.

"And yours is just a bunch of made-up bullshit created by your psychotic dad."

My eyes meet hers, confirming the outrage I intentionally put there. I only hope my timing was right.

She leans toward the sculpture and heaves an exhale so forceful, the heat from the flames causes the rope holding the dagger to instantly snap, allowing it to career straight for Dace's soul.

I watch the progression.

I don't dare blink.

With my hand held open before me, I beg another silent plea.

Calling on my powers of telekinesis, which lately have been tenuous at best. But right now, it's all that I've got.

Well, that, and my intent. Which, according to Paloma, is magick's most important ingredient.

And yet, despite my best intentions, despite my fervent prayer, the dagger, now just a razor's width away from Dace's soul— refuses to alter its path.

It slams straight down.

Straight into the space where Dace's soul once stood.

I scream an unearthly involuntary sound. Gape in outraged disbelief.

Silencing when I see the way Phyre stares at me and I follow her gaze to my hand.

My intention was to save Dace's soul, and it appears I did exactly that.

My telekinesis didn't fail me.

It merely forfeited the dagger in place of the object that truly mattered most.

While the dagger fell, the soul found its way to my hand.

With eyes blazing as bright as the flames that she set, Phyre lets out a horrible wail and charges straight toward me. The force of her body slamming into mine knocks the air flat out of me, as the soul slips free of my grasp.

It hovers above us, as we both desperately claw for it. Though it's not long before it begins to drift into the sky.

Phyre shoves off me, jumps to her feet. As I scramble to catch up, keep her from claiming it.

Because of the fires she set, the once heavy blanket of snow is now melting around us. Turning to a thick, viscous mud that bungles the chase, leaving us slipping, sliding, losing our balance but never our will in pursuit of Dace's soul.

"You can't save him," she shouts, racing before me. "It's the Word. It is written. It is already happening. There is nothing you can do to change it."

I lengthen my stride, fight like hell to overtake her. And when my feet finally hit a patch of dry land, providing me some much-needed traction, I leap toward the sky, leap toward Dace's soul—only to watch as Phyre reaches it first.

She captures it in her outstretched hands. Pulls it in close to her chest. The sight of this crazed, unhinged girl handling something so fragile, so delicate, so precious, so easily destroyed—leaves me breathless and horrified.

She stares at it with wide, dreamy eyes, transfixed by the sight of it. But when she notices my approach, she pulls it even closer. Wrapping a protective arm around it, she clucks her tongue and says, "I wouldn't do that if I were you."

I lift my palms in surrender, stand silently before her. Watching as she snakes a hand into her pocket and retrieves the turquoise-and-silver lighter she lifted from Cade.

"Did you know my middle name is Oleander?" Her eyes briefly meet mine. "Phyre Oleander Youngblood. How's that for a mouthful?" she muses, idly flicking the lighter's ribbed metal wheel with the pad of her thumb. "Although I wasn't given the name until I was sixteen. That's when my destiny was sealed. Though it started way back when I was eight. My father told me it was a great honor. One that I should bear proudly. Never mind that it nearly killed me on more than one occasion. But, as it turns out, when it's all said and done, my father was right. Then again, he usually is." She reaches into her pocket again. This time retrieving a perfect pink blossom with a short, thin stem she props between her front teeth.

At first I assume she's going to swallow it whole, but a moment later I watch as she pulls the flowerless stem from her lips and uses the lighter to set it ablaze. The mere act of flame meeting stem is enough to cause a thick cloud of acrid smoke to surround me, leaving me gagging, choking, blurring my vision until everything around me begins to shimmer and halo. Rendering it nearly impossible to keep an eye on Dace's soul when every single thing is glistening, glimmering with a nimbus of light.

"It's really too bad it had to end this way." Phyre assumes a thoughtful expression, as hundreds of brilliant orbs dance between us. "Under different circumstances, I'm sure we could've been friends." She smiles briefly, purses her lips, and exhales a deep breath she directs right at me. Engulfing me in a cloud so noxious I can't help but fall to my knees.

My body seized by convulsions, my vision swimming with the illusion of glimmering orbs, I clutch hard at the ground and claw my way toward her. Stealing a moment to jerk the neck of my sweater up past my chin, until it covers my nose and my mouth, hoping it will filter the smoke long enough for me to defeat her.

When I face her again, I'm amazed to see a whole host of spirit animals are beginning to creep out of hiding.

The snow is melting.

The earth is warming.

Their forced hibernation has come to an end.

I count rabbits, skunks, squirrels, and sparrows among them. Yet still no one I recognize. No one with any obligation to help me.

I continue to squint through the smoke and haze, as Phyre

moves tantalizingly close, Dace's soul precariously balanced on her palm.

"Beautiful, isn't it?" Her fingers flex, soften, then flex again. Leaving no doubt that one solid squeeze will see that it's done. "It's so fragile. So delicate. So easily . . . *crushed*." She curls her fingers. Looks right at me. "So strange to hold the soul of the boy you love in the palm of your hand. I'm afraid this is it, Daire. He belongs to none of us now."

Her fingers clench.

Her eyes fill with tears.

And I use the moment to duck my head low and barrel straight toward her. Knocking her right off her feet, sending her soaring into the sky, her arms windmilling wildly. Until she slams hard into the ground, with me right on top, and the force of the jolt causes the soul to slip free, just as I'd hoped.

I push off her and watch its progression. Hoping with everything I have in me that the familiar presence I spotted in the distance is still on my side.

Catch it! Oh please, catch it!

Phyre leaps to her feet, tries to get past me, but it's too late.

Raven has already swooped down.

Already caught it in his opened beak.

And by the time he makes the handoff to Horse, I turn back to find Phyre has fled.

thirty-six

Dace

"How do you feel?" Daire hugs me tight at the waist, resting her chin on my shoulder in a way that causes her soft strands of hair to brush over my cheek. Our bodies swaying in tandem to Horse's easy gait.

"Good. Still good." I crick my neck just enough to take in her glittering green eyes, the rosy flush of her cheeks, captured by the absolute wonder of her.

"Like your old self?" She narrows her eyes. Gnaws hard on her lip. A move I recognize for what it is—an attempt to keep her joy contained—her hopes well in check.

I flatten my lips, and stare straight ahead. "No. Not yet," I say, preparing for the lie to come. "But someday. Someday soon. I'm sure of it." I nod to confirm it, but the truth is, I have no proof whatsoever to back up my words.

While I may have gotten my soul back, it still bears Cade's mark.

The day I took a soul jump into my twin, I came away changed.

There's a good chance I may never find my way back.

"Dace—can I see your eyes?" Her voice is both forceful and tentative. And I'm amazed yet again at her ability to do that. To ease my fears as though they never existed, convincing me to do the one thing I'd prefer to avoid.

With a heavy heart, I allow my gaze to meet hers, only to see her flinch in response.

"Oh." She drops her gaze to her lap, unsure what to make of it—make of me. As though she needs some time to process and think.

I heave a ragged breath, preparing myself to lose her again. But there's no way to prepare for something like that. I can't imagine my world without Daire.

"I thought maybe . . ." Her voice fades. There's no need to finish when the unspoken bits are easy to guess.

"Daire—" I pause, backing away from the lie I told earlier. It was a cowardly, self-serving act. If nothing else, I owe her the truth. "I'm afraid it won't be that easy. Now that I've stolen a piece of Cade, I have no idea how to get rid of it."

She absorbs my words with a serious face, a determined tilt of her chin, as she asks, "What can I do? How can I help?"

I squint. Not sure I heard right.

She wants to help? Does that mean she's not looking to leave?

"There must be something I can do," she says. "And, if not me, then maybe Paloma will know of something—or even Chepi, or Leftfoot, or Chay. Between the four of them, the elders are like a storehouse of remedies and magickal secrets."

I swallow hard. Feeling a little choked by her words. And more than a little ashamed for doubting her. Daire's a fighter. Loyal to a fault. She doesn't give up on anyone.

I reach behind me, cup a hand to the outside of her thigh. "This is not one for the Seeker," I say. "This is my mess to fix."

"But—you're still *you*, right?"

I gaze straight ahead, tracking the path Raven sets. "Yes," I say, voice barely audible. "I'm still me—though a slightly changed version of me. I'm no longer pure goodness and light. The darkness inside causes me to feel differently—see differently . . ." I squeeze her leg, needing her to understand the magnitude of my words. "But there's one thing that will never change."

She stiffens behind me, as though prepared for the worst.

"My love and devotion for you."

She exhales a soft breath, presses tightly against me, until I'm keenly aware of the swell of her breasts pushing hard at my back.

I close my eyes and release an involuntary groan. Wondering if she has any idea of the way her nearness affects me.

I've been weak for so long. Immersed in a bleak hellish world, haunted by regrets. But now, with my soul intact, with my life force thrumming within me, and the heat of Daire's body insistently pressing against me, it's all I can do to keep my desire contained.

I inch my fingers up the length of her thigh, cup a hand around her backside, and pull her even closer. Torn between reveling in the sensation of every curve and valley of her body conforming to mine, and trying to shield her from the depths of my need. Not entirely convinced I should initiate this when I'm not entirely me.

But when she slips a warm hand under my sweater and finds my flesh eager and willing—I forfeit the struggle. The world suddenly reduced to the only thing that really matters—the two of us being together.

"Daire—" My voice is hoarse, thick with craving. "Before we head back, what do you think about taking some time for ourselves? Take a little break from our problems? It's not like they're going anywhere."

"You mean the Enchanted Spring?"

Her lips smile into my neck. Her fingers snake under my waistband, mold warm to my flesh. Her touch so sure and insistent, I'm hers to command.

"I'm pretty sure Horse and Raven are way ahead of us."

With her free hand, she points straight ahead, and that's when I realize that all of this time, our spirit animals have been leading us to these magickal waters.

Horse and Raven wander away, as Daire and I shed our clothes quickly and wade into the spring. She smiles, her face bright and happy, then placing a hand on each of my shoulders she dunks me under the water until we're fully submerged. Only to emerge a few moments later, notably stronger, rested, and healed.

"Despite what happened last time we were here, I refuse to let Cade tarnish the magick we've shared here." Her voice is soft but determined, her astonishing green eyes flashing on mine. "I refuse to let him dictate our memories, or the way we perceive things."

I couldn't agree more. But the sight of her standing before me—bared, glistening, and glorious, with droplets of water clinging like jewels to her skin—has rendered me speechless.

"I just want this place to be ours once again."

She inches toward me, but like the starving man that I am, I get to her first. My fingers hungry for the feel of her flesh, my lips seeking hers. We kiss fully, deeply, our need for each other equally matched. And though I've yearned so long for this moment, it's not long before I begin to want more.

I want to taste her sweet skin.

Immerse myself in her flesh.

Still, I wait until I'm sure that she's ready. Until she whispers my name in a voice thick with need.

I lift her into my arms and out of the spring. Placing her upon a soft patch of grass, I steal a moment to admire the long, languid sight of her body, the sweep of her hair clinging damp to her shoulders, before I swoop down to join her.

"Dace," she whispers, her lips teasing my ear. "What if it wasn't a mistake? What if the darkness now living inside you is part of your fate?"

I pull away, peer deep into her eyes.

"If darkness defines the light—perhaps this will make you shine even brighter?"

I'm not sure if the words are meant to assure me or her, but her willingness to accept me, to seek the goodness in me just as I am, sends me over the top.

I curve my body over hers. Sink into her arms. Desperately seeking the sweet scent of her skin, the taste of her lips, the mysteries of her flesh.

And when she smiles and nods, inviting me in, I fall deeper into her than ever before.

thirty-seven

Daire

By the time we make it to Leftfoot's all of the elders are gathered around the kitchen table, as though they've been not so patiently waiting for us.

Everyone except Paloma, that is.

She's the only one missing.

Chepi's the first to react. At the sight of Dace, she bolts from her chair, and hurries toward him in a blur of whimpers and tears. She hugs him tightly, murmurs softly in their native tongue. Then draws away, cups her palms to the sides of his cheeks, and carefully studies his eyes.

"You are back." Her voice rings surprisingly steady and sure, defying her highly emotional state. "Yet a darkness remains."

Dace averts his gaze, extricating himself from her grip. His features softening in relief when Leftfoot pulls him away and says, "Come on, let's have a look at you." The old medicine man leads him into the spare room to check his vital signs, and Chepi's quick to follow, leaving me alone with Chay.

I claim the seat beside him and say, "Where is she?" My gaze skims over his broad nose, defined cheekbones, and hooded brown eyes, before coming to rest on the dark glossy ponytail that hangs just past his collar. "I assumed Paloma would be here, awaiting our return with the rest of you."

Chay hesitates. Making careful study of the intricate silver eagle-head ring he always wears with deep golden stones standing in for the eyes. "Paloma stayed back at the house," he finally says, the words as guarded as the expression masking his face.

"Why?" I lean toward him, alerted by the nagging twinge that pulls at my gut, along with his clouded gaze and grim lips. Chay's far too honorable to be a good liar. Deception is not a sport that comes easily to him. If he's not lying, at the very least, he's holding something back.

"She's not feeling well," he says, exhaling deeply as he squares his gaze on mine. "I urged her to rest. Promised her I'd hold vigil until you and Dace returned."

I splay my hands on the table and take a series of slow steady breaths in an attempt to center myself and quell my growing alarm. It's more than that. Something's wrong. I can tell. Chay is far more concerned than he lets on.

"Okay," I say. "Now that I've heard the story you've both agreed on, what's really going on with Paloma? C'mon, Chay. I need you to tell me the truth. I can handle it, whatever it is."

"It's nothing that can't be remedied," he says, but again, the words ring untrue. "Leftfoot has tended to her. And he will do so again as soon as he's finished with Dace. I'll head over there as well, and stay through the night in case she needs something." When that clearly doesn't quash my fears, he creases his brow and goes on to say, "Look, Daire, Paloma's been under a lot of stress, as you already know. Stress that began sixteen years ago with the death of your father. The stress of losing her only child, the stress of keeping the Santos legacy alive far longer than normal, along with the stress of keeping the Richters contained, especially with Cade coming into his own and branching off from Leandro's more modest goals in the way that he has—all of it's contributed to the way she's feeling now. But make no mistake, your arrival in Enchantment was the best thing to happen to her in a very long time. Your work as a Seeker has not only relieved the burden she bears, but you've also made her inordinately proud."

I sit quietly before him, taking a moment to weigh his words. No matter how guarded his message, I see right through him. He's trying to assuage my worst fears. Insisting that I'm not one bit responsible for Paloma's failing health. But I won't take the bait. Unfortunately, I know better.

"I was a reluctant Seeker." I frown, plagued by the bitter memory of my ill-fated attempt to run away. "And because of it, I put her through hell. Delayed the whole process. From the moment I finally got my act together, I've had the undeniable feeling we're in a race against time. Time that was lost because of me."

"You did nothing out of the ordinary," Chay says, covering my hand with his own. His palm is warm, welcome, but it fails to provide the comfort intended. "Your reaction was perfectly normal, understandable. Your father did the same thing."

I dismiss the words with a defiant shake of my head, refusing to be let off so easily. Learning from my failures requires me to face my failures. Not to hide behind a bunch of convenient excuses.

"Paloma didn't rebel against it. She embraced her destiny right from the start. I saw the whole thing. She gave me a lineage transmission. Shared her entire life's journey. It was amazing. Awe-inspiring. And I was humbled by the level of personal sacrifice she endured for the greater good of all—" My voice falters, needing a moment before I can continue. "Her life's contained so much hardship and loss, and I—" Before I can finish, Chay interrupts.

"All life comes with hardship, Daire. That's just the nature of things. Every difficulty, every struggle, serves as a signpost that leads us to the ultimate truth that none of us stands alone. There is no *us* versus *them*. There is only *we*. We are as connected to this earth as we are to each other. But, for most of us, the journey to enlightenment begins with despair. The moment we're brought to our knees, left with no choice but to admit that the old ways are no longer working, serves as a portal to a greater understanding. Paloma has always been aware of the perils of her position. She was well prepared by her mother, the Seeker before her. She's always understood that great privilege comes with great responsibility. She has never dwelled on her tragedies. Same way she doesn't gloat over her triumphs. She stays steady, humble, and present. With one eye fixed on the horizon ahead. And I'm sure I'm not remiss in saying she would wish the same thing of you." He gives my fingers a reassuring squeeze. The cool silver band of his spirit animal ring pressing into my skin. "She's stronger than you think. I'm sure she'll get through this in no time. She's just a little under the weather, that's all."

"Paloma doesn't get under the weather." I slip my hand from his, and rock my chair back on two legs. Allowing my gaze to wander, seek solace in the handwoven Navajo rugs hugging the dark wood floor, the short, sloping ceiling overhead, the deep niches carved into the walls filled with all manner of crosses, fetishes, hand-carved santos, and other powerful objects of worship that Dace always refers to as *the tools of the light worker trade*. "She's immune to things like cold and flu. She only falls ill when she's been impaired in some way. Which means there has to be a reason for this. Is her soul still intact? Cade didn't manage to steal it again, did he?" I return my focus to Chay, relieved to see he's quick to rebut it with a firm shake of his head. "Well, maybe it's Wolf then . . ." My voice fades as I try to make sense of the idea that just occurred to me.

Chay swivels in his chair, tracking my progress as I push away from the table and roam about the room. Stopping before the niche that holds the beautiful wolf fetish carved from a single, shiny, white stone.

"For the last week, up until today, the Lowerworld was in an icy, frozen state that forced all of the spirit animals into hibernation so they weren't available to guide us. So I'm thinking that maybe Paloma was adversely affected by Wolf's absence." I fold the stone in my palm, surprised by its heft and warmth, as Chay leans back in his chair and takes a moment to consider my words.

"Daire, while I can't know for sure if Wolf's lack of influence is to blame, what I can say is that the last week without you has taken its toll. In an attempt to hasten your return, Paloma entered into a deep state of fasting and prayer—as did Chepi and Leftfoot—while I was in charge of holding down the fort. I'm sure the fast left her a bit weakened. I'm also sure that now that you're back, she will start to mend. But remember, you only just returned. It's going to take some time for her to regain her strength." He nods as though he's convinced, but I can tell that he's not, and neither am I.

I'm about to press further, when I notice a new furrow etched at his brow that makes his eyes appear even deeper, more hooded. This talk isn't just to quiet my fears, it's to quell his as well. Paloma is his lover, his partner, his closest companion, and friend. The mere thought of losing her is a burden he's not ready to bear.

I return the wolf to its niche and cross the room to the sink where I pour Chay a glass of water and place it before him. "Change of subject," I say, eager to move on to less emotional ground.

He takes a grateful sip and says, "Shoot."

"What do you know about Oleander?"

"Oleander—as in the plant?"

I nod, watching as he adopts a thoughtful expression as I reclaim my seat. "Phyre made a weird reference to it. Going on about how it's her middle name. Given to her by her father on her sixteenth birthday. It seemed so strange. So completely out of context, yet she clearly wanted me to know. Is there something unusual about it? What are its properties? What makes it unique from other shrubs that you'd name your daughter after it, other than the fact that the name itself is kind of pretty?"

"Well, I'm a veterinarian, not a botanist," he says, fingertips tracing the table's rough wood grain. "But I think it's safe to say that it's a common, ornamental shrub that's considered to be extremely toxic. It'll kill a horse easily. A person too. What else did she say?" Chay sits up a little straighter, eyes glinting, jaw clenching, granting me his undivided attention.

"About the Oleander—nothing. Though I did watch her pull a bloom from her pocket and eat it. "

Chay leans toward me. "Describe it."

"You think it was an oleander?"

"Maybe."

"Well, as someone who never had a home, much less a garden, I can't say for sure. I'm not that great at identifying different species of plants, but it certainly could've been. Especially considering the way she made such a big deal about it. But honestly, there's not much to describe. It was small, pink, pretty. But when she lit the stem, it emitted this horrible cloud of noxious smoke. Come to think of it, she also had a torch of dried twigs that did the same thing."

"Were there any other effects?" Chay's posture grows stiff, his voice tense.

I think back. "While it didn't seem to affect her at all, for Dace and me, it was rough going. The smoke was acrid and heavy. And it wasn't long before I started to grow really dizzy, and my vision went all blurry and weird to the point where everything around me bore this sort of strange halo-effect. I figured it was the influence of the Lowerworld. But you think it might be the oleander?"

"And you watched her eat the flower?" Chay dodges my question for one of his own. Nervously working the eagle ring on and off his finger.

I lean forward, needing to know what he knows. "Chay, what are you thinking? Does all of this actually mean something?"

Without answering, he pushes away from the table and

peeks his head into the back room where Leftfoot is still examining Dace. "Chepi," he calls. "I need you to come out here and join us. I need you to tell us everything you know about poison women."

thirty-eight

Daire

"There hasn't been a poison woman for years," Chepi says. "So many years, most assume it's a myth. Why do you ask?" Her eyes dart suspiciously toward me. As though she suddenly suspects I might be one.

I locate her son and restore his soul, just like I promised, and she still doesn't trust me! What more do I have to do to gain her approval?

"Many cultures have stories of poison women," Leftfoot says. Having finished examining Dace, he comes in to join us as Dace follows behind. "In Eastern Indian culture, they're known as Vish Kanjas. Japanese myth features them as well, they're called Dokufu. As the myth usually goes, a poison woman is chosen from infancy when she begins receiving small but regular doses of the poison in order to build up a tolerance. Over time, her bodily fluids become so contaminated that making physical contact with her becomes extremely dangerous, if not fatal."

"But surely an oleander isn't capable of that—aren't they the landscaping plant of choice on the L.A. freeway system?"

"Oleander is highly toxic," Chepi says, sliding her arm around Dace and pulling him close. "One of the most poisonous of all the common garden plants. Ingesting the nectar from the flower or chewing the leaves can prove fatal."

"And when burned, it emits highly toxic fumes that can impair vision, cause dizziness, and worse," Leftfoot adds.

Dace and I exchange a look. Between our dizziness and impaired vision, coupled with Phyre's bizarre fascination with her saliva, the way her breath alternately inflamed and tempered the fire—it jells.

This has got to be it.

Phyre Oleander Youngblood is a poison woman.

"Her dad's that crazy snake-handling prophet," Dace says. "You remember, Suriel Youngblood. The one who used to live on the reservation that everyone sought to avoid? The one who handles the rattlers to prove how righteous he is? Claiming God would never allow him to get bit—and if by chance he did, it would only be to prove his powers to the disbelievers when he was instantly healed."

"The one who took his wife's maiden name?" Chepi makes a disapproving face.

"So, you think maybe he's been feeding her a mix of rattler venom and oleander sap since she was a baby, in place of the pureed bananas and carrots the rest of us were raised on?" I ask, my gaze darting between the elders, before settling back on Dace.

"It's possible," Leftfoot says. "But a lifetime of ingesting distilled oleander extract alone is enough to do considerable harm to anyone who became intimate with her. The snake venom would almost be overkill. Though I'm not sure it matters either way. Phyre is poisonous, of that I am sure."

I picture her waiting outside of Cade's house, purposely moistening her lips before moving in to kiss him—and I'm convinced Leftfoot's right. Or at least until I remember Phyre's intimate history with Dace, and the theory crumbles just as easily.

I turn to Dace, hating to do it, but it has to be asked. "Did anything weird happen to you after you two were together?" I ask, surprised to find that I am apparently the only one who was aware of their history.

Chepi balks, gaping incredulously at her son, as Dace drops his chin and studies the cracked tile floor.

While I'm sorry I've made them uncomfortable, now more than ever, I need to get to the bottom of this. Need to either prove or disprove this horrifying new theory that just popped into my head.

"Listen," I say. "I know this is awkward, but I think by this point, we should all be far beyond embarrassment. The fact is Dace was with Phyre, however briefly, and I need to know if—"

"No," Dace says, icy-blue eyes meeting mine. "I suffered no ill effects, other than a lingering case of regret."

I screw my lips to the side, trying to make sense of it. But then I remember something Phyre said.

"I wasn't given the name until I was sixteen. That's when my destiny was sealed."

Which is most likely the same year she became toxic.

The same year she moved back to Enchantment.

The same year her father ordered her to fulfill her destiny by killing either Dace or Cade Richter, thereby commencing the Last Days.

My eyes grow wide. I can't believe I didn't see it before.

"What day is it?" I cry, frantically searching for a clock. It's impossible to keep track of time in the Otherworlds, and I have no idea what day it is, much less how long Dace and I have been gone.

"December thirty-first," Chay says. "New Year's Eve."

I swallow hard, attempting to ease a throat gone suddenly dry. My voice so gruff I hardly recognize it as mine when I ask, "What time, specifically, down to the exact minute?" I look to the window, horrified to find the sky draped with night.

"Eleven fifteen. Why?" Chay leans toward me, starts to put a comforting hand over mine, but I'm already out of my chair.

Already grabbing Dace by the arm and pulling him along with me, as I race for the door.

"Phyre's going to kill Cade," I say, glancing back one last time. "And she's going to do it with a single fatal kiss at the stroke of midnight!"

serpent's kiss

thirty-nine

Daire

"What's the New Year's Eve tradition at the Rabbit Hole?" I grip the edge of my seat in an attempt to keep from vaulting into the roof, as Dace maneuvers his old white truck with the worn-out shocks over bumpy dirt roads. "Since every holiday seems to be celebrated there, I'm wondering if there's something different about the way they observe it. Something we can use."

"It's the usual routine." Dace pulls a hard right, his fingers gripping the wheel so tightly his knuckles go white in sharp contrast to his gorgeous brown skin. "Decorations, noisemakers, stupid hats, music, food, mayhem, chaos, drunkenness, and the countdown to midnight when everyone makes a mad grab for someone to kiss." He comes out of the turn and punches hard on the accelerator again. Sending the truck rearing and bucking onto another dirt road that's in even worse shape than the one just before.

"And Phyre will make a mad grab for Cade. It's the deadline her father gave her when he said, 'See that it's done by midnight . . . Any later is too late.' It's her last chance to prove herself worthy of her made-up destiny." I peer out the side-view mirror, watching the dust swirl in our wake.

"Then she better get in line." Dace glances my way. "Girls have always been drawn to my brother."

"It's the mind control. He's altered their perception." I make a frowny face, quick to dismiss it.

"And here I thought you were going to say it's because he shares my good looks." He lifts a brow, flashes a grin. And while I'm glad to see he hasn't lost his sense of humor, it takes a moment for me to lighten my mood and join in.

"You look nothing like Cade." I make a point to avoid his eyes when I say it, so I can pretend that it's true. "You're a zillion times hotter than he'll ever be."

Dace laughs—the sound deep and true—adding a welcome bit of levity to an otherwise somber mood.

But the effect is short-lived. Another moment passes, and once again, our problems intrude.

"Every year it's the same, but Lita was always there to fend them off, keep them away. This year, without her, it could be a problem."

"No one stands a chance against Phyre. If our theories are correct, she'll make sure she gets to him first. She's beyond determined," I say. "And it would be a mistake to underestimate her. She's smart, cunning, and desperate—it's a deadly mix. She's also on a major losing streak. Having failed at everything else, this is her last chance to make her dad proud." I frown at the clock on the dashboard. Less than forty minutes to spare. "Not a lot of time to get the job done." I pat my pocket for reassurance, grateful for the athame I stashed there.

"And we may have even less. Suriel is convinced the New Year serves as a herald for the Last Days. And while he's charged Phyre with the task of killing Cade, he's also lost faith in her ability to get the job done. He might not want to chance it. He might not even let it get to that point."

"I've no doubt she'll go through with it. You should've seen her face right before she fled the Lowerworld. By now, it's become a matter of principle. If nothing else, she's tired of being thwarted at everything she sets out to do. If we find Cade, we find her."

"Or Suriel." The look Dace shoots me is as ominous as his voice.

"Either way, it's over by midnight."

"And we'll be so busy stopping her, I won't be able to kiss you. Can our luck get any worse?" He stops at the far end of the alleyway, kills the engine, and swivels toward me with deep haunted eyes.

"It can always get worse. If we're unable to stop them—"

He leans toward me and presses a finger to my lips, snuffing the words before I can speak them. "We'll stop them," he says. "I'll make sure of it. Now that I have you back, I have no plans to lose you again." He hesitates for a moment, as though wanting to replace his finger with his lips, then abruptly draws away and jumps free of his truck as I do the same. "If Cade was a reasonable person, we could just warn him that Phyre's a poison woman and her sudden interest in him is all part of her dad's crazy, Apocalyptic vision, and get on with our night. But it's never that easy, is it?"

"That would only spike his suspicion and spur him straight into her arms. He'd never believe that I'm actually out to save his horrible, worthless, wretched excuse for a life. I can hardly believe it myself." I peer down the alleyway, seeing a small group of people gathered at the far end. "Why'd you park here—is this a legitimate space? And why so far away? The last thing we need is to get towed."

"Trust me, no one's getting towed. There are a few nights every year when the rules are suspended. This is one of them."

"Let me guess, the other is on the Day of the Dead."

"Except the New Year's party at the Rabbit Hole is like the Day of the Dead on steroids." Dace catches my incredulous look, and captures my hand in his. "I figured it was better to park out of sight and slip through the back. The bouncers may be off duty by now, but why take the chance of them alerting Cade that we're here? Better to slip in unannounced."

We make our way down the alleyway. Guided by shouts of revelry seeping from the building, and the dull glow of the single streetlamp casting an odd shadow that at first glance I mistake for an animal.

A rather large animal. Like a big coyote, a fox, or possibly even a wolf.

I stop in my tracks, blinking at the space. I could've sworn I saw it returning my look with bright flashing eyes.

"Did you see that?" I whisper, alternately staring and blinking at what is now clearly empty space looming before me.

Dace shakes his head. Studies me with concern.

"You didn't see anything?"

He lifts his shoulders in response. "You okay?" he asks, lacing his fingers with mine.

"Yeah. I'm fine." I rub a hand over my eyes. "Wouldn't be the first time I thought I saw something out here. Last time it was glowing people and crows."

"And this time?"

"A coyote, a wolf, a fox, a Labrador retriever?" I lean into his side and start walking again. "Hard to say for sure."

"Trick of the light," Dace says.

"Must be," I murmur, matching my steps to keep pace with his. With so much at stake, there's no time to delay.

He stops before the back door, about to push it open when he says, "The Rabbit Hole's New Year's Eve party is pretty much a free-for-all. Brace yourself for just about anything."

He's not kidding. From the moment we step inside, it's like crashing into a wall of noise that smells vaguely of popcorn, beer, and the sour promise of vomit. And that's just the first impression coming from the back entrance. I can't even imagine what I'll find once we're deep in the thick of it.

He leads me through the maze of the kitchen. Having spent the past year working here, he knows his way around much better than me. And when we burst through the double doors, it's exactly like he said—a vision of absolute chaos surrounds us.

The club is swarming with bodies. Their noisemakers, air horns, whistles, kazoos, hand clappers, tambourines, and maracas, clashing badly with the band on stage. A hail of balloons continuously fall from the ceiling, while fog and bubble machines pump from alternate corners. And after a quick glance around, it's clear the drinking age has been lifted and most everyone is taking advantage. Unaware that in Enchantment, there's no such thing as a free pass. The Richters prey on people's weak mental states—drunkenness being chief among them. They thrive on the uninhibited, reckless, indiscriminate behavior it provokes. All it takes is one drink too many and the next thing you know, you're Richter bait.

"Even more crowded than last year, if you can believe it." Dace shouts to be heard over the din. Scanning the crowd as he adds, "It's like every single citizen of Enchantment is here. Maybe even some out of towners as well."

"Why would anyone choose to come here to ring in the New Year? Talk about depressing." Dace and I exchange a quick look, as he grips my hand tighter and pulls me through the mad crush of bodies.

The two of us ducking clouds of confetti and clock-faced balloons that drop from the ceiling like giant chunks of hail. Passing walls plastered with black-and-silver banners proclaiming HAPPY NEW YEAR! as a hidden projector sends an image of a neon coyote swirling through the room.

It's madness.

So much sensory overload, I'm not even sure where to look. Which is probably why we've made it all the way to the center before I realize that along with all of the noisemakers and glow sticks, everyone present is wearing a mask.

"What is it with these people and masks?" I glance all around.

Unlike the masks worn on the Day of the Dead, none of these are skull masks, but they're elaborate all the same. Some covered in lace, some with intricate feather headdresses attached, some harlequin-style, some ribboned and jeweled, some in the shape of butterfly wings, some bearing giant, hooked noses, some with horns, some crafted from slim pieces of silk intended to obscure only the surrounding eye area and nothing more.

"As if it wasn't hard enough to find Phyre and Cade in this crush. This makes it nearly impossible!" I shout to be heard above the noise.

"Originally, the masks were meant to represent the darkness dwelling inside. Their removal during the midnight kiss symbolized an act of purification, a chance to begin anew. But the Richters aren't much for tradition. They're always driven by their own sordid agenda." Dace presses his lips to my ear, his touch brief but welcome. "Wearing a mask lessens the inhibitions. Which in turn, inspires the susceptible state the Richters manipulate."

"Everything they do has an angle." I continue to survey the room. The constant swirl of flash and noise, bubbles and fog, make it impossible to discern anyone in particular. "How are we supposed to find our friends, much less our enemies? Lita said they'd be in the usual spot, but I can't even tell where that is."

"We'll find them the same way we always do," Dace says. "Tune out the noise, and tune in to what your gut already knows." He swipes two masks off a table and hands one to me.

"Got anything a little more discreet?" I eyeball the plain black mask he slips over his face, preferring it to the bright turquoise one with the silver-and-gold feathers he gave me.

"It suits you," he says, carefully arranging it to cover my eyes, before adjusting the strap to lie smoothly against the back of my head. Then pressing his lips to my cheek, he says, "C'mon, Santos. Follow me."

Glittering bits of confetti rain down all around us as Dace pulls me through the slam of bodies. Leading me halfway across the room to where Xotichl is sitting with Lita as Auden stands off to the side with his mask pushed back on his forehead, caught in an intense conversation (or maybe that's just because of all the yelling required to be heard in the crowd) with a man I don't recognize.

"I just read your text for the hundredth time." Lita glances up from her phone. "And while I'm glad you're still alive and your soul is returned," she directs the words at Dace, "I think the real headline here is that Phyre Youngblood is a poison woman!" She shakes her head, and pulls her Marilyn Monroe mask back down to cover her face. "Did I tell you, or did I tell you?" She speaks through molded, puckered lips.

"Did you tell us what?" Xotichl says. Having forfeited wearing a mask for her own, natural, clean-scrubbed good looks, she scrunches her nose in amusement. "I don't recall you ever mentioning that particular theory."

"I said I didn't trust her." Lita pushes her mask up again, pointedly looking at each of us. "I said she was up to something. And this proves I was right!"

Xotichl shrugs, not entirely convinced, while Dace jabs a thumb toward Auden and says, "Who's he talking to?"

"You mean the guy with the ponytail and the double hoops in his ears?"

It takes a second for us to catch it, but when we finally do, Dace and I lean toward her and say, "Xotichl—can you see him?"

She takes a deep breath and nods ever so slightly. But before I can react, she's quick to add, "I can see him in the same way I did in the Lowerworld. The outline of his shape, the color of his energy. Stuff like that. Figured those things swinging from his neck and ears was either a ponytail and hoop earrings, or he's just another Rabbit Hole demon."

"So the magick did stick." I study her closely. I didn't think it was possible. Then again, if there's one thing I know for sure, it's that there's way more to the world that I've yet to discover.

"I didn't say anything earlier because I wasn't sure if it would last, and I didn't want to get anyone's hopes up," she says. "But now, I'm thinking maybe after this whole mess is settled, we can go down there again and see if it improves."

"Count on it." I raise a grin. Grateful for one good thing in a big, fat pile of awful.

"Anyway, ponytail man is from a record label. Auden met with him earlier. He's interested in signing Epitaph. Isn't that great?"

Xotichl is brimming with excitement, so I do my best to match it. But part of me can't help but question why anyone would come to Enchantment on New Year's Eve to scout bands. It seems strange. Doesn't really make sense. But Xotichl is so adept at reading energy, I'm sure if there was anything strange about it, she would have caught on immediately.

"Any sign of Phyre or Cade?"

"They're both here. Suriel too," Xotichl says.

"They got here just before me. I was about twenty people behind them in the line to get in," Lita says. "So that's when I decided to go through the back."

"Did they see you?" I ask, an idea forming in my head.

"They saw me and snubbed me. Not like I care."

"What kind of mask is Phyre wearing?"

"She's wearing a cat mask. Not a full face mask, just a half mask. Oh, and she's wearing a tight, pink T-shirt that says: KISS ME—IT'S MIDNIGHT SOMEWHERE!" She rolls her eyes. "Crickett and Jacy are wearing them too. I swear, they're such lepers."

"I think you mean lemmings." Xotichl laughs.

But Lita just shrugs. "All I know is it's creepy as hell once you realize what she really intends to do with that kiss."

"Did she get any takers?" Dace asks.

"The bouncer tried to take her up on it, but she just laughed and said, 'Don't believe everything you read.'"

"Well, at least she's not planning a massacre." Xotichl makes a face, continues to survey the room.

"Yeah, we've got enough of a boy shortage in this town." Lita groans. "Anyway, last I saw, Jacy and Crickett were over there." She motions toward the far wall that from here looks like a haze of fog, bubbles, balloons, and confetti. "But Phyre moved on."

"I've been trying to get a read on her," Xotichl says, "but what with all the noise and chaos—it's taking a little longer than usual to get my abilities up to their usual speed."

"When's Epitaph going on?" Dace asks.

"Soon," Xotichl says, giving a quick glance to where Auden is standing.

"So they'll be playing at midnight?"

She nods.

"Who does the countdown to midnight?" I ask. "The band?"

"Depends," Dace says. "Sometimes Leandro chooses to handle it. If for no other reason than it allows for one more opportunity for him to remind everyone who to show fealty toward. But sometimes, he blows it off and lets the band handle it. Depends on his mood."

"Well, we have to find Cade and Phyre long before that. I can't take the chance that she'll wait for the countdown to begin."

"I know where you could start," Lita says, instantly claiming our attention. "Every year the Richters throw their own private party within the party. Cade took me the last couple years."

"Where?" I lean toward her.

"Well, that's the thing, I don't know."

"You were there and you don't know?" Xotichl frowns.

"They make you go through this weird initiation involving cigarettes and blindfolds. Looking back, I can't even believe I did it. But, at the time, it seemed so covert and exciting . . . Anyway, it's supposed to be some big honor to be invited. Or at least that's how they sell it. And believe me, it works. No one ever declines."

Cigarettes and blindfolds—Dace and I exchange a knowing look.

"Did you walk down a long tunnel that leads to a really bizarre luxury cave?" I ask, knowing the answer long before Lita nods to confirm it.

"You've been there?" She glances between us, sending a tumble of curls to fall over her cheeks.

"Once or twice." I look at Dace. "And it looks like we're going again. But if you happen to see them out here, be sure to text me immediately."

"That's it?" Lita shakes her head, purses her lips to match the ones on her mask. "That's my job? Texting? Is that all you think I'm capable of?"

"You already did your job. I think you may have located them." Turning to Xotichl, I say, "Keep scanning the room. If the energy in any way starts to feel strange—stranger than it already does—then do whatever it takes to get the hell out. Don't worry about Dace and me—just grab Auden, and Lita, and whoever else is nearby, and run like the wind. Okay?"

"Got it." She nods. Her voice betraying her growing anxiety when she says, "You guys don't think there's anything to Suriel's crazy doomsday talk, do you?"

Lita's eyes widen as she looks between Dace and me.

But I'm quick to dismiss it. "On a mystical level, no. But I also wouldn't put it past him to do something completely insane in order to live out some semblance of his messed-up fantasy. So whatever you do, be safe."

I look at my friends, ensuring they're on board, before I say, "Oh, and one more thing . . ." I snatch Lita's mask from her head and replace it with mine.

"What are you doing?" She casts a mournful look at her Marilyn mask, clearly not comfortable seeing it clutched in my hands.

"Pretending to be you. Phyre knows Cade's still into you, so wearing your mask might draw her to me. Cade too, for that matter. I figure it's worth a shot."

Lita places a defiant hand on her hip, as offended as she is unconvinced. "Okay . . . not to be rude, but I'm not sure you have what it takes to pull it off. It's not all that easy to be me. There's way more to it than an obsession with Marilyn. It's not nearly as effortless as it seems."

"I've no doubt." From behind the mask I sneak a half-grin and start to turn away. "But you know what they say—people tend to believe what they see."

forty

Dace

"You sure about the mask?" I study Daire with concern. Watching as she fiddles with the strap, adjusting it to better cover her face. "It puts you at risk. Makes you a target for both Phyre *and* Cade."

"Believe me," she says. With the mask firmly in place, she walks quickly beside me. "As both the Seeker and your girlfriend, I'm more of a target without it. Besides, if what you say is true, better me in danger than Lita. At least I have the skills to defend myself with. Still, if it comes down to it, and we somehow end up separated, I'll deal with Phyre and you deal with Cade. He wants to kill me. She wants to kill you. Let's not give either one of them the opportunity. And whatever you do, steer clear of Suriel as well."

"I can handle Suriel," I say, needing her to believe it. But the firm shake of her head tells me she's far from convinced.

"Now that you have your soul back, he'll go after you just as easily as he'll go after Cade. He doesn't care which one of you goes down—just as long as the other one follows."

I could continue to push it, try to sway her to my point of view, but when we reach Leandro's office and the door is ajar, allowing muted voices to drift from inside, I motion for her to keep watch while I venture a look.

Last time I was here, I made a soul jump into Cade and came away with a stolen piece of his darkness. A souvenir that, once lifted, I can't seem to shake. And after talking with Leftfoot tonight, I'm not sure I should try.

There are positive and negative aspects to everything, he said, the moment Chepi left us alone in the room. *The breeze becomes a tornado—the ocean's swell a tsunami—a campfire an inferno—a snowflake a blizzard—and man is no different. Perhaps this isn't a curse like you think. Perhaps you've merely become fully human for the very first time.*

I'd never thought of it that way. Never thought to view it as anything more than a burdensome mistake.

But now that he's presented it to me in that way, well, I can't help but wonder if he's right.

Maybe the darkness I willingly ingested isn't some colossal mistake.

Maybe it just makes me normal.

All I know for sure is that now that it's in me, I have to find a way to use it. If there was ever a time to call upon the darkness within, it's tonight.

I raise a flattened palm to the door and push hard. Ready to face Leandro on my terms, my way, only to find myself squinting at a desk left in chaos and an empty leather chair. The voices I heard are coming from the large flat-screen TV.

After a quick search of the room, looking for anything that might prove to be useful, and a glimpse of the security monitors that only proves how impossible it is to single out anyone in particular, I exit the room, grab hold of Daire's hand, and race for the vortex.

Cigarettes at the ready, we're primed to face the usual beast brigade, only to find the veil wide open and wavering before us, not a single demon to guard it.

No demons.

No beasts.

No Coyote.

No Richters.

Almost like it's daring me to breach it.

Like it's some sort of trap.

Daire and I exchange a brief look, and I know she's thinking the same thing as me.

Is this a challenge—a trick—or are they just that overconfident we wouldn't dare try to crash?

Figuring we'll find out either way, we push through the wall that's not really a wall, and creep through the tunnel with a step that, while purposely light, still manages to amplify in a series of dull, heavy thuds that are sure to alert them.

It's not by coincidence that the Richters crafted the entrance of tin.

Nothing they do is an accident.

Nothing except me, that is.

According to Cade, I'm the biggest, most regretful mistake Leandro's ever made.

And if I do nothing else with my life, I vow to prove him right.

He has no idea just how much he'll come to regret the violence he wrought on my mother the day he conjured me.

Has no idea of my vow to make sure he pays.

My hands automatically curl into fists. The thought alone enough to spark the bit of stolen darkness within me.

It begins with a glimmer that soon morphs into a deeply rooted thrum that continues to grow and expand until my entire body is alive with a buzzing intensity that's hard to contain.

I fight to steady my breath—settle my limbs. With Daire right beside me, I can't afford to let on.

Still, this must be what Cade feels when he transforms into the demon version of himself.

Uncaged.

Liberated.

Released of all moral obligations—exceeding all physical limits.

"You okay?" Daire asks, her voice no more than a whisper, but still it seems to echo off the walls, and reverberate in my head.

I inhale a deep breath, steal a hasty glance at my body. "Yeah. Fine," I mumble, surprised to find I'm still me. Black sweater. Dark jeans. No talons—no tail—no scaly feet—and yet, there's no denying the presence of the creature now awakened within me.

Daire casts a concerned look my way, but continues toward the mouth of the den, where the two of us stand in the entrance, observing a party in full swing. Everyone oblivious to our presence.

Everyone except Coyote, that is.

With a snarling snout and red glowing eyes, he springs into the air and lunges straight for my throat. His irrepressible blood-lust fueled by the memory of the prior feasts he's made of my flesh.

Somewhere nearby a girl screams.

Another one squeals.

As the growling beast roars toward me with the sole intent to kill.

Instinctively, Daire leaps between us—tries to intervene. Spurred by the knowledge that as Cade's spirit animal, the wounds Coyote inflicts on me bear no effect on my twin.

But the darkness inside me is strumming.

Thrumming.

Leaving me with unknowable strength, and lightning-fast reflexes.

Long before Daire can inject herself into the fight—long before Coyote can sink his fangs into my flesh—I catch him in midflight and shove my way through the crowd. Shouting, "Where's Cade?" as the snarling Coyote hangs from my fist.

The drunken throng parts before me, leaving me a clear view of Leandro lounging in an oversized chair with two scantily clad women perched one on each leg.

He tilts his head back, appraises me from over the bridge of his nose. Unceremoniously unloading the women so carelessly they fall to their knees.

"Cade's not here," he says, switching his gaze from me, to Coyote, to Daire just beside me. Settling on my creepy cousin Gabe sitting on the couch just opposite, sandwiched between two attentive blondes, each massaging a shoulder, and another standing behind him, softly kneading his neck. His fiancée Marliz nowhere in sight.

With a pointed look from Leandro, Gabe unloads the women in a similar fashion. Sending them away without a second glance, he leaps from his seat as though he's about to evict me, when Leandro orders him to stand down.

"Where is he?" I ask. "Where's Cade?"

Leandro settles deeper into the cushions, folds his hands behind his head, and looks between the two of us as though deeply intrigued by the scene unfolding before him.

"Where is he?" Daire scowls. "Taking the night off along with all the other demons?" She widens her stance, fists her hands by her sides. Wanting him to know that while she may be deceptively slim of build, while she may be a girl, she is not one to be messed with.

Coyote continues to whimper and thrash, but my grip is strong, it's a minor irritation at best. "I don't have all night," I say. "Tell me where Cade is, and Coyote *might* live."

At that, Gabe cracks a slow, feral smile that never comes anywhere close to reaching his eyes. "You're funny." His gaze rakes a steady path from my head to my feet. Nodding toward Leandro, he adds, "I had no idea he was so funny."

"There's a lot you don't know about me." I clench my fist tighter, squeezing Coyote so hard, his tongue flops uselessly out the side of his snout as his eyes begin to bulge from their sockets.

"I'm beginning to believe it," Leandro says, studying me with renewed interest. "You sure you want to kill him?" He motions toward Coyote as though he has no real stake in the outcome either way.

He's bluffing. I've no doubt. He must be aware of the connection between Coyote and Cade.

I glance at the beast. Reminded of his savage attacks. How he dumped me in the most hellish dimension imaginable, and how he seemed to relish the task.

While the urge to see the light in his eyes permanently dimmed is certainly strong, in the end, common sense wins.

My goal is to keep Cade alive. Or at least it's my goal for tonight. Which means I can't risk killing Coyote until I'm sure it won't bear me any ill effect.

"Not today." I drop the beast to my feet, grinning with pleasure as I watch him slink and cower away.

"A wise decision." Leandro steeples his hands at his chest as he continues to appraise me. "So, it seems another one has risen from the dead."

He shifts his focus to Daire, staring at her with an intensity that makes me regret letting go of Coyote. If nothing else, I could've used him as leverage. But now, if he tries anything, I'll have to rely on my wits, my strength, and the beast now awakened within me.

"First your girlfriend, the Seeker, and now you. And yet, it seems you've come back new and improved. How'd you manage it, anyway? I truly am curious." He folds his hands around his knee, as though settling in for a really good yarn.

"Guess your prodigal son failed. *Again*," Daire says, glaring at him with a hate-filled gaze.

"And it seems I've underestimated his twin." Leandro uncrosses his legs, slides to the edge of his seat. "Believe me, it's a mistake I won't make again." He shifts his gaze to his flashy gold watch, rubbing his palms together as he says, "Year's almost over." He looks right at me. "Still, it's never too late to make a new start.

How 'bout I give you your old job back? I'll even throw in a pay raise. What do you say?"

If I didn't know what I know, if I was still blissfully uninformed of how I came into this world, the offer would be undeniably tempting. I'm desperately in need of a large cash infusion. Rent on my shithole apartment is about to come due, and I have no idea how I'll cover it. Still, there's no going back. No way to un-know what I know.

"What's that they say about friends and enemies and keeping them close?" I hold his gaze for a moment, then peer past his shoulder, trying to see into the rooms just beyond, wondering if Cade might be hiding in one.

"You calling us enemies?" Leandro looks thoughtful, if not vaguely offended.

"We're certainly not friends." I lift my shoulders, take a quick glance at Daire who's still glaring between Leandro and Gabe.

"How about family?" Gabe says, his burst of laughter cut short with a sharp look from Leandro.

"I'm a Whitefeather, not a Richter," I say.

"You're half Richter." Leandro's eyes grow dark as a deep crease forms over his brow. "I brought you into this world. Never forget that."

"I don't think you have to worry about that. The truth of my existence is not something I'm apt to forget." My tone holds the unmistakable promise of the threat I plan to make good on. "Besides, the half you're talking about—it's not the half that counts." I narrow my lids until my gaze becomes as hooded as his.

"Don't be so sure." Leandro leans back again, seemingly satisfied with the exchange, which irks me to no end. Making him happy was never my intention. Destroying him is.

"I'm the mistake you will live to regret." I shoot him a challenging gaze, hoping he'll take the bait.

Unable to put a name to the vague flicker of emotion that crosses his face when he says, "Don't be so sure of that either." He surveys me a long moment, then switches his focus to Daire. "He's not back there."

Daire ignores him, moves to slip past him.

"I already told you, he's not here." His voice betrays his growing annoyance with her.

"Yeah, well, you're not exactly a fountain of truth," Daire says. "So I figured I'd see for myself."

"And you weren't exactly on the guest list," Leandro snaps. "And it's not our policy to tolerate crashers."

His words hint at an unspoken threat, and I insert myself between them, poised to intervene. *Just give me a reason.*

"But, in this case . . ." Leandro's lips widen into a smile, though it starts and stops there. "I'll make an exception." His gaze settles on me. "I'd hate to get Dace any more worked up than he already is. I'm not sure any of us are ready to see his inner beast."

His eyes flash on mine and all I can think is, *he knows!*

He knows what I've done.

He can sense it inside me.

And the worst part is, he likes what he sees.

I glance at Daire, nod for her to proceed. Just about to join her, when I say, "Cade and Coyote travel as a pack. You can't tell me he's not here."

"Not tonight, bro." Gabe snorts, the sound loud, crude, and rude, just like he is. "Dude's got a date."

I can feel Leandro studying me, and though I do my best to hide my alarm, I'm not sure it worked.

Especially when I see the way his eyes glint when he says, "Coyote tends to scare the girls away. So Cade decided to move his private party elsewhere."

I take a moment to absorb the words, searching for even the slightest speck of truth. "And yet these girls aren't scared?" I motion to the surrounding crowd that's just now starting to venture back into the room.

"This is no ordinary girl." Leandro shrugs, studies me through slitted lids. "She hasn't been, how should I say—?" He looks to Gabe to supply the word for him, as I peer past his shoulder to see Daire sneaking into and out of the back room with empty hands and shaking head.

"Indoctrinated." Gabe leans forward, takes a sip of his drink.

"Indoctrinated." Leandro bobs his head as though he's still not quite satisfied. But then deciding to go with it, he says, "Anyway, you should know all about that. If I'm not mistaken, and believe me, I never am, the two of you were once an item."

Daire looks at me with a wide, stricken gaze. And it's only a second later when she's spinning on her heel, racing from the room, as I linger long enough to shout, "Where'd they go? Tell me— now!"

Leandro meets my demand with an empty grin, as Gabe laughs into his drink.

Without another word, I'm chasing after Daire, with Leandro's voice calling out from behind me, "You can't escape me, son! Like it or not, you wouldn't be here if it weren't for me. I made you. I'm in you. Anyone can see it. Even with the mask, it's right there in your eyes."

forty-one

Daire

When Jacy and Crickett turn the corner before me and push into the bathroom, I tell Dace I'll be right back, and push in behind them. Thinking that as Phyre's new BFFs, there's a pretty good chance they might be able to tell me where to find them.

They settle before the mirror. Removing their masks, they place them on the long metal shelf and tend to their hair. Jacy adjusts the slant of her side-swept bangs, while Crickett fluffs at her ends, and I stand just behind them, trying not to choke on the perfumed puffs of alcohol fumes wafting off them.

"Where's Phyre?" I ask, sparing no time for small talk.

They continue their primping, allowing a few beats to pass before I can truly confirm they are bent on ignoring me.

"Just tell me where to find her, and I won't bother you again," I bargain, only to have them pretend not to hear.

If I wasn't so pressed for time, I'd probably be impressed with their level of deep concentration and commitment. But, as it stands, I'm a little under the gun. And while I know I shouldn't do it, while Paloma warned me early on about the dangers of using my magick in immature ways, I can't think of any other way to get through to them.

So the second the lip gloss wands emerge from their respective purses—perfectly timed, as though they rehearsed it (which is amazing in and of itself considering their current state of drunkenness)—I steel my focus, raise my hand, and drag both those wands clear along the sides of their cheeks. Painting wide stripes of berry and pink that drag from lip to ear, before flinging them to the opposite side of the room where they crash against the wall and land on the filthy tiled floor.

"You ready to acknowledge me and tell me where Phyre went with Cade?" I allow two full seconds for them to consider. "'Cause if not, the purses go next. And you'll quickly follow."

They look at each other in silent communion, and Jacy is the first to fold. "She's taken *your* place," she says, scowling as she overenunciates the third word.

My place?

I glance in the mirror, surprised to see what they see. I'd almost forgotten I'm wearing Lita's Marilyn mask. And they're so far gone, they've mistaken me for her.

"She's hooking up with Cade—not like it's any of your business. I mean, excuse me, but—aren't you the one who dumped him?" Jacy places her hand on her hip, teeters on her heels, and uses that same hand to right herself again.

"Exactly where is she meeting him?" I switch my focus between them, voicing it more like a demand than a question.

They glance at each other, silently weighing whether or not they should tell me. So I give them a little nudge and lift Crickett's purse right off the sink's edge and into my hand. Planning to hold it hostage until someone responds.

"Outside," she says, warily eyeing her faux designer handbag now in my possession.

"Where outside?" I dangle the bag before her.

"Outside by the chain-link fence. Supposed to be some kind of sacred, romantic space or something. Look—whatever. Just—can I have my freaking purse back?"

I'm about to hand it over, when I notice the shiny blue tourma-line pendant she wears at her neck. "Where'd you get that?" I ask, having to force my gaze away in order to return my focus to them.

Cricket shakes her head and rolls her eyes. "Sheesh, were you always this annoying?" She looks to Jacy for the answer.

"Where'd you get it?" I lift her purse higher, swing it from its short vinyl strap.

"The swag bag. Everyone got one at the door. Okay? Happy now?" Crickett heaves a dramatic sigh, and swipes a hand forward, snatching her purse from my grip.

"No," I say, that doesn't make me happy at all. "But it helps." I race out the door, eager to tell Dace what I learned—only to find Dace isn't there.

I push through the mob of inebriated New Year's revelers, searching for Dace among them, but he's nowhere in sight. And now that I know what I know, there's no time to search for him. All I can do is hope he's okay as I make for Phyre and Cade.

I plow through the exit, racing for the chain-link fence with the small gold lock clinging to it. Phyre must've been watching us the night I put it there. There's no other way she could've known it held any significant meaning.

And sure enough, the moment it springs into view, I find her right where I expected.

Her back pressed against the fence, her cat mask discarded at her feet, as Cade looms before her.

She hooks an arm around his neck and pulls him in close, an-gling his face toward hers, about to make contact, when I rush up behind them, yank hard on Cade's coat, and jerk him right off her.

"What're you—crazy?" she shouts, her expression ranging from startled to fury, the moment she sees that it's me. Appealing to Cade when she says, "Do something! Stop her—make her go away!"

But Cade just stands there and grins. "Never figured you for the jealous type, Santos." He dips his head, swipes a hand through his hair. "But I'm afraid I have a bit of bad news. Thing is, I'm just not that into you." He blows his cheeks out, pausing long enough for the words to sink in—the better to devastate me. "Yes, I know it's you, Seeker. Nice try with the switching of the masks. While you might be able to fool dumb and dumber in there." He hooks a thumb toward the club—a thinly veiled reference to Jacy and Crickett that doesn't make sense.

How could he possibly know they directed me here?

Though I barely have time to ponder, before he goes on to say, "Your little ruse is far too sophomoric to fool someone like me. You see, I can smell your Raven scent a mile away. And I have to tell you, Seeker, this game you insist on playing is getting more than a little tiresome. That's the second time you've interrupted Phyre and me, and it's really beginning to grate. If you want to sit back and watch, I got no problem with that. Hell, you might even learn a few things. But if you interfere one more time—you die. And this time for good. Understood?"

With an annoyed shake of his head, he turns back to Phyre who's waiting for him with glassy eyes and glistening lips.

He centers himself before her, and she hooks a leg around his, pulling him in, as he angles in for the kiss. And despite his warning, I yank on his coat once again, shouting, "You kiss her—*you* die!"

Phyre secures a tight grip on his collar, her fingers digging into the cloth, urging him closer. But Cade places a hand on her chest, holding her at bay as he glances over his shoulder.

"Her kiss is lethal. She's a poison woman. Trust me, you do *not* want to do this. I'm sure there are plenty of other girls you could make out with." The words come out in a rush.

"Hundreds," he says, eyes flashing, tongue working the side of his cheek. "Thousands."

I roll my eyes. "Whatever. Just know, it you insist on kissing this one, it'll prove to be your last."

His face creases with rage, as he hisses a stream of curses under his breath. Turning to Phyre, he shoves a hand hard against her chest and pushes her into the chain-link fence.

I heave a little sigh of relief. Ready to turn my focus to locating Dace, when Cade looks over his shoulder again and shoots me a wide feral grin.

"Just how long did it take you to figure it out?" His fingers inch toward Phyre's throat, squeezing so hard most of her air is cut off. "'Cause I've known since the first day she got back in town. I could smell her oleander breath a mile away." He switches his focus between the two of us, and I struggle to stifle my growing alarm.

He knew all along!

This whole thing's a setup!

I think about the athame in my pocket, longing to use it—but what good would it do? Hurting Cade means hurting Dace—it's a truth I can't afford to lose sight of.

"It's like I've told you before, Seeker—Coyote has formidable senses. It's to your great disadvantage that you always seem to forget that. And as you're about to see, underestimating me will prove to be deadly. I've been planning this ever since that unfortunate incident when you set me on fire." He clicks his tongue against the roof of his mouth, emitting an ominous, ticking-clock sound. But whether it's meant to scold me or scare me, I can't say for sure. "This will prove to be a big night for me, and—spoiler alert!—it will go just like this: I kill you—Suriel kills Dace—and no one kills me." He punctuates the news with a wink and a grin. "In case you've forgotten, all I have to do is shift so that my brother's demise doesn't affect me."

Despite all that followed, I'm still stuck on the part about Suriel killing Dace.

I glance behind me, glance all around, but we're the only ones here.

Surely Dace will steer clear of Suriel—like I warned him to do?

Cade's calculating, beautiful, monstrous face looms before me—an exact replica of Dace's, and yet so entirely different. "Nothing happens in Enchantment without my knowing. I'm always dismayed at what a slow learner you are. You should know that by now. I control this town and the people within it. And as it turns out, Seeker, that includes you." He clenches and unclenches his fist, grinning with great amusement as Phyre gasps and sputters for each shallow breath. Finally tiring of the game, he releases his hold and, bored, watches without interest as she sinks to the ground in a spasm of coughing, before turning his attention to me. "I'm tired of you messing in my business. I'm tired of you skulking around my club and my town." He takes a step toward me, then another, until we're nearly touching. "I'm tired of *you*, Seeker. And you know what happens when I tire of something?"

"You donate it to charity?" I quip, seeing him standing before me with his arms raised to his sides, his eyes red and blazing, all too aware of what happens next. Massive growth, followed by clawed feet, scaly skin, and two-headed snakes shooting from the place where his tongue ought to be.

I take it as my cue to leave.

I've no interest in fighting him. While I don't doubt for a second his intention to kill me, I also know he'll do whatever he can to delay the deed. Keep the fight going, drag it out much longer than necessary, if only to allow Suriel enough time to kill Dace without my interfering.

Not on my watch.

With only a breath spanning between us, I slip off my mask and toss it at him. An act that's undeniably lame, but it does buy a few seconds' delay which allows me to spin on my heel and run like the wind.

Racing across the snow-covered field, following the frenzied tracks Phyre left in her wake.

forty-two

Daire

When I reach the mouth of the alleyway, Phyre's tracks vanish into a wasteland of crumbly asphalt and well-trampled snow. Leaving me with no way to discern which way she went.

I curl my fingers around the soft buckskin pouch that hangs from my neck. Summoning the wisdom and strength of the elements, my ancestors, and the animal spirits that guide us, when I'm alerted to the crash of breaking glass—the screech of raised voices. One in particular rising above all the rest.

"The blasphemous will not be tolerated! Repent now, before it's too late!"

Suriel.

I bolt down the alleyway to where a disorderly crowd is beginning to form. Edging up alongside a trio of drunks, I stoop my shoulders and duck my head low. Careful to stay sheltered among them, until I can get a sense of what's going on.

"Those who follow false prophets, do so at your own peril!"

I slink a bit closer, lifting my chin just enough to make out Suriel dressed in his usual stark black suit, scuffed shoes, and white shirt, preaching from his place behind the pulpit. A makeshift plywood stage and podium to match, bearing all manner of strange,

Apocalyptic images crudely painted on its front and sides. Snakes with sharp fangs and hungry eyes, horned beasts with spiked tails, angels with drooping halos and broken wings, crying copious rivers of blood while a sea of flames licks at their feet.

My gaze roams the stage, expecting to find Phyre right alongside him, and having to stifle a gasp of surprise when I find Dace in her place. Bound to a chair placed at center stage, he's surrounded by a number of tall cathedral candles with smoky, hissing wicks.

"It's not too late—there is still time to be saved!" Suriel steeples his hands to his chest as one of his rattlers slithers around his shoulders and neck.

But despite the deliberately dramatic tableau and the ominous tone of his well-rehearsed speech, the crowd's more interested in drinking and heckling than taking his message to heart.

Someone laughs.

Another yells something foul.

While someone else flings an empty beer bottle at the side of Suriel's head.

But Suriel doesn't so much as flinch.

He's a man of conviction. Truly believing his own undeniable righteousness will save him from any abuse a sinful mob can hurl.

In that particular case, it does. Well, either that or a little thing called gravity combined with a really poor aim. The bottle veers wildly, landing several yards away from Suriel's stage.

I return my focus to Dace, trying to get a read on why he'd choose to be up there.

Surely he chose to be up there?

He's so much bigger and stronger than Suriel. There's no possible way Suriel forced him.

Even so, what the heck is Dace thinking?

With unwavering concentration, Dace focuses hard on the writhing, hissing snake, oblivious to Suriel standing beside him.

"Don't be fooled by outside appearances!" Suriel's voice booms and pitches, his limbs shake with fury. Pointing an accusing finger at Dace, he urges the mob to move forward, get a better look.

The crowd quickly obeys, surging toward the stage while I remain firmly in place. Reluctant to make myself known until I have a better idea of what Dace has planned.

"Demons rarely appear in true form. They come in all manner of disguises, and one must remain vigilant at all times. Come now, boy." Suriel retrieves a dagger from the top of his podium that reminds me of the one his daughter used when she tried to annihilate Dace's soul. Thumping it hard against Dace's shoulder, he prods at him roughly and shouts, "Show yourself to the crowd. Let these sinners see the true face of a demon!"

To my dismay, Dace is quick to submit. Rendering the drunks temporarily sobered as they watch Dace smile and wave.

"That's not a demon, that's Dace Whitefeather!" someone shouts, causing the crowd to roar, as another beer bottle is flung toward Suriel's head, this one narrowly missing.

"This is a demon disguised as a human!" Suriel shouts. "And I'm here to prove it!"

The crowd, hungry for a spectacle worth watching, begins chanting, *"Prove it—prove it—prove it!"* As I stand shadowed among them, my fingers instinctively squeezing the pouch at my neck, desperate for answers.

What the heck is Dace doing? What is he thinking? And why is he staring at the snake when he should be watching Suriel?

"A righteous man, a truly righteous man of the Word, is always protected. I myself am living proof. Thirty years of handling the most venomous snakes in the world, and I've never been bit. But you, boy . . . I'm afraid you won't be so lucky." Suriel turns to Dace, places a hand on each of his shoulders, and gazes intently into his eyes. "Well, look at that!" Suriel lifts his chin, stares down the bridge of his nose. "Seems you got your soul back." He flicks his tongue twice around his lips. Wipes his palms down the front of his cheap, poly-blend suit. "Don't know how you managed it, but as far as I'm concerned, the pot just got sweeter!"

"Demons don't have souls!" someone yells. "You're a false prophet! You're a—"

Before he can finish, Suriel shouts, "Demons are tricksters—abominations! And demons with souls are the most dangerous of all because they're free to walk among us in human form!" Satisfied by their stunned silence, he returns to Dace and says, "Boy, I've just accused you of being a demon. Would you agree that my assessment is true?"

Dace shrugs. His vision not once veering from the snake, he says, "Guess we'll find out."

It's a crowd-pleaser. Prompting the mob to break into loud, roaring laughter, whooping and cheering and egging him on. A few even run inside the club to tell their friends to come outside and watch.

"Don't be swayed by what you see and hear before you!" Suriel cries, desperate to regain control of the mob. "A demon, a true beast, would never admit to his true identity. There's only one way to separate the righteous from the sinful . . ." He carefully uncoils the snake from his neck and offers it to Dace. And that's all I need to see to begin shoving my way to the front of the stage.

Maybe Dace isn't up there of his own accord.

Maybe he really was coerced.

While I have no idea how he got there, I'm determined to stop this madness before it can escalate further.

I jostle against the bloodthirsty crowd, gagging on sickly puffs of ethanol that waft from their lips, seep from their pores, as I make my way to the front. Only to watch Dace willingly lower his head, allowing Suriel to drape the hissing, writhing rattler around his neck, as a hand clamps down hard on my arm, dragging me back into the belly of the masses.

"Almost time for me to shift." Cade tightens his grip. His fingers leaving sharp imprints in my flesh, his fathomless, icy-blue eyes meeting mine. "And just as I planned, my timing is perfect. Seems you and Dace really are fated. Destined to die at the exact same time. Tragically romantic—all the way to the bitter end." He uses his free hand to shove a cold sharp knife hard against my side, before I have a chance to reach for mine, leaving no doubt of his intention to use it.

I push against him in protest.

Jab my elbow smack into his gut as my foot finds his shin.

But Cade's freakishly strong. He just laughs in my ear and holds me in place. "Watch," he hisses, twisting the knife until it pierces the tight weave of my sweater, rips a hole in the tank top I wear underneath, and pricks at my flesh.

At the moment, the state of my flesh bears little consequence. With only the vaguest awareness of the shock of icy-cold metal piercing my skin, the warm trickle of blood that streams down my side, I continue my struggle against him in a desperate fight to reach Dace, as I gape in horror at the spectacle unfolding before me.

Dace.

Tied to a chair.

With a venomous snake draped over his neck.

"One strike and he's history!" Cade's voice buzzes with excitement. His words reverberate hard against my cheek. "It's all over, Seeker." He focuses hard on the snake with an intense, burning red gaze. Waiting for just the right moment to complete the shift, cleave his blade deep into me, and claim the ultimate Coyote victory.

If I had any clue what Dace was doing, or how he ended up there, I might have a better idea how to help. But while I don't know a thing about reptiles, I do know that animals tend to strike when they feel hungry, threatened, or both.

Which means I need to rethink my earlier plan to ambush the stage. I can't risk startling the snake when doing so could cause it to turn against Dace.

Left with no choice but to trust that Dace knows what he's doing, I turn my focus to summoning my athame into my hand.
While I'm committed to not killing Cade, if he goes too far, injuring him is not out of the question.

From somewhere within my back pocket, the blade begins to
vibrate and move, as Suriel stares transfixed at Dace, and Cade's
hot, labored breath pelts hard against the back of my neck—the
second sign (after the glowing red eyes) that the shift is at hand.

He adjusts his grip, digs the blade deeper into my flesh, as I steal
a moment to close my eyes and call upon my collection of helpers
and tools. Using every bit of magick I possess to ask for their help
in moving the athame from my pocket to my hand.

The blade flips out of my pocket. Finds its way to my palm. As
Cade curses under his breath, and Dace says, "I think he likes me."

What?

My lids snap open, my athame all but forgotten, when I see
Dace still on the stage, still tied to the chair, a good-natured smile
lighting his face as the venomous rattler lovingly nuzzles his
cheek.

"Does this mean I can keep him?" Dace lifts his gaze to meet
Suriel's, laughing when the snake creeps up to his head, coils itself on the crown, and hisses at Suriel when he tries to snatch it
away.

"Did you see that?" Outraged, Suriel whirls on the crowd. His
voice thick with indignation and fury, he shouts, "Did you see the
way he looked at that snake? He has possessed it with his demon
spirit—just as he will soon possess all of you. None of you are
safe!" His eyes bulge, his crooked index finger stretches toward
the sky. Only to have the mob respond by sending a half-full beer
bottle soaring toward his head, this time grazing his ear.

But Suriel's so far gone, so unhinged, he remains completely
unaware of the wound—the jagged flag of flesh left bloody and
dangling, dripping onto the frayed white collar of his shirt. He
stoops toward the large basket he's placed by his feet, dips a hand

in, and faces the crowd with a feverish gaze, and an armful (seven if I can trust my hurried count) of venomous snakes.

"Still feeling brave?" He dangles the nest of snakes before Dace. "You'll never survive this one, boy. You can't get to them—they know who you are!"

Dace flinches. The move slight, nearly imperceptible, but I caught it. And from the way Cade laughs under his breath, he saw it too.

"Here comes the money shot!" he sings. Having regained his confidence, he inches the knife deeper into me. "I change, and the Seeker and my abomination of a brother say bye-bye forever."

Cade's eyes glow a deep burning red, as he watches Suriel toss the tangle of hissing, venomous snakes into Dace's lap. And I know I have just a matter of seconds to use my weapon against him while I still can.

"Sure you want to do this?" I say, my eyes never once leaving Dace, as I tighten my grip on the hilt. "Sure you want all of these people to see you in demon face?"

"You kidding?" He laughs, the sound he makes somewhere between animal and human. "They're so ripped they won't know the difference. Besides, they're about to get used to it. As soon as I rid the world of you, I plan to spend most of my time in my altered form. I'll have no further need to blend in." He pushes the knife just a little bit deeper, but still enough for me to let out a small squeal of pain. The sound as startling to me as it was to him. And I know that no matter what happens on stage, it's time to fight back. It's just a matter of time before Cade punctures something, does serious damage.

I pull a slow quiet breath, aware of his body shaking in anticipation of the change about to take place. But I can't let him get there, can't let him reach his demon state. The moment he transforms, I won't stand a chance. None of us will.

Intending to wound just enough to delay him without causing any real harm, I lift the knife and sink it into his forearm.

Using his moment of shock to jerk free of his grip and bolt for the stage.

By the time I reach the platform, Dace is sitting silent and rigid, dripping with snakes. As Suriel stands right beside him, lips parted in anticipation, eyes wide and glittering, waiting for the first one to strike.

I push against the platform, about to shout Dace's name, when he turns to me with a strange silver gaze warning me to stay where I am. But I'm not sure I can do that. While I want to trust that he knows what he's doing, I've yet to see any real evidence to prove that he does. For all I know, the first snake could've been a fluke. And, from the deep, guttural roar coming from the crowd, his brother is in the midst of transforming.

I step onto the stage, ready to deal with Suriel on my own terms, when a lone voice from the crowd rises above all the rest, urging them to join in.

"They're fake! You're a fake!" they all shout in unison, as though singing the chorus to the latest hit song. "You've removed their venom glands!"

And that's when I notice what Dace was urging me to see.

Just like the rattler before, instead of striking, instead of sinking their venomous fangs into his flesh, these seven deadly snakes choose to slither lovingly over Dace's shoulders and neck. Sidling up to his face, where they fondly flick their forked tongues at his cheek.

"Looks like I win," Dace says, gazing upon an outraged Suriel. "So what do you say we end this charade, so we can all go inside and celebrate the New Year in peace."

The crowd is enraged. Furious at Suriel for wasting their time, it's not long before a hail of beer bottles soar toward his head, along with a fresh slew of insults, deeming him a fake, bogus, fraud, disassembling as quickly as they came.

But Suriel won't go down easily. Having lost none of his fire, despite losing his audience, he reaches for the dagger and advances on Dace as I leap onto the stage, wielding my athame.

"Daire, I got this," Dace says, his voice barely a whisper, though loud enough for me to hear. Still, I can't help but look skeptical. He's swarming with seven varieties of the world's most venomous snakes, who despite their friendly appearance, can turn on him just as easily. "Trust me," he says, through tightly clenched teeth. "I know what I'm doing."

Taking him at his word, I lower my athame. Remaining on high alert as Suriel charges toward Dace.

Enraged at his snakes for turning against him, enraged at losing his crowd, he's immune to his daughter's desperate call, begging him to halt.

"Daddy—stop! I can do this!" she cries, her voice too close for my comfort. While Suriel may be able to ignore her, I can't.

I whirl toward the empty space where the crowd once stood and find Phyre with Cade right beside her.

"The righteous will ascend—the Last Days are here!" Suriel looms before Dace, dagger at the ready.

Dace breaks free of his binding with a surprising lack of effort, and in a steady voice says, "It might be your last day—but it's not mine." With a curt nod of his head, all seven snakes fling themselves off Dace and land hard at Suriel's neck.

Phyre screams.

Cade looks on with burning red eyes.

Suriel drops to his knees, face turned skyward, convinced he'll prevail. Until all seven snakes sink their fangs into his flesh at the exact same moment, as though they'd struck a previous agreement. Leaving Suriel gasping and railing against the utter betrayal they've wrought upon him.

With a bloodcurdling shriek, he crumples into an agonized heap as the snakes continue to attack. Seven sets of fangs repeatedly biting into his skin, depositing lethal doses of poison into his body until they tire of the game and slither away. While Dace looks on with wide silver eyes. His entire body trembling, shaking, as though he's caught in the grip of something extraordinarily powerful and completely unknowable.

Phyre leaps onto the stage. Wailing with grief, she flings her blood-spattered form to cover her father's.

Blood-spattered?

Whose blood?

Despite her deep state of grieving, she appears physically fine.

And that's when I see the blood-soaked dagger she grips in her fingers.

That's when Cade's voice awakens me with his screams.

"What the hell have you done to me, Seeker? I will *kill* you for this!" He lumbers toward the stage, his entire left side drenched in red.

"Change!" I shout, racing toward him. Horrified to see his eyes wild and blazing, but otherwise looking very much the same. "Change—*now!*" I scream, as though I could actually command such a thing. Unable to comprehend the scene unfolding before me, when Cade shakes his head, falls to his knees. For some reason he can't make the shift.

"Whatever you've done, take it back!" His voice is fading, along with his life force. But the truth is, I haven't done anything. If I ever needed to see his demon self, it's right now.

I whirl toward Dace, afraid of what I might find—only to see him still caught in that strange, hypnotic, silver-eyed state.

Strangely still. Strangely unharmed. Looking as though he's on the verge of transforming into something I can't even begin to imagine.

I turn my focus to Phyre and race toward her. Determined to wrestle the dagger away, unwilling to take the chance that she'll use it again.

She lets it go easily.

Too easily.

Freeing up her hand to reach into her father's suit pocket, and retrieve the detonator he'd stashed there.

A single glimpse of that small, electronic device is enough to make all of the pieces fall into place.

The explosives Dace told me he saw in her father's shed are now stashed inside the Rabbit Hole.

I whirl on Dace, desperate to awaken him from his strange, hypnotic state. "The club!" I shout. "The club's going to blow! You *have* to warn everyone to evacuate!"

Dace shakes his head, looks at me with wide glittering eyes making a slow return to their usual icy-blue. Seeing the detonator in Phyre's hand, his blood-soaked brother falling against the stage, gasping for breath, he turns on his heel and races for the Rabbit Hole. While I lunge toward Phyre and tackle her to the ground. Effectively pinning her down, only to realize too late that the button is blinking.

She's already pressed it.

Already started her own New Year's Eve countdown.

"You should've listened to me while you had the chance," she says. Her neck visibly bruised from Cade's hand. The absurd message on her T-shirt illuminated by the haphazard row of candles that continue to flicker around us.

Her words punctuated from the countdown coming from inside the club.

Ten!

You can hear the swell of excitement from here.

Nine!

Phyre looks at me, her eyes a mess of mascara and tears, making her look like the villain of some tragic cartoon. "The last days are here." She shrugs as though she's not the least bit responsible for what she's just done. Putting hundreds—possibly thousands of lives in ultimate danger, as behind us, the crowd counts down from eight to seven. "Better make your peace now. There's no more avoiding it. No time for forgiveness."

Six!

I punch her hard in the jaw. Slamming her cheek deep into the ground, more out of frustration than anything else. A move I instantly regret the second I see the way she grins in response.

Five!

I push off her, longing to rush inside, help Dace clear the place, but I can't afford to leave her with Cade. Can't afford to let her finish him off. Now that Dace is back to being himself, I can't be sure he'll survive it.

Four!

The next thing I know, the alleyway is teeming with bodies. Once-happy revelers now frantic in their need to evacuate the party. Oblivious to Suriel's prone body. Cade's perilous state. They storm the stage, causing me to lose sight of them in the chaos. But when a space is suddenly cleared, I find Cade gasping for breath as Phyre looms over him, grabs hold of his shirt, pulls his face to hers, and centers her mouth over his.

The countdown in the club may have halted—but in my head it continues.

Three!

I leap onto her back, and pull her off him, jamming my athame hard to her throat.

Two!

"Do it!" she screams, her neck arced in offering. "Put me out of my misery! Please—I never asked for any of this!"

My hand hesitates, not sure I can go through with it, when something off to the side catches my eye. The same luminous animal I saw before, just moments after we arrived.

With silky white fur and a piercing blue gaze, I instantly recognize it as Paloma's Wolf.

It's a sign.

But what kind of sign? What does it mean? What is it she wants me to do?

Cade is gasping, wheezing, inching away, as Phyre lies prone in my arms, waiting for me to deliver her.

I grab hold of her T-shirt and yank her back to the ground.

Forgive me. I direct the words to Wolf, to Phyre, to the universe. *One!*

I slip the knife farther down, pressing the tip against the place where it says KISS on her T-shirt. Watching Phyre's eyes widen as a soft smile crosses her lips.

"She's here," she whispers.

"Who?" I ask. "Your mother? Is she here to meet you?"

Phyre shakes her head, parts her lips to speak. Looking at me when she says, "You can't do it, can you?"

Her eyes meet mine, and we both know the truth. She's not a demon. She's just a sad, troubled girl who never stood a chance in the world.

She heaves herself out of my grasp and staggers toward the club. And I'm just about to go after her, when Dace appears before me, grabs hold of my arm, and shouts, "Run!"

I point toward Cade, lying in a half-dead, bloody heap beside us. And we pick him up between us, and drag him toward safety.

Having just cleared the edge of the alleyway, when the Rabbit Hole explodes.

forty-three

Dace

When the first blast hits, I push Daire to the ground, and throw my body over hers, in an effort to protect her from the barrage of shooting flames and flying debris. The series of explosions seeming to go on forever, coming one after another, punctuated by only the briefest of lulls.

"What happened to our friends?" Daire shouts to be heard over the noise. "Did you get them out? Are they okay?" She lifts her head, squinting through swirling gusts of black smoke.

"They're fine," I say. "Safe." Careful to keep her body contained, until I'm sure that it's over. "Before I even got there, Xotichl was already herding everyone out. She must've sensed it." I lift my body from hers, and help her to her feet. "They went out through the front. I told them we'd all meet by my truck."

"And everyone else?" Daire looks at me with red-rimmed eyes and an ash-smudged chin, her hair falling in limp tangles around her cheeks. But to me she's never been more beautiful, and I have to resist the urge to pull her into my arms and kiss her. "You didn't have much time, were you able to get them all out?"

I rub a hand over my chin, a long-time habit I can't seem to shake. "I don't know," I admit, the words thick with the burden of truth. "It's impossible to say for sure. While I couldn't care less about the Richters, there were all those people at Leandro's private party who aren't guilty of anything other than having their perceptions altered without their consent. But there was so much pandemonium and so little time, it was impossible to get close enough to the vortex to properly warn them."

Daire meets my words with a sobered gaze. Her chin lifting in earnest when she says, "Still, you did good." She nods to confirm it, but I'm too absorbed by the possible loss to acknowledge the kudos. "You did the best you could. Without you, it would've been worse."

I shrug. Look away. My mind swimming with the determined look on Phyre's face as she pushed past me. Racing to get inside the very place all the others were fleeing.

Despite her earlier attempt to kill me, I tried to stop her. Tried to convince her not to do it. But she just looked right through me as though it were already done.

"What happened to Phyre is not your fault," Daire says, accurately reading the look of loss on my face. "You're not responsible for her. If anyone bears that burden, it's me. She begged me to finish her and I was unable to do it. Unable to keep her from rushing into the building, determined to do what I couldn't."

"You did the right thing," I tell her.

"Then why do I feel so conflicted?"

"Because watching a life self-destruct is never supposed to feel good. Unless you're Cade Richter."

Or me.

Though I fail to put a voice to it, there's no denying the surge of power I felt when those snakes flung themselves from my neck to Suriel's.

No denying the ripple of delight when I watched as they repeatedly sunk their fangs into his flesh.

No denying how those same feelings were connected to the mystical shift occurring within me.

But I keep all of that to myself.

Wrapping an arm around her, we begin the walk back to my truck when we come upon my bloody, injured beast of a brother, who looks at me and says, "You're supposed to be dead! What the hell did you do?"

I stare at him with changed eyes. A slow grin creeping onto my face when I see the way he cowers away.

He struggles to rise, eager to make an escape, but one swift kick from Daire puts him right back in place. She kneels down beside him, grabs hold of his shirt, and drags him up to her face. And though this is her fight, I still stake a position beside her, in case she should need me.

"I saved your life tonight," she hisses, practically spitting the words, leaving no doubt just how much she wishes it had been otherwise. "But I only did so to spare Dace. Consider it a one-time pass, Coyote. Next time, you're dead."

Her hands shake with rage, and I know she's tempted to finish him now. But I can't let that happen. The beast is settling inside me. There's no guarantee it'll rise up to save me again.

A flurry of fire engines, police cars, and assorted emergency vehicles begin to arrive in a blur of blaring sirens and flashing lights.

"Daire." I coax her away from her rage. "Enchantment's finest are here. Most of who are Richters. It's time to move on."

With obvious reluctance, she lets go of Cade. Watching with glaring eyes and grim lips as he scrambles away, disappearing inside the smoldering club.

"You planned that whole thing, didn't you?" she says, inexplicably transferring her anger from my brother to me. "Suriel, the snakes, all of it—why didn't you tell me?"

She's only half interested in the details, the other half is steeped in feeling deceived, and it's the part I set out to quell first. "It wasn't nearly as planned or strategic as you think," I say, urging her toward my truck. Wanting to get as far from the club as we can before the authorities find us, the questions begin, and they find a way to blame us. "I figured Suriel was gearing up for some big reveal, and I knew I wanted to be there. The only reason I didn't mention it is because I didn't want you to worry. But, Daire, you need to know that my life was never in jeopardy—getting killed was never a remote possibility."

She ducks out of my reach. Standing stubbornly in place with an accusing gaze and arms crossed defiantly, she lifts her chin and says, "Are you that righteous?" And though she does her best to commit to her anger, I know she's fueled more by the fear of almost losing me, after all she went through to find me.

Since she deserves no less than the truth, I meet her gaze and say, "I used to be. I used to be made of the purest white energy. But I think we both know that's hardly the case anymore."

She swallows hard, drops her focus to her feet. Seeming to direct the words to the scuffed toe of her shoes when she says, "So why didn't they bite you? Clearly the venom glands weren't removed." She shifts her gaze toward the place where Suriel's lifeless body lies, now a trampled, pulpy mess thanks to the frantic exodus of the panicked masses.

I place a hand on her arm, steering her away from Suriel's grisly remains. When I'm sure I have her attention, I say, "Suriel believes in a world of us versus them—where everything exists separately from each other. Whereas I believe in a world of complete and total connection—one where we are all a part of the same, unifying source. Which means I'm as connected to those snakes as I am to you. Thing is, in order for it to work, you have to truly believe it in the deepest part of your soul."

"So why did Suriel last so long without getting bit?" The determined tilt of her chin tells me she's not fully convinced.

"Because Suriel's the hand that feeds them," I say. "Problem is, he let too much time pass between meals. Those snakes were starving, and they blamed him."

"Speaking of being connected," she says, once I have her moving again. "Cade was unable to change." Her voice quickening along with her pace when she sees our friends waiting next to my truck. "He couldn't shift past the glowing red eyes, and he didn't seem to know why. He even tried to blame me, but I'm wondering if maybe you had something to do with it."

"I didn't," I say. "Or at least if I did, it wasn't deliberate. Weird thing is, while he couldn't shift, I started to." The look that meets mine isn't one bit surprised, so I take a chance and offer my hand. Pointing out the spot where the small remnant of a talon remains, noting the way her eyes widen as a flurry of soft white feathers drift from my sleeve.

"What is that?" she asks, voice hushed with a combination of awe and uncertainty.

"I don't know. Something very powerful though."

"Has it happened before?"

I shake my head in reply.

"Does it worry you?"

I rub my hand over my chin, unsure of the answer. "I'm not sure," I admit. "It certainly didn't feel bad. Actually, it felt quite the opposite—amazing and good. It took all of my strength to stop the progression. And the only reason I did, is because I had no idea where it would end. While I'm sure it saved me from suffering the same fate as Cade, I couldn't risk riding that wave all the way. Daire—" I take her worried face in my hands. "All I can say for sure, is that it felt like I'd swallowed a bolt of lightning. It was the most tremendous surge of power I've ever experienced. It's hard to describe . . ." My voice fades when I see the way she focuses hard on my eyes.

Afraid that I've said something to scare her, I start to turn away, eager to get to our friends, leave the gaffe behind, when she holds me in place. Her soft hands cupped to my cheeks, she says, "Whatever it was, it can't be all bad. For the first time in a long time, I can see myself reflected in your eyes."

forty-four

Daire

I rush toward our friends, never so glad to see them. "Thank God, you're okay!" I hug each of them to me. Focusing on Xotichl when I say, "You sensed it, didn't you?"

She nods, burrowing deep into the shelter of Auden's shoulder. "But it took me a while—longer than it should have. I was almost too late. For some, I was too late."

"You did the best you could, flower." Auden's quick to comfort her. "None of us would be here if it wasn't for you."

"Don't forget about Dace," she says, looking right at him.

But Dace is quick to brush it off, preferring to give the credit to her. He lifts his shoulders and says, "It's been a wild night."

"Yeah," Xotichl agrees. "And for some, it's not over yet." Her attention drifts to the far side of the alleyway as she burrows deeper into Auden's chest.

And I'm just about to ask her what she meant, when Lita says, "Xotichl's way more of a hero than she lets on. After I jumped on stage to tell Auden to yell *fire* to get everyone out, Xotichl centered her energy on the doors and blew them all open, making for a quicker getaway."

"You did that?" I study her with open admiration.

Lita nods to confirm it, as Xotichl works her jaw, and continues to gaze toward the alleyway.

"What is it?" I ask, disturbed by the look on her face. Xotichl never looks frightened, and while she doesn't exactly look frightened now, it's the next best thing. I follow the length of her gaze, but I'm unable to make out anything other than a team of emergency workers hovering over Suriel's remains.

"The preacher is stuck." She fields our collective blank stares when she adds, "His spirit is hovering near his body, and he's angry as hell. Can't believe what became of him. It's only a matter of time until he sees us and exacts his revenge. I just hope his spirit guide gets to him first."

"Why wait?" Lita makes a beeline for Auden's wagon. "A scary preacher in limbo, and a blown-up version of the Rabbit Hole that's even creepier than the non-blown-up version—never a better reason to *vamanos* as far as I'm concerned!"

We head for our respective cars, having agreed to meet at Paloma's. And once I'm inside Dace's truck, I slide across the worn leather seat, eager for the comfort of his body beside me.

He shifts into reverse and backs onto the street. And after he's put a good distance between us and the Rabbit Hole, I look at him and say, "Not to sound callous, but . . ." He turns to me, eyes creased with curiosity. "Do you think it's too late to claim that New Year's Eve kiss? I hear it's bad luck to miss it, and I don't think either of us can afford to risk it."

Without another word, Dace pulls to the side of the darkened dirt road and drifts toward me as eagerly as I drift toward him.

At first, I keep my eyes wide, stealing a moment to revel in the sight of his beautiful face looming before me, his lips angling to meet mine. Then my lids softly drop as I merge into the kiss. Savoring the heated press of our bodies coming together after what feels like so long apart.

His mouth moves on mine, and I meet his tongue with an earnest intensity matched by his own. Relishing the moment for all

that it is—a welcome reprieve from a life fraught with problems—a just reward after a battle hard-won—a New Year's Eve
tradition meant to bring good luck—a life-affirming action in the
face of senseless death.

But more than anything, it's the promise we give to each
other—to never give up on ourselves.

His arms providing safe haven. His lips offering the sort of
comfortable permanence I've never been able to claim until I met
him.

Here, in his arms, it feels like I'm home.

A low groan escapes from his lips as he molds his body hard
against mine until there's nary a breath spanning between us. His
touch growing urgent, heated, as our hearts thrum in tandem.
Rising and falling in deep fervent melody, as though keeping time
with the chiming and swishing of the keys at our necks.

I settle into his warmth, linger on the sweet deliciousness of
his tongue. Ready to act on the heated desire rising within me,
when he draws away and says, "Listen, my place is a mess, but—if
you don't mind." His heavy-lidded gaze displaying the depths of
his need.

"I can't imagine I'll notice." I kiss him again. And though it's
meant to be brief, once there, I find it hard to leave. "After Paloma's.
I'll sneak out if I have to, but I doubt that I'll have to."

Planting a final kiss on my cheek, he settles back into his seat,
and heads for my grandmother's. That luminous white wolf with
blazing blue eyes appearing before us throughout the entire ride.
Its spectral form bobbing in the headlights' glare, almost as though
it's leading us home.

"Tell me you can see that," I finally say, plagued by the fear
that the hallucinations that landed me here have returned. But
when I see the way Dace reluctantly nods, gripping the wheel so
firmly his knuckles leach of all color, it leaves me so uneasy, I ask,
"What do you think it means?"

He sits silently beside me, pressing hard on the accelerator.

"Dace—" I swivel in my seat until I'm fully facing him. "What do you think it means?"

He lifts a hand from the wheel, rubs it over his chin. "I'm not sure," he finally says, purposely avoiding my gaze. "Just . . . we'll be there soon. I'm going as fast as I can. So . . . here . . . here we are . . ."

From halfway down the street, I can already see that all the lights are on and Paloma's blue gate is wide open. And before Dace can properly stop, I bolt from the truck.

My feet barely hitting the ground when that luminous, blue-eyed, white Wolf appears right before me. His ears perked, his eyes bright and glistening, he throws his head back and lets out a long mournful howl that lasts until he centers his eyes on mine and urges me toward the doorway, vanishing the moment his paw crosses the threshold.

I race into the house, my vision swimming with blurred images of Chay, Leftfoot, Chepi, Cree, and—Jennika and Harlan?— all of them rushing toward me.

Chay reaches me first. Wrapping a solid arm around me, he whispers my name.

But it's Jennika's tearstained face looming before me that tells me the story I never wanted to hear.

"Where is she?" I cry, pushing past the hands that try to hold me, comfort me. Try to stop me from seeing what I don't want to see. "Tell me where she is! What happened? Bring me to her—*now!*"

My gaze moves among them, taking in a sea of grief-stricken faces. And when I hear that plaintive howling again, coming from the direction of Paloma's bedroom, I race toward it. Praying for a miracle—praying to disprove what I know in my soul. The truth I've fought to deny since the moment I first saw Wolf at the Rabbit Hole.

When I reach the doorway—when I see my *abuela* lounging peacefully—with her eyes closed, hands softly folded over her chest—I allow myself to live in the lie.

I pretend all is well.

I pretend that she's napping.

Dace calls my name in a voice choked with emotion, but I'm not yet ready to heed it.

"Someone get her a blanket!" I shout, reaching for Paloma's cold hand. I rub it furiously between mine in a futile attempt to warm her cold flesh. "She's freezing! Why won't you help her? What's wrong with all of you?"

I glare at them accusingly, but the truth is, I don't really see them. Can't make out much of anything.

Only vaguely aware of Dace standing helplessly beside me, as Jennika soothes a comforting hand over my hair, mumbling an incoherent stream of explanations and apologies.

"I'm so sorry," she murmurs, her voice like a soft, distant hum that bears no real significance. "I wanted to see you, the flights were all booked, so Harlan and I drove instead. By the time we arrived, we found Paloma like this."

"You mean, sleeping?" I turn to look at Jennika's grief-stricken face, as Harlan stands with his head bent behind her. Watching as she chews on her lip, swipes a finger over the fresh purple crescents hanging under each eye.

Still, her gaze never leaves mine as she says, "Daire, Paloma's not . . . sleeping."

I look at her for a long moment, then I focus back on Paloma. The reality of the situation looming before me—exposing a truth that cannot be denied—I hurtle headfirst into the dark madness of grief. Which for me, looks nothing like I would've expected.

After a few long moments, I lift myself from Paloma's lifeless form, and replace her hand to the space where I found it. In a foreign, almost robotic voice, I say, "Exactly how did you find her?" I turn my attention to my mother, sparing only the briefest glance at Dace standing beside her.

"I found her lying unconscious. I tried to revive her, but it was already too late, and so I called Chay."

"Did you move her?"

She plays with the small diamond stud flanking her nostril. Striving to match my serious tone, she says, "I couldn't stand to see her like that . . . and since it didn't appear to be a crime scene, we lifted her onto the bed."

"So she was in here?"

Jennika nods, motions toward Paloma's effects. "It seemed like she was getting dressed, getting ready to go out, or something. I found her lying in front of the closet."

I whirl on Chay, disbelief marking my gaze. "Were you two going out? I thought you said she was ill?"

"We were planning to stay in and wait to hear from you. I was already on my way over, parking my truck in the yard, when Jennika called."

I glance around the room, avoiding the place where my grandmother rests. Trying to wrap my head around the impossible. None of it makes any sense.

"We've been trying to reach you," Jennika says. "And then, when we got the news about the Rabbit Hole—I was determined to go down there—but Chay insisted I wait."

I survey the room once again, seeing Paloma's espadrilles left discarded before the closet, as her winter boots lie at the ready. The red wool cardigan Jennika gave her for Christmas abandoned on the back of her chair, as her heavy winter coat waits at the foot of the bed.

She was ill. Waiting for Chay. Yet determined to leave.

Something happened.

Something she was eager to tell me about.

Without a word, I bolt from the bed, pass through the den, and race up the ramp that leads to Paloma's office.

At first glance, it's as neat and orderly as always. Everything in its place and a place for everything. Except for the book she left lying open on the table, the blue tourmaline stone I gave to her to inspect, placed right on top as though marking the page.

I slide the stone to the side.

Skim the passage beneath.

My knees are the first to go.

Buckling right out from under me, forcing me to grasp the table's edge to keep from falling.

My sanity is next on the list, but I fight like hell to hang on to its tenuous hold.

It's only a few seconds later when Dace is beside me. Hauling my body against his, he reads the text from over my shoulder, and curses under his breath long before reaching the end.

Seems Xotichl was right.

As it turns out, the tourmaline does emit a troublesome energy.

According to the book, some gems are cursed.

Embedded with a sort of psychic hook that enables the giver to exert complete control over the receiver. Enabling them to manipulate the body, mind, and soul.

And, in many cases, to extinguish life itself.

My body goes rigid.

A single name swirls in my head.

Cade.

All along, it was him.

Showing the kind of patience I never would've expected, by slowly and systematically weakening Paloma's defenses.

First by stealing her soul.

Then by making her think I was dead.

And finally by ensuring she ended up with the tourmaline—the recipient he intended it for all along.

Lita and Xotichl were merely pawns in his game.

He knew Lita wouldn't want it.

Knew Xotichl would read its strange energy.

He also knew she'd easily convince me to give it to Paloma to study.

The whole time I sought to save him—if only to save Dace—Cade was plotting against me.

Seizing control of Paloma's mind, body, and soul through a shiny, blue stone.

I shut my eyes against the scald of unshed tears forming under my lids. And though I long to give in to them, long to sink to my knees, throw my head back, and wail until I'm hollow and empty—there's no time for that.

Now, more than ever, I need to keep a cool head. Can't afford to be weakened by loss.

Refusing to indulge in despair—refusing to experience it from the inside—I direct my grief outside of me—eager to be rid of it.

Causing Wind to lash at the windows and howl at the doors.

Causing Fire to spark and hiss so loudly in the kiva fireplace, I can hear it from two rooms away.

While Earth trembles, shaking jars from shelves and pictures from walls.

As mad sheets of rain pelt hard against the flat adobe roof.

The magnitude of my grief alone enough to manipulate the elements—and yet, I couldn't stop Cade from manipulating me.

"Daire, please stop." Dace's touch is gentle, his voice soft and coaxing.

But I can't stop.

Won't stop.

Not until I stop Cade.

"Daire."

It's another voice this time. One I haven't heard in a while.

Dace mumbles under his breath.

Lita gasps.

As the rest look on in confusion.

His deep purple gaze meeting mine, he motions toward the chaos I've caused. And with a single sad shake of his head, and a pleading look in his eyes, he convinces me to stop.

"Are you here to take her up?" I ask, seeing no other reason for his return.

"No," he says, the word alone containing countless layers of untold sadness tinged with regret. "Paloma's in good hands. She's already moved on. As for me, I'm afraid I've made my choice. It's no longer home."

I should feel bad, but I don't. It's like he said, Axel made his choice. Now I'm making mine.

With a weary gaze and a heavy heart, I stand before my family and friends, feeling as though I've grown several decades in the space of one night.

"She'll want to be buried beside Django." I speak with the kind of hard-earned authority that no longer surprises me.

Jennika whispers my name, starts to move toward me, but I hold up a hand to keep her at bay.

"I see no reason to delay. Paloma wouldn't want a big, formal affair. Everyone she loved and cared about is already here. Besides, I want it done before the news spreads and the Richters catch on. I don't want to give them the opportunity to interfere, or find a way to desecrate her memory before we've had a chance to properly honor it."

"Daire, you're tired. It's late. There are professionals you can call upon to handle these things," Chepi says, softening toward me for perhaps the very first time since I've known her.

But it's Chay who steps in. He and I now partners in grief, he looks at me and says, "Daire's right. Paloma would've wanted it this way. I see no reason to delay."

forty-five

Daire

By the time it's all said and done—by the time Paloma's grave is properly dug and we're gathered around it—the first light of dawn is beginning to break. The shell of sky cracking into a riot of color that drips toward our heads, as we lower my grandmother's body into the earth, putting it to its final rest beside her only son.

I watch the progression with dry eyes and a scratchy, parched throat. Remembering what Paloma told me the first time I came here—that I shouldn't confuse it with my father. That he no longer remains in this place. It's merely a place for the body to rest. The soul has moved on.

"*Your father is everywhere,*" she said. "*His soul's been released, freed from the earth. Left to become one with the wind that blows through your hair, the dirt that shifts under your feet. He's the rain in the storm cloud that hovers over those mountains beyond . . . he's the bloom in every flower. He is one with the energy of the earth. He is everywhere you look. Which means you can speak to him here, just as easily as you can speak to him anywhere. And, if you go very quiet, and listen with care, you just might hear his reply.*"

I focus on the Sangre de Cristo mountain range with its snow-capped, meringue-like peaks. Remembering the reverent set of

Paloma's gaze as she turned to face them that day. Then I search among my friends, seeing Xotichl huddled under the reliable shelter of Auden's love, as Dace keeps a close eye on me while supporting Chepi, his mom. Leftfoot and Cree, faces slick with the effort of digging, wipe beads of grime from their chins as they take a few moments to honor Paloma. As Lita stands beside Axel, keeping a respectable distance, though there's no denying the spark that sizzles between them. While Harlan provides comfort to a sobbing Jennika, and Chay, stoic as ever, stands beside me.

My family and friends all relying on me to keep them from the same fate as my *abuela*.

But how can I possibly do that when the one person whose guidance I most depend on is no longer here?

"And, if you go very quiet, and listen with care, you just might hear his reply" . . . Paloma's voice sounds in my head.

If the words hold true for my father, then I can only assume they hold true for my grandmother as well. And now, more than ever, I need to hear her reply.

Need some proof she's still with me.

I tilt my face skyward, desperate for answers.

Seeking guidance, an omen, or, at the very least, some hint of acknowledgment.

The clouds gather and spread.

Somewhere nearby a bird chirps, greeting the day.

Then, seemingly out of nowhere, a murder of crows bursts into sight. Soaring in slow perfect circles right over our heads.

"Your birth was heralded by crows," Chay says, as a sniffling Jennika blows into her wadded-up tissue and nods to confirm it.

I keep my gaze trained on the birds, watching as a lone black figure breaks free of the flock.

This one bigger.

Its wingspan wider.

Its beak distinctly hooked.

And when it lets out a long, plaintive caw, the sound is guttural and deep.

A raven.

The thought confirmed by the single black feather that drifts from the sky and lands at my feet.

"It's a sign," Chay says, watching as I stoop to examine it. "An omen if there ever was one."

I swallow hard, start to ask what it means, but the answer is clear.

With Paloma gone, I'm the last of the Santos.

It's time for me to stand in her place.

Time for me to fly solo.

forty-six

Daire

With the last bit of dirt tossed onto the grave, it's time to move on. While it's tempting to linger, there's no denying the truth of Paloma's words. I shouldn't confuse this place with her. She's returned to her origins. She is now a part of everything.

We head for our cars with Chepi clutching at Dace, and Jennika clutching at me. And while I know she's exhausted from the drive, and wracked with loss, while I know she longs to provide comfort, I'm not the daughter she left behind just two weeks ago. With Paloma gone, my responsibilities just multiplied tenfold, and it's Dace I need most.

While it may be my turn to fly solo, Dace and I will face this together.

I hug my mother tightly to me. Comforted to know that Harlan is with her, that she's giving him the chance he deserves. Then I draw away, promise to meet up later in the day, and follow Dace to his truck.

"Can we swing by the Rabbit Hole?" I ask, as he holds the door open and helps me inside. While I long to get to his apartment, while I can't think of anything better than to spend the night huddled in the warm shelter of his arms, there's another stop I need to make first.

He shoots me a curious look and slides in beside me. The truck humming to life after a few insistent turns of his key.

"I just need to see it one more time before sleep," I tell him.

We're more than halfway there when I remember the scene in the bathroom with Crickett and Jacy. So much has happened between now and then, I'd almost forgotten Crickett's glimmering tourmaline pendant. How she claimed they were in the swag bags everyone got at the door.

"Dace . . ." My voice sounds smaller than I'd like as I state my concerns.

"You don't think he's going to try to kill everyone, do you?" Dace looks at me with hooded eyes, and a deeply creased brow. "What good would that do?"

I shake my head and squint into the distance, recognizing the truth of his words. But then I remember that strange look in Marliz's eye every time she gazed at her brilliant blue tourmaline engagement ring.

"No," I say. "I don't think he's trying to kill them. I think he's found another way to control them. It's just like Paloma's book said—the tourmaline serves as a hook, providing the Richters a way to control the recipient's energy."

Dace looks at me with a gaze so weary, it's clear neither of us will be fit to deal with much of anything if we don't get some rest.

When he reaches the Rabbit Hole, he slows the truck to a crawl. Rolling past the smoldering remains of a building reduced to a burnt-out carcass of rubble.

"Do you think any Richters were among the casualties?" he asks, eyeing the trio of police cars parked out front—all the other emergency vehicles long gone. "Or, at the very least, Cade's crazy Coyote?"

"I don't know if we're ever so lucky." I frown, searching for signs of them, but mostly just seeing a building in ruins.

"Do you think they'll rebuild?" Dace turns to me, places a hand on my knee.

"I have no doubt." The sardonic grin that follows leaves a sour taste on my lips. "They may be defeated for now, but it won't last. If I know one thing for sure, it's just a matter of time before they regroup. And this time around promises to be far worse than any other that's come before . . ." My voice fades along with the last remaining vestiges of night.

The sky blooms wide.

A new year has dawned.

And when Dace squeezes my knee and steers away from the club, I slide across the cracked leather seat until my thigh pushes up against his. Then I lean my head on his shoulder, and allow myself to fall into a deep dreamless sleep.

Don't miss the magnificent final book in

The Soul Seeker Series

horizon

Coming November 2013

DAIRE SANTOS CAN NAVIGATE BETWEEN THE WORLDS OF THE LIVING AND THE DEAD. Now she must find out if the boy in her dreams is her one true love . . . or the enemy she must destroy.

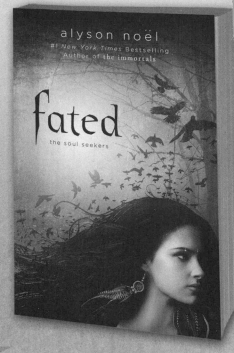

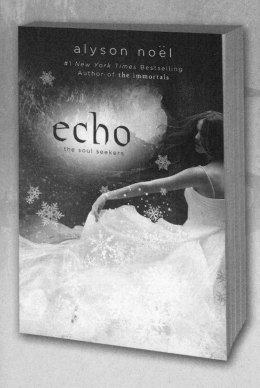

A DARK FAMILY OF SORCERERS HAVE BEEN LET LOOSE in the Lowerworld, and Daire and Dace must find them before they upset the balance between good and evil and destroy the world.

the soul seekers series continues
MYSTIC, *available Spring 2013* • HORIZON, *available Fall 2013*

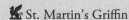 St. Martin's Griffin